Hidden Assets

By Leeann Betts

Book 6 of the By the Numbers series

Featuring Carly Turnquist,

Forensic Accountant

Copyright: 2017

ISBN: 978-1-943688-31-9

Cover art by: Donna Schlachter

Published by: PLS Bookworks, Denver, Co

Other Books By Leeann Betts:
Counting the Days: a 31-day devotional

By the Numbers series
No Accounting for Murder
There Was a Crooked Man
Unbalanced
Five and Twenty Blackbirds
Broke, Busted, and Disgusted

Books by Donna Schlachter:
Second Chances and Second Cups; A sweet collection of stories
of second chances from a second-chance God.
The Physics of Love: where the past, present, and future collide
Echoes of the Heart in The Pony Express Romance Collection

Mended by God series
Broken Dreams, Mended Heart
Broken Dreams, Mended Family
Broken Dreams, Mended Marriage

By Leeann and Donna:
Nuggets of Writing Gold -- a compilation of articles and
essays on the craft of writing.

All books are available at Amazon.com in print and digital

Follow us:
Donna: www.HiStoryThruTheAges.wordpress.com
www.HiStoryThruTheAges.com
Leeann: www.AllBettsAreOff.wordpress.com
www.LeeannBetts.com
We are also active on Facebook and Twitter

Dedicated first and foremost to the glory of God.

Without Him, no story is worth telling

To Patrick, who is the evidence of God's love for me.

To Terrie Wolf, my agent, my friend, one of my biggest fans.

Please leave an honest review at Amazon.com and Smashwords.com

Danforth Wyoming is caught in the 1880's,

Where it all began.

Carly Turnquist is caught in 2004,

right where she belongs.

May 2004

Chapter 1

On a train in eastern Wyoming

Carly Turnquist, forensic accountant by day, satisfied diner by night, patted her stomach. She was right. Dinner on the train was every bit as good as she'd hoped. Tonight, in celebration of the fact they were in beef country, they'd had a choice of rib eye steak, prime rib, or barbecue beef ribs.

After several agonizing minutes of indecision, she chose the ribs, and Mike went with the prime rib.

She eyed the pile of bones on her plate, stripped clean. Just the ribs alone would have been enough, not to mention the three sides, appetizer, and dessert.

Had she died and gone to heaven?

Mike smiled across the table to her, warming her heart and sending an electrical shock all the way to her toes. "Did you want coffee?"

She shook her head. "I think I'm already drunk on food. And I want to sleep tonight."

"You could have decaf."

"True, but I'm so full, I think I'd have to carry it in my pocket."

He chuckled at her words. He said it often after eating one of her down-home-cooking meals. "Shall we retire?"

"Sounds good. But first I want to stop in the gift shop and see if they have a novel I haven't already read."

Mike groaned. "You need to bring a library along with you just to keep yourself occupied."

She smiled. "Go on. Turn down the bed, switch on some nice music, and I'll be along presently."

He stood and offered her a hand, which she accepted. "Fine. But if you're not back by breakfast, I'll come looking for you."

He headed to the far end of the car toward their sleeper about six cars back, and she headed to the front of the train. The gift shop occupied the next car, which was marketing genius. Passengers with seats or sleepers in the first class section of the train, toward the front, had to pass through that car six times a day if they ate their meals on the train.

Must have been designed by the same guy who came up with the idea to put milk and bread at the back of the grocery store. Irritating, but genius.

Carly pushed through the door into the small foyer between cars, and paused. The sun was well set now, and their train seemed to be slowing. She stepped nearer the window and raised the glass. A porter passed by, and she turned to him. "Excuse me, why are we stopping?"

"Nothing serious, Miss. Just to let the express westbound train pass."

"Okay, thank you."

She turned back and breathed in the smells and sights of the train. Diesel. Squealing brakes. The smell of hot metal. Cool evening air. Apparently, May in Wyoming wasn't as warm as May in Bear Cove. And as the train settled to a halt, the hissing of steam, the groaning of metal coming to rest.

Faint at first, then building in volume, metal wheels on metal tracks drew closer. A train horn, low and mournful, recognizable anywhere, sounded from behind her train. And then the westbound express streamed past. In one of the passenger cars, a small boy waved at her, and she waved back. In another, somebody pulled down the blind. In yet another, two men struggled on an open platform between two cars before one fell over backwards on the opposite side of the train. The remaining man peered over as he gripped the ladder leading to the roof of the car, then adjusted his jacket and stepped back inside the car.

She gasped. And blinked. And craned her neck to look at the train passing by again.

Had she seen what she thought she saw?

Surely her overactive imagination was simply playing tricks on her.

And if not, somebody would raise the alarm and stop the express train.

But the final car passed her, and all she saw were the tracks, glinting dully in the moonlight, and a foot, propped at an odd angle, the rest of the body out of sight on the slope running down and away from the track bed.

The diesel engines on her train revved and moaned with the effort of starting their forward momentum again, until finally the wheels beneath her spun, gathering speed, and her train pulled out onto the main track once more.

Hurry, hurry. Catch up with it! Her mind screamed, but her body froze in place, her fingers gripping the bottom ledge of the window.

Her heart pounded in rhythm with the powerful diesel engine pushing and pulling her train. For several moments, she was certain she would faint.

But she was not the fainting type.

She was the action type.

She glanced from left to right, hoping Mike had come back looking for her.

But no, he wouldn't. He couldn't have been gone more than three or four minutes. He'd think she was still trying to decide which book to buy.

She stepped into the gift car. Maybe if she changed her surroundings, she'd realize her imagination had almost run away with her. Because otherwise, what she'd seen was too horrible to even consider.

To throw a man like a piece of trash off a fast-moving train was unthinkable.

Inhuman.

She needed to find someone to help her understand what had happened.

There had to be a rational explanation.

There had to be.

Because otherwise, that reality was just too much to consider.

Chapter 2

A young woman behind the sales counter turned in Carly's direction. "Can I help you?"

Carly sidled up to the counter, checking to see if anybody else was within earshot. No point in panicking everybody.

She was already panicked enough.

Satisfied the car was empty, she leaned in closer and lowered her voice. "I need to speak with a conductor. Somebody in authority."

The woman glanced around as though expecting that person to materialize. "Is there a problem?"

Carly straightened. "Are you a supervisor or a manager?"

"No. Just a clerk." The woman smiled, revealing a mouthful of braces. "I could call my supervisor."

"Would he have the authority to stop the train?"

"She."

"She?" What was the woman doing? Arguing political correctness in the midst of murder? "Sorry, would she have the authority to stop the train?"

"Stop the train?" The woman's brow pulled down. "Why should she?"

"Because I need the train stopped. Now." Carly looked above the windows. No emergency cord. In the movies, there was always a way a passenger could stop the train without having to go through this interrogation. "A conductor, perhaps?"

The woman, whose nametag read Susie, gestured toward the front of the train. "He just went into First Class to alert the passengers that dinner is ready."

Carly nodded and headed that way.

"But you can't—"

Carly waved off Susie's words and continued through the connecting doors and into First Class. She paused to get her bearings, impressed with the upgraded surroundings. Ambient lighting instead of fluorescent track fixtures. Crushed velvet upholstery instead of sturdy vinyl. Patterned carpet instead of the industrial-grade in her car. Not to mention the uniformed attendants and a drinks cart.

Never mind. She didn't need all this luxury. Might spoil her. She'd get used to it and want to travel First Class all the time.

She spotted the conductor—Henry was his name, she recalled—at the far end of the car, and made a beeline for him. Background music playing some classical tune she vaguely recognized—the one drawback to First Class apparently, but only because she didn't like the music of the masters—covered the hushed voices of the attendants and passengers.

Feeling a little like she was back in the grade school library and shouldn't raise her voice, she whispered as loud as she could. "Henry."

The older man didn't even slow down.

She tried again. "Psst. Henry."

Conversation ceased and all heads turned to her. She lifted a half-smile and shrugged. Still they stared.

An attendant at the far end of the car tapped Henry on the shoulder, and the conductor turned around. After a few whispered words between them, Henry met her gaze. His head tipped in question, then he scurried toward her. "Mrs. Turnquist, are you lost? This is First Class."

"Yes, I know where I am, Henry. We must stop the train at once."

His brow pulled down. "Stop the train, madam? Whatever for?"

A man and woman sitting near them listened in. Carly glanced at them, then touched Henry's forearm and directed him toward the doors leading to the rear of the train. "I can't tell you here. We don't want to panic the passengers."

"Panic the passengers, madam? I don't understand."

She leaned in, catching a whiff of his aftershave. Not citrusy like Mike's. Something more outdoorsy. And spicy. Her nose tickled. She preferred the one Mike used. Which reminded her, she needed to buy—

Back on track, girl.

"I saw a man throw another man off the train."

His eyes widened. "Off this train?"

"No. The other train."

Once again, his brow pulled down. That man's eyebrows traveled more miles in a day than he did. "The other train?"

She exhaled. Harrumphed was actually more like it. "When we were stopped." She hooked a thumb behind her. "Back there."

"When the express train passed us?"

"Right."

"And you saw this, madam?"

"Yes. I was standing between the cars. And I saw two men struggling as their train went past. And one man pushed the other man off the train."

"You saw this man hit the ground?"

"No. He pushed him off the other side of the train. Away from me. Down over the bank." She gripped Henry's sleeve. "We must hurry. He might still be alive. Although how somebody could survive such a fall, I don't know. He rolled down over the bank. He might have hit his head. He could be bleeding to death right now."

"You saw a lot for being on the wrong side of the train, madam."

She peered at him. "You don't believe me."

"Was anybody else with you when you saw this?"

Her shoulders slumped. Why was it people didn't believe her when she said she saw a crime being committed? Like the robbery in Bear Cove. Which turned out to be true. Sort of. "I was alone. That doesn't mean I didn't see it."

"Madam, we cannot stop the train simply because you think you saw something. What I can do is alert the previous station to send someone out to look at approximately where you think you saw—"

She planted her fists in her hips. "I did see."

He nodded. "And I can send a message to the next station. Perhaps they can detain the passengers a short time to ask if anybody on that train saw anything."

"So you're not going to stop the train? Pull a secret cord or push a hidden button? Send us careening into each other? China and crystal sliding off tables?"

He smiled. "No, madam. That would be dangerous, disruptive, and costly, wouldn't you agree?"

She dropped her hands to her sides. "Not if it saves a man's life."

He nodded toward the door. "Now, madam, if you will return to your seat. This section is reserved strictly for First Class passengers."

She glanced over his shoulder. "Are you saying I'm not allowed in this car?"

"Strictly speaking, no, madam, you are not."

She harrumphed again. Really, she couldn't recall a single day where she'd used that particular expression of exasperation more than once. And now here she'd gone and done it twice in just a few minutes. She turned and headed for the door. "Fine. You know where to find me when we get to the next station. I'm sure the authorities will want to talk to me."

"Yes, madam. I'm certain they will."

For some reason, his words were of little comfort to her.

+++++

Mike sat in the easy chair in their sleeping room, tapping his toe. Where was Carly? How long did it take to pick out a book? Knowing Carly as well as he did, she had probably read every book they carried and was now instructing the person in the gift store on which books to stock.

Or how to shelve them by title. Or author name. Or genre.

He chuckled. Carly always seemed intent on changing something, wherever she went. Like the time they went to the art museum and she almost got arrested for reaching over to straighten a painting that hung slightly askew. According to her. He couldn't see it.

Then again, he didn't always see things the way Carly saw them.

Take this train trip, for example. Recalling the time they became embroiled in a murder investigation before they even got off the plane, he thought traveling by rail was a good way to keep her out of trouble. She could truly take a few days off work. Bury her nose in a book. Or three. Let somebody else do the cooking for a change.

A real vacation before they got to Wyoming and she started delving into her friend's financial affairs.

But at every turn, Carly seemed intent on thwarting his plans.

She listened in on the conversations of their fellow passengers. She looked for reasons why folks got on at one station and off at another. Made up stories about their lives. Wondered about their occupations.

Seriously, the woman was better suited to be a writer, the way she loved making things up.

But where was she?

He stood. Well, he'd just go looking for her. Maybe she'd gotten ill. Maybe she was stuck in a conversation with a long-winded passenger and would appreciate him rescuing her.

He smiled. For someone who got herself into as much trouble as his wife did, she was an introvert at heart.

Mike slipped on a sweater. Moving between the cars, although most of the landings were enclosed, still meant cooler temperatures.

Most of the passengers were already in their sleeping room, the blinds pulled down as they settled in for the night. The dining car was quiet and dark, a thin ribbon of light marking the pathway. From the kitchen area, the tinkling and clinking of dishes and crystal mingling with lowered voices and the occasional chuckle.

He was about to push through the door toward the gift car when he caught sight of movement at the last table. He slowed. "Carly?"

His wife sat in the shadows, staring out the window, but she jerked at the sound of her name.

"Oh, Mike. I didn't hear you."

He slid in beside her and laid an arm across her shoulder. She was cold. "Are you okay?"

She nodded. "Fine."

Oh no. *Fine* didn't really mean fine, at least, not in Carly's vocabulary. *Fine* meant she wasn't fine, but didn't want to talk about it. *Fine* meant she had gotten herself into something but wouldn't share it with him. Yet. Because that was another thing he knew for certain about his wife—the time would come when she'd 'fess up about the trouble she'd gotten herself into.

He pulled her close. "Want to go to the room?"

She shook her head. "Not just yet. I need to think."

"What happened?"

Instead of answering him, she dropped her hands into her lap and tied her fingers into knots.

Another sign she was worried. Thinking through another mystery.

He groaned.

Not again.

She looked at him. "What's wrong?"

"Exactly what I was going to ask you."

"Why does there have to be anything wrong?"

He smiled down at her. "Because I let you out of my sight for five minutes. Which has turned, by the way, into at least twenty. I was worried when you didn't come back. Thought you might need rescuing."

"Oh, Mike."

"Am I right? What have you gotten yourself into this time?"

The door slid open and the conductor—Henry?—stepped into the dining car. He paused at their table. "Madam, I wanted to let you know—" His eyes slid from Mike to Carly, and he hesitated then tipped his hat to them. "I wanted to let you know that we'll arrive at the next station within about ten minutes."

Mike looked from Henry to his wife. "And you needed to know that because?"

She patted his arm. "No reason, dear. Henry was telling me just as he would tell any other passenger." She looked at the conductor. "Isn't that right, Henry?"

Again, the glances from one to the other. These two were definitely up to something. What, he could only guess.

Then again, maybe he didn't want to know.

Mike sighed. Yes, he did. He couldn't let this go any more than she could. "Okay, what's going on?"

The tenor of the train changed, and Henry planted his feet a centimeter wider apart. "We're preparing for our entry into the station. You might find it more comfortable to go to your compartment. If anybody needs to speak with either of you, I'll direct them there."

Carly pushed at Mike. "Good idea, Henry. I'm looking forward to relaxing."

Mike slid out of the booth. "And reading?"

Carly glanced around. "Reading?"

"You went to the gift car to buy a book. Or did you forget why you were there?" He peered at her. "Or did you really disappear for another reason?"

"No, I needed another book."

Mike looked past her at the table and seat. "Where is it?"

"I didn't buy one."

"Read them all, did you?"

She chuckled, that disingenuous noise she made when she'd been found out. "Nothing interested me. No big deal." She headed for the back of the car. "C'mon Mike. I'm sure Henry needs to get back to work."

Mike followed her, but she didn't fool him. Not for one minute. Not to say she never fooled him, but this time, he was on to her.

He just wished he knew what she'd gotten herself involved in.

+++++

In response to the invitation from the railway police at the next train station, Carly and Mike waited in the small depot to answer questions about her allegation of the man she saw thrown from the train. She turned the incident over and over in her mind, struggling to recall details which might aid the police in their investigation. Apart from dark profiles of two men struggling and one man stepping back into the car, nothing surfaced. So far, she'd managed to defer Mike's questions by claiming she was tired and would rather go through it once when the police arrived, but he wouldn't be put off much longer.

A younger man in a dark blue uniform approached, the overhead lighting reflecting off the badge on his chest and his regulation police-style cap. He nodded to each in turn. "Mr. Turnquist. Mrs. Turnquist. I'm Tom Cook, railway police."

Mike shook the man's hand. "Sorry to drag you out so late at night."

"No problem. I'm always happy to look into a passenger's concerns. Part of the job." He gestured toward a small room off the main lobby area. "Shall we go to my office?"

Carly stood and followed him, with Mike close behind. Very close. So close, in fact, she felt her husband's breath on the back of her neck, and while under other circumstances she'd have found that incredibly sexy, now was not the time.

Tom Cook led the way into the room, walked around his desk, and indicated two chairs on the other side. "Please."

Feeling like she'd been called to the principal's office, she sat. Mike scooted his chair several inches closer and grasped her hand. His touch lent her courage, and she was glad he was there.

Even though he was likely going to explode when he learned why.

Cook folded his hands and looked to Mike. "So I understand you saw two men fighting on the train?"

Mike shook his head. "Not me. My wife did."

She breathed a sigh of relief. At least he believed her. "Yes. Me."

Chief Cook nodded and pulled a sheet of paper toward him. "You wouldn't believe the forms we have to fill in when somebody wants to make a report." He looked up, his pen poised in mid-air. "Whenever you're ready."

Carly leaned forward. "Like I said, I saw two men fighting, and one man went over the side."

Cook scratched a few words then paused. "Let's start at the beginning. Name?"

She sighed. This was going to take forever. She glanced at Mike, who relaxed in his chair, arms crossed, eyes drooping.

If he starts snoring. . .

She replied to the railway detective's introductory questions of name and contact information, but stopped when he asked about level of education and employment. "What difference does that make to what I saw?"

He smiled and set his pen on the desk. "You'd be surprised. Folks who don't work but stay home all day watching True Crime TV or Perry Mason think they know all there is to know about crime and the law. So when they see something, what they've seen on television tends to color their evidence."

She huffed. "I am far too busy to sit around watching trashy daytime television."

At this, Mike roused. "But you do love those prime time forensics shows."

"But those are real, Mike. Just last week, they showed how—" She paused at the slight lift to the corner of his mouth. "You're teasing me."

He straightened. "Yes, I am." He patted her arm then turned to the officer. "Proceed."

"Education?"

"College graduate. Forensic accountant. I look for—"

The chief interrupted. "Yes, I know. I have a niece who does that. She works for the FBI. We kind of joke about it at family gatherings. She's always looking for a mystery."

Mike nodded. "Just like Carly."

She mock-punched her husband's arm. It was one thing for him to say that, quite another to agree with a complete stranger. "I wasn't looking for a mystery on this train, Mike."

"Like you weren't looking for a mystery on the plane?"

"That was different. That woman killed her husband."

"And you just happened to see her do it."

"Well, it's not like I knew what she was planning. You make it sound like I let her kill the poor old man."

The chief stood. "Wait. I feel like I'm at a tennis match watching you ping-pong the ball back and forth." He sat. "What does the dead man on the plane have to do with the two men on the train?"

Mike sat back again. "Nothing. Just an example of her looking for mysteries."

"Not fair. I didn't look for a mystery on the train. I was simply standing at the window to get some fresh air."

"You were supposed to be on your way to the gift shop to get another book. I don't know why. You'd already read four since we've been on the train."

The chief piped in. "Mysteries?"

She glared at him and his smile slipped. "Why would I waste time reading anything else? It's good research to see where criminals try to hide things from detection."

Cook nodded. "Tell you what. I'll be back in a minute. Let's take a quick break and draw a few breaths."

He stood and exited the room, leaving Carly and Mike in silence.

But not for long.

After about thirty seconds, she shrugged the kinks out of her shoulders, releasing the tension. "That man is hard on the nerves."

Mike chuckled. "He'd probably say the same thing about you."

"He probably already is. Telling somebody what a crazy woman he has to deal with. Who wants to answer every question with another question."

"So when he comes back, just answer his questions so we can get out of here. Our train already went on without us, and I don't want to miss the next one."

Carly checked her reflection in the window behind the chief's desks and patted a couple of stray locks of hair into place. "I'm so looking forward to getting to Anne's, sleeping in a real bed, showering in a full-size shower."

Mike waggled his eyebrows in her direction. "Maybe she has a shower with room for two."

Carly knew where this was going. Well, two could play that game. "Maybe she does. If so, you're welcome to invite whoever you like to share your shower with you. Me, I'm showering alone."

His shoulders fell and he clasped a hand to his chest. "Oh, my broken heart. When did the romance die?"

She shoved him playfully. "Romance, nothing. Privacy, everything. After racing across the country for four days where I haven't had room to change my mind alone, I need me space."

Mike looped his arm across her shoulders and pulled her close. "I know. Just teasing."

And that's where she would have been happy to spend the night, snuggling with Mike.

Except Tom Cook chose that moment to return.

He set his paper on the desk. "So, Carly Turnquist, forensic accountant. Seems you've been involved in a number of criminal investigations. Ones in which you always seem to figure prominently."

She sat up straight. "It's not like I was the criminal."

"No, but you always seem to be in the wrong place at the wrong time."

"I'll have you know I was in the right place at the right time when I saved my boss from being cooked alive in a furnace."

He scanned the page in front of him. "Right. I see that."

Mike laid a hand on her arm, and she clamped her mouth shut as he leaned forward. "Chief, I'm sure a call to the police chief in Bear Cove, Maine, will straighten all this up."

"Already called him. Roused him from his bed. He wasn't happy." Cook looked at her. "You can probably expect some hard feelings over that, but it couldn't be helped."

Great. Just what she needed. Chief Donovan upset with her through no fault of her own. She sighed. "Are you going to throw me in the hoosegow?"

Cook sighed. "We don't use that old word for jail anymore."

"Then can we leave?"

"Not yet. Got to get the details of what you saw."

She crossed her arms over her chest. "Really? Why bother? I'm simply a nosy old woman who pokes into places where she doesn't belong."

Cook held up one hand. "Don't get me wrong. Just because the chief wasn't happy about being roused at two in the morning doesn't mean you're in trouble. Rather, he encouraged me to listen carefully to what you say, because you're more often right than wrong. Said you sometimes get the details wrong, but your ability to jump to conclusions on very little evidence is astounding. So he said."

"Jump to conclusions? Well, I never—"

Another touch from Mike. "I think the chief meant that as a compliment." He looked to Cook. "Please, ask your questions."

Over the next twenty minutes, Carly explained—and in some cases, elaborated—on what she'd seen through the window. How she'd managed to see it at all—her train was stopped at the siding. Why she was there—on her way to the gift shop and saw the movement. Details—not much, except the impression that there were two men, struggling. And one man straightened and returned to the car on his left. No, she didn't see the man fall. No, they were facing away from her, toward the woods side of the tracks. No, she didn't hear any voices. No, she didn't see the beginning of the fight. No, she didn't know why they were fighting. All she saw was the foot as the train moved away.

At the conclusion of the interview, she sat back, exhausted. "I can't think any more tonight. Please say we're done."

The chief finished with his notes and stood. "Let me check on one more thing and I'll be right back."

She laid her head on Mike's shoulder and sighed. "Are we done?"

He stroked her cheek with a finger. "Almost. And the next train comes through at five, so we won't have long to wait."

"Good. I could do with a cup of coffee and a snack."

The door opened and Cook returned and sat. "I wanted to check with the other offices. Searchers have not located a body."

The words slammed into Carly's chest like a pile driver, pushing the air from her lungs. From the room.

From her universe.

No. Not a repeat of the bank robbery she saw, which nobody else saw.

Except that time, she did. Despite what anybody else said, there *had* been a robbery.

Sort of.

Her next question was useless—she knew before she even uttered the words. "Are you sure?"

What did she expect him to say? No, sorry, made a mistake. We did find a body.

He blinked a couple of times as he held her gaze. "No body means no body."

Mike stood and offered her his hand. "Right. Time to get something to eat and catch our train." He turned to Chief Cook. "We are free to leave, right?"

The chief indicated the doorway. "Absolutely. Sorry we couldn't help."

Oh, he'd helped plenty. He'd made them miss their train. He'd made them wait in this drafty depot for hours. He'd kept them awake all night. And now she'd have to settle for a greasy burger or something which would probably make her sick and would ruin the rest of her working vacation and—

She stopped in her tracks. Was that quiche she detected? Light, flaky pastry with just the right combination of ham, peppers, onions, and eggs? And fresh-brewed coffee?

Things were looking up.

Finding a dead man and identifying a murderer could wait.

Chapter 3

A full tummy overrode the effects of three cups of coffee and lulled Carly to sleep almost before their train pulled out of the station. Mike smiled at her peaceful expression.

He'd love to see her like that more often.

Not fretting over missing bodies or missing money or nasty divorce cases.

Why she had to look for a mystery everywhere she went was beyond him.

He pulled out his laptop and tapped his fingers on the tray table while waiting for it to boot up. The rolling landscape unfolded through the window like a giant mural. Cattle, sheep, and horses grazed in fields with antelope and deer. White tails flicked as the deer took notice of the train speeding past, but the antelope gave little indication, apart from a few raised heads.

A cowboy on horseback urged a flock of sheep through a gate, while a couple of sheepdogs nipped at the heels of the stragglers. Wyoming seemed prime sheep country, although why, Mike wasn't certain. Perhaps he'd find time research that while his wife worked part of their vacation.

Except if he knew her—which he did—she wasn't likely to settle for looking for hidden assets.

No siree, she'd be looking for murders and bodies.

Mike pulled out his file containing copies of the client specs regarding the program they wanted him to write. The employees of Financial Freedom Inc owned a hundred percent of the company, with profits paid in the form of dividends. Mike liked this idea—a reduction in taxes and the owners knew the profitability of the business on a timely basis.

He chuckled. This format should ensure the employees worked hard to generate income and reduce expenses to maximize profits and their proportional share. However, he doubted this concept would work. In his experience, there were two kinds of employees—those who generated income, and those who generated expenses. The former kept the latter in a job.

So he'd been hired to write a program to measure individual and group productivity against expenses, so profits were more equitably allocated. The result, in effect, would rewrite the ownership agreement, which the bylaws permitted once every five years. The first term expired next year, in 2005. This program would determine whether to keep the current system or make changes.

But something wasn't setting right in his mind. His job involved taking the original allocation program and writing in new modules for tracking income and expenses. A stickler for details, Mike's habit was to create a virtual version of the original program and run it under a test shell to see what it did in different circumstances.

And this one accessed credit card accounts, emulated recurring charges, and transferred those funds to offshore accounts.

Strange.

As a tracking program, designed to determine how much an individual received in dividends, this program should not have access to accounts outside the company structure.

He closed the lid on his computer and sat back to ponder the situation.

Maybe a bug existed in the program, or perhaps an accounts receivable account linked to this program in some way. But why? He couldn't fathom. Did they send him two programs that ran in tandem? That didn't make sense, either. An allocation program, similar to a payroll program, would pay monies out, not attempt to withdraw funds.

He shut the computer down as the train whistle sounded, alerting passengers and employees they neared the Danforth station. He nudged Carly until she opened her eyes and blinked at him. "We're here."

"Huh?" She straightened and rubbed her eyes. "Where?"

"Danforth. Anne. Remember?"

She smiled. "Right. I knew that." She quirked her chin toward his computer. "How is that program coming along?"

"You know how it is. I do most of my programming with my eyes shut."

She elbowed him in the ribs. "Right. Accompanied by snoring."

"It's how I work best."

This particular jab was one of her favorites. She always insisted there was no way he could program while sleeping on the sofa or in his lawn chair. To which he replied that he did his best work in that position.

Carly smoothed down her wrinkled shirt and fluffed her hair with her fingers. "When I called Anne last night, she said not to worry about getting here late. She'd pick us up and we could start the day fresh." She sighed. "Right. Fresh as a three-day-old fish."

Mike pulled her close. "No worries. You can always get a shower and have a nap when we get to Anne's." He waggled his eyebrows. "I could help you take a nap. And a shower."

She pushed him away. "Michael Turnquist, you're incorrigible."

"Not incorrigible. Insatiable when it comes to my beautiful wife."

She shook her head. "Not a chance. I have assets to find, and you have a program to write."

He sighed. "Hopefully we'll get some time to relax and—um, nap while we're here. It is supposed to be a working vacation, remember."

"Right." She stood as the train slowed to a stop. "Working for me, vacation for you."

"Doesn't seem much like a vacation for either of us. I still can't figure out what this client is trying to do with the program. Might take me a few days to sort that out."

Carly shrugged into her light jacket and slung her oversized purse over one shoulder. "Sounds good."

He sighed again. She wasn't listening to one word he said.

Which meant she was already off and running on something else.

Most likely related to what she thought she saw last night.

Some vacation this was going to be.

+++++

Carly stepped down from the train and scanned the platform. Would she even recognize Anne Torbin after all these years? College was a long time ago. Almost— she shuddered. She didn't want to count that high.

A woman with long graying hair, wearing a tea-length denim skirt, checkered shirt, and cowboy hat, waited near the depot doors. When Carly's feet hit the wooden surface, the woman took a couple of steps toward her and raised a hand in greeting.

Through sleep-deprived eyes that probably resembled a raccoon's, Carly squinted then hurried to close the distance between them. "Anne. My goodness. You haven't changed a bit."

Anne pulled her into a close hug, patting her back several times before releasing her. Anne's hugs were one of the reasons she and Carly were such good friends. Carly felt so safe with her friend and college roommate. "Carly, I'd recognize you anywhere."

They held each other at arm's length and surveyed the passage of time on the other.

Carly broke their appraisal by turning to indicate Mike. "This is my husband, Mike. Mike, Anne."

Mike bowed slightly and offered his hand, but instead of shaking it, Anne used it to pull him into her arms. Over her shoulder, Mike's eyes widened as he begged Carly with his expression to get him out of this, but she simply smiled.

Served him right for not believing her when she told him about the man falling off the train.

Sure, he'd eventually come around, but maybe next time, he'd be quicker to credit her with good eyesight and a not-so-vivid imagination.

After about fifteen seconds, however, she took pity on him and patted Anne on the shoulder. "We're really looking forward to spending time in bustling downtown Danforth."

Anne released Mike, who filled his hands quickly with their suitcases. Carly smiled at him. He was a quick study. Much more difficult to hug someone whose arms were full.

"Forgive me. I was so excited to see you again, Carly." She turned to Mike on her other side. "And meet you, Mike, that I forgot you might be tired from your trip." She looped an arm over Carly's shoulder. "Tell me all about this delay."

Carly groaned inwardly, but Anne had been persistent in college and didn't look like she'd changed much in the intervening years. She gave a quick replay of how she'd seen the fight, saw the man go overboard, reported the incident, and was treated like a crazy woman while being interrogated all night.

She concluded her story with, "And if it wasn't for the great food at that last station, I don't know what I would have done."

Anne's eyes crinkled with laughter. "Don't forget their exquisite coffee."

"You're right. And their coffee."

Anne nodded toward the depot building as they headed for the parking lot. "The diner here isn't half so good. Sometimes I take an afternoon and ride the train back up the line just to check out the café and see what's new on their menu." She leaned in closer, smelling slightly of lavender. Anne's favorite scent. "I've been known to borrow a recipe for the B&B."

"Sounds like a marvelous way to spend an afternoon."

Anne's smile slipped. "I don't get to do it as often as I used to. Or as often as I'd like to." Her face brightened. "Maybe you and I could take the trip while you're here."

"Sounds like a plan."

Anne led the way to a newer pickup, and Mike deposited their suitcases and computer bags in the back. She indicated the spacious four-door cab of the truck. "Organize yourselves. It's literally a three-minute drive."

Carly slid into the rear seat. "I'll sit in back. I was the best backset driver in college."

Anne laughed. "You were in college, that's for sure."

Mike turned in his seat. "Sounds like there's a story behind the backseat driver thing."

Anne nodded. "There is."

Carly leaned over the seat and laid a hand on her friend's arm. "Don't tell him all the stories on the first day, Anne."

Anne laughed again. "Okay. I'll limit myself to one per day."

Mike leaned back and groaned. "If you do that, we'll need to stay here at least a year."

Anne touched her chin with a forefinger. "Now, that's a thought. Maybe you will."

Carly sat back. She wasn't afraid of running out of things to talk about.

She wanted to censor the stories.

Mike didn't need to know *everything* about her.

Three minutes later, they pulled up to the rear of a large Victorian-style house. The forest green paint with burgundy and cream accents was a delightful contrast to the rather ordinary bungalows and craftsmen-style houses on the street. Lilac bushes, in full bloom, encircled the house like a shawl, releasing their delicious scent and coloring the garden. The matching garage—formerly a carriage house as Anne explained—housed more vehicles.

Anne pointed out a smaller version of her own pickup. "I'm happy to drive you wherever you want to go, but if you'd like to explore on your own, or if I'm not available, you're welcome to take the little grasshopper."

Carly chuckled at the name. The pale green mini-truck did remind her of the insect. "Is that a service you extend to all your guests?"

Anne nodded. "Most travel here by train, and there isn't anywhere to rent a car in Danforth, so I like to offer little amenities where I can. I can't compete with the larger resorts, so this is a homey touch. Like borrowing the car from your dad."

Mike pulled the suitcases from the bed of the truck while Carly hefted their computer bags. They followed Anne across the yard, scattering chickens in their wake. One particularly stubborn bird, however, refused to give way to Carly, and they stared at each other for several long seconds before Carly gave up and went around the creature.

Anne chuckled. "Don't let Gertrude get the best of you. Threaten her with the stew pot. Don't know why, but it always works."

"Do you raise them for the eggs?"

Anne nodded. "And the stew pot, eventually."

Carly grimaced. "I've never personally known my dinner. Especially not its name."

Anne opened the old-fashioned screen door and held it ajar for them. "Seems wrong not to name them. And up here, most everything has the potential to become dinner. Like the line in the old Clint Eastwood movie, when he was asked why he called his horse, Horse. He said he didn't like to name anything he might end up eating."

Mike stepped through the doorway, but Carly paused and surveyed the yard. Chickens pecked at the ground. A small hutch near the carriage house held several rabbits. A goat or two occupied a lean-to in the far corner of the property. If a horse and a cow had sauntered around the corner, she wouldn't have been surprised.

She turned to Anne. "I guess I wasn't picturing such a rural setting. I really did think we'd be in the middle of downtown Danforth."

Anne indicated the yard. "We are, but downtown Danforth is in the middle of nowhere. Except for the train depot, I don't think this town would have made it. It's been here since the 1880's, but it didn't get its first church until 1925. Before that, everybody went up the road or down the road on Sundays."

"Hard to imagine a place without a reason for being." Carly followed her friend into the house, pausing to allow her eyes to adjust to the darker interior. "Something smells good."

"That's dinner. I have a lady who comes in and takes care of meals, cleans rooms, does a little housekeeping around the common areas. That way, I can see to the business, the animals, and the guests."

"Goodness. Sounds like you're busy. Do you ever get to take a vacation?"

Anne's lopsided smile communicated more than her words. "If I want to take a day here or there, I have a neighbor who looks after the animals. But I don't take off much time."

Narrow wood planking floors spread before them, gleaming with care and polish. The back door entered through a mudroom into the kitchen, and Carly glimpsed tall wooden cupboards stretching toward the twelve-foot ceilings. Modern appliances and fixtures populated the area, as well as a granite countertop and island that wasn't original to the house.

Through the dining room, past a living area and into a hallway leading to the front of the house, however, other original touches remained, including brass light fixtures now converted to electric, a quaint runner of Oriental design on the floor, and pineapple-shaped finials on the stair posts.

Carly paused and turned around in a circle. "This is truly lovely, Anne. I think it's great how you managed to modernize the necessary while keeping so much original."

Anne smiled. "It's been my pride and joy for many years. Before I married Gary, even. Thankfully, the house isn't considered a marital asset. Only the appreciation is. I paid for all the upgrades and maintenance myself, so I get to deduct that from any increase in value." Tears filled her friend's eyes. "I might have made a huge mistake in marrying him, but I didn't make any mistakes in the pre-nup. My attorney says I have an iron-clad agreement."

Carly laid a hand on Anne's arm. "I'm so sorry you are going through this."

"I know. Thank you." Anne indicated the stairs. "Your room is on the second floor."

Mike set the suitcases at the foot of the stairs. "Do you have other guests?"

"Not right now. I didn't want anybody here in case Gary caused a scene. He just moved out last week, but he's been hanging around. Another couple arrives in a day or so. They weren't positive when last I spoke with them."

Carly's mind cast back to her own unhappy first marriage, thanking her lucky stars her husband died before things got too ugly. Anne's first marriage was good but her husband died young of a heart attack. She remarried the same year as Carly and Mike, but according to her Christmas cards, it sounded like they were never truly happy.

The complete opposite to Carly's own experience.

Mike hefted the suitcases then waggled his eyebrows. "More privacy."

Carly's cheeks heated. It was one thing to insinuate his intentions when they were alone, but in front of her friend. . .a friend who was going through a divorce. Well, she'd get back at him. "Right. More privacy to work. To program. To *snore.*"

Mike glanced from her to Anne and back again. His smile slipped. "Right. Exactly what I meant."

She tossed him the *Gotcha!* look she'd perfected, and he laughed as he headed up the stairs. She followed with Anne close behind.

Once again, the second floor retained much of its old-fashioned charm. Their room, the first on the right of the stairway, looked out over the yard. The scent of lilacs wafted in through the open window covered with lace curtains. The double bed, complete with four posters and a handmade crazy quilt, looked comfy enough to collapse on right now.

About the only thing that looked out of place was a vaguely familiar motel-style print over the bed.

Then again, what did she know about artwork? Not much.

Anne opened a door on one wall. "This is the walk-in closet and master bath. You should have enough towels and supplies, but if you need more, there is a linen closet in the hallway with extras."

Carly peeked in. She liked a bathroom with all the modern conveniences such as running hot and cold water, a jet tub, and a high efficiency, dual-flush toilet. Latte-colored tiles covered the walls and floor, and cream-colored fixtures gleamed in the sunlight from a window near the door. An oversized mirror ran the length of the vanity, and the other side of the bath held an oversized shower stall with matching showerheads. A jet tub big enough for two nestled nearby.

Great. If this bathroom didn't give Mike ideas, nothing will.

Anne tugged at a corner of the duvet. "I hope you'll be comfortable here." She gestured to a desk next to a window. "Mike, I knew you'd be working, so I had a desk moved in. Hopefully the view won't distract you."

Mike crossed the room and set his laptop bag on the surface then peeked out through white lace curtains. "I see what you mean. I can see a fishing spot from here."

Anne laughed. "And it's no catch-and-release pond, either. You get to keep—and eat—the fish. Bring 'em home, and I'll fry 'em up for you."

Mike tossed Carly a smile. "I might have to spend some time on that lake programming."

Carly groaned. "Sounds like an excuse to go fishing."

Anne stepped toward the door. "Hopefully the other table will work for you, Carly."

"It all looks great. Thanks, Anne."

"Well, I know you had a rough night. How about we meet in a couple of hours for coffee in the kitchen?"

"Around ten? Sounds like a plan."

Anne paused, her hand on the original cut glass doorknob. "And if you ask, I'll tell you about the legend that there are bodies buried in the basement."

Carly perked up, all thoughts of a nap evaporating. "Bodies? In the basement?"

"Thought that would catch your attention. More to follow. Get some rest." She looked toward Mike. "We have secure internet. The login and password information are in the top drawer of the desk."

"You've thought of everything, Anne." Mike sat on the bed and patted the cover. "Rest, Carly. I'll set the alarm on my phone. We'll see you at ten, Anne."

"Mike, we don't need an alarm. It's almost eight now."

Despite her words, he went ahead and punched in numbers. "I'll give us fifteen minutes to wake up and get downstairs."

Carly couldn't—or didn't want—to rest right now. She had hidden assets swirling in her head, not to mention bodies in the basement. How could anybody think of sleeping?

A soft snore came from the bed. He lay on the bed, eyes closed, his phone still clutched in one hand. Maybe he was programming. Although, she doubted it. No matter what he said.

Still, she could put her feet up for a few minutes as she puzzled through what she knew about Anne's situation. She'd think through some strategies, make a list of who to contact, decide what documents she'd like to look at. . .

Chapter 4

The fire alarm sounded, buzzing and screaming in her ear, and Carly bolted up from the bed. Mike. Where was Mike?

When she finally regained her senses, she realized it wasn't the fire alarm, but Mike's phone, buzzing at her from the table on his side of the bed.

But he wasn't there.

Sounds of running water came from the bathroom.

Right. She drew a deep breath and exhaled.

The alarm she didn't think they'd need.

Which apparently she did.

Now she wished she'd had him set the alarm for thirty minutes so she could have showered, too.

Carly followed the off-key singing and torrential downpour melody into the bathroom and stood before the mirror. Her hair, now grown out to shoulder-length as she waited for inspiration on a new hairstyle, lay flat on one side and ruffled to frizziness on the other. Her shirt was wrinkled—she'd change that, although her stretchy jeans were okay for now. She could change for dinner.

Maybe a little mascara and a hint of lip-gloss would brighten her appearance.

By the time Mike stepped out of the shower, a bath towel wrapped around his middle, his skin still pink from his choice of super-hot shower, she was heading for the bedroom to change her top. His drunken caterpillar eyebrows tried to hypnotize her to bend to his will, but she waved off his advances.

"Later, Mike."

He groaned. "But we've been on a train for two days, plus a night in a train station. This is our first time alone since we left Portland."

She glanced at the clock. "We're going to be late."

"I don't think Anne would mind."

Carly's cheeks colored. "Since we can't claim we were stuck in traffic, she'd know what we were up to."

"Well, we're married. She shouldn't have a problem with it. She's probably done it a few times herself."

Carly tossed a clean shirt and underwear to her husband. Her incorrigible husband. "Get dressed. We'll have plenty of time later."

Mike's groan would have fit right in with an amputation without anesthetic, but he returned the towel to the bathroom and came back, then ran a comb through his greying hair. Carly buttoned her shirt and spent a few minutes setting up her laptop and connecting to the internet, which was even faster than their service at home. She checked emails while he dressed.

Mike stood behind her and rubbed her shoulders. "Ready?"

"Yes." She stood and turned to face him. "But first things first."

She stood on tiptoes to kiss him, resting her hands on his shoulders. He leaned in, pressing the full length of his body into hers, and they held that position for a long minute.

When they came up for breath, his eyes twinkled. "Sure you won't change your mind?"

She pushed him away. "Just wanted to remind you what's waiting for you. Later."

He clasped her hand. "Then let's hurry through this day so we get back before we're exhausted."

She laughed. "I know you too well, Mike. You are never too tired for *that*."

Giggling like schoolchildren, they descended the carpeted stairway to the main foyer.

Anne called to them. "Down the hallway to the kitchen. It's a lovely day. We'll sit in the sunroom."

A short hall connected the foyer to the kitchen. Off the foyer were two doors, one leading to a formal living room, the other a parlor-type room. The library, dark with wood and deep blue curtains, upholstery, and carpets, books lining the walls. A room she'd choose to spend a lot of time in. She lingered there for an extra moment, savoring the smell of old paper.

Past the library, a formal dining room, a pantry, and the open kitchen. Sunlight brightened the room, as did the pale yellow paint and duck and chicken accessories. A black and white tile floor, reminiscent of the original linoleum pattern, created a sense of symmetry. The only concessions to modernity were the stainless steel appliances and the chic pot-filler faucet.

An electric percolator bubbled on the counter, emitting coffee-scented steam.

And a tray of cinnamon rolls warmed in the oven.

Carly's nose tipped her off to that fact.

Anne stood from her seat at a white wrought-iron table in the sunroom. Resembling a greenhouse, with glass on all sides and the roof, the room would be inviting even on a cold winter's day, warmed by the fire pit in the corner when the sun wasn't strong enough.

Carly poured coffee for Mike and herself, doctored each according to their preferences—double cream for him and single for her—then carried their mugs to the table, which was already littered with files, statements, and correspondence.

Anne's lopsided smile saddened her. "If you're hungry, I could get you a cinnamon roll."

Mike pushed Carly's chair in for her. "Let me. You ladies can get started."

Anne's mouth drooped a notch further before she straightened her shoulders and pasted on a smile. "Sounds wonderful. Thanks, Mike."

Carly recognized the signs of putting a good face on a situation.

She'd done it often enough herself.

Before she met Mike.

Carly sipped her coffee then smiled at Anne. "This is a lovely house."

Anne nodded. "It really is my dream. After my first husband died, I wanted something that would last. Not just a new car or a vacation. Something real. I came through Danforth on the way to visit friends on the west coast, and this house was on the market. It was such a great price that it didn't really matter whether I ever made a go of it as a B&B." She toyed with her coffee cup. "But surprisingly, many people like to vacation in out-of-the-way places. I'm booked as much as I want. Maybe a little more."

Mike set a plate before her, and Carly's mouth watered. She smiled her thanks at him.

He cleared his throat softly. "I'm going to take my coffee and cinnamon roll to the room, if you don't mind. Thought I could get a head start on my project."

Anne tipped her head. "Don't let all our girlie talk scare you off."

He patted Carly's shoulder. "It would take more than girlie talk to scare me. But seriously, if I can get this job off my plate, Carly and I will have more time to spend with you."

Carly rubbed his hand. "Sounds like a good plan. Off you go. I'll see you later."

Mike balanced a plate with two cinnamon rolls and fruit on his oversized coffee mug, and headed up the stairs, humming his never-ending song.

Carly waited until he was out of earshot. "So why do you need me?"

Anne's smile slipped. "Things haven't been good between Gary and me for a while. I think I mentioned it in my Christmas letter to you."

"You didn't say much, but I suspected as much." Carly covered Anne's hand with her own. "And I went through some of the same things with my first marriage, so you didn't have to leave much of a trail of bread crumbs for me to follow along."

"He told me about six months ago that he didn't want to stay. I said fine, I'd help him pack his stuff."

Carly spluttered on the coffee she was sipping. "How did he take that?"

"You know the saying 'his jaw dropped'?"

Carly nodded, a picture building in her mind.

"Well, his did. I thought he'd crack it on the floor." Anne leaned in. "We'd had this discussion several times in the past, and I always begged him to stay. Which he did, promising things would be better." She sat back. "But this time I was done."

"Had something specific changed?"

Anne nodded. "Money was missing from the bank account. The cash box was always short. He said it was to pay for materials for repairs on the house. But it was too much money over a long time. And then I got the credit card bills and the materials were on that."

"Sounds like he was skimming from you."

"Stealing is the word I used, and he didn't like it. Said it was our money. But when I asked why his paycheck wasn't our money, too, he blew up."

"Why didn't he leave then?"

"My guess is he hadn't taken as much as he was hoping for."

"Did he bring assets into the marriage?"

Anne nodded, toying with the saltshaker. "He had a large chunk of cash from selling his business before he moved here. And he had one or two paintings. Nothing much."

"You said he worked?"

"Past tense. When he filed for divorce, he quit his job because he said he wasn't going to pay me maintenance. I didn't want support from him. I just wanted him out of my life. Forever. But before that, he worked over at the train depot as a ticket agent and maintenance man. Made a decent living."

Carly stood. "Okay. Let's see the papers you have. Bank statements. Financial records. Tax returns. Whatever you have that shows Gary's assets and income."

Anne refilled her cup. "Sounds good. I have it all here in boxes in the dining room. I'll set you up there since I don't plan to use that room this week." She snapped her fingers. "Oh, I just remembered. The other couple called. They're checking in the day after tomorrow. Once they get here, we'll move you somewhere else."

"Great. I like to do my preliminary work with pencil and paper, then I'll transfer it to my computer for the final report. After that, I can move to the table upstairs. I'll just need the boxes handy so I can refer to them as needed."

Anne chuckled. "You don't need to give me a report. Just tell me what to do."

"As a forensic accountant, my report can be used as evidence in the divorce trial."

Her friend shuddered. "I hope it doesn't come to that. I guess I was thinking I'd just tell him what you found, and he'd back down and tell the court the truth."

"And if he doesn't, you'll need my report. I don't have to do a report, but if I start with the notion that I will, I've already laid the groundwork."

Anne led the way to the dining room table. "I put pencils and paper there, along with accounting paper, legal note pads, erasers, and a calculator for you to use."

"You thought of everything except two important things."

Her friend's brow lifted in question.

"Coffee and cinnamon rolls."

Anne laughed. "Coming right up."

Carly settled into a chair that faced away from the garden outside. No point in looking for distractions. No, she'd work diligently to earn her keep and to help her friend.

Although she'd never met Gary Torbin, already she didn't like him.

And Diligent was her middle name.

+++++

Mike paced the bedroom, his mind whirling. The more time he spent on this program, the less sense it made. While the intricacy of the charges had raised his curiosity, the accounting trail was as convoluted as a plate of spaghetti, and about as difficult to unravel.

Credit card charges amounting to hundreds of thousands of dollars a month. Refunds amounting to just a few thousand. Perhaps credit card customers who noticed the charge and challenged it? In many cases, a customer's only recourse was to cancel their credit card, which most people were reluctant to do, at least in his experience.

The strange thing was why he'd received a copy of the main program with this particular hidden module. Had he been sent the wrong code by mistake? Or did the company have a more sinister motive? Were they planning to make him a scapegoat if found out? Did they intend to lay the blame at his doorstep?

Only one way to find out.

He returned to the desk and searched through the folder for the contact information for Philip Osgood, the man who'd hired him. If anybody knew, he would.

He punched in the numbers on his cell phone and resumed pacing. While he waited for an answer, he realized he was doing what he accused his wife of doing so many times: jumping to conclusions without enough information.

Four rings. Five rings.

Well, he'd get the information. Straight from the horse's mouth.

Seven rings. Eight.

A click, and he drew a breath to ask for Osgood, when a voice message filled his ear, telling him they were sorry but they couldn't get to the phone and for him to leave a message.

"Mr. Osgood, Mike Turnquist here. I received the program code. Thank you. I have a couple of questions about some things that just don't add up. Give me a call at your earliest convenience. Thanks."

Mike included his cell number, then disconnected.

Osgood would call and explain the mystery, and Mike could continue the job.

Unlike Carly, he believed in simple explanations.

Now, time to relax. He downed the last mouthful of cinnamon roll, polished off the last of the grapes, and washed it all down with his tepid coffee.

The lake—and a fishing pole—called his name.

+++++

Carly sat back in her seat and studied the columnar sheets before her.

Something didn't add up.

And no, she hadn't made a mathematical error. She could do long addition in her head.

But based on Anne's meticulous records of income from guests and expenses for upkeep, supplies, utilities, and the myriad other details involved in running a bed and breakfast—wait. Quality pillows and towels didn't cost that much. A lot more money should remain than showed in the bank account.

The money Gary took—stole—wasn't a trifle amount. He was closing in on a hundred thousand dollars very quickly.

No wonder Anne wanted him gone for good.

Included in the materials Anne provided was an inventory of long-term assets such as the house itself, furnishings, and artwork she'd purchased both to decorate and use as a longer term investment. Carly pulled the first page toward her, a list of every item and the room it resided in.

She scanned the list. Dining room. Cherry sideboard. Check. Antique brass chandelier. Check. Antique rose patterned Oriental carpet. Carly glanced at the floor. Check. Original numbered bronze sculpture of "Long Road Home" by Remington. Carly rose and picked up the somewhat familiar piece, turning it over to check the number.

Strange. It didn't feel heavy enough to be a bronze. She scratched at the bottom surface with a fingernail.

Brass-colored paint flecked off, revealing a white surface.

Some kind of resin, by the looks and feel of it.

She checked the list again. Maybe she'd read it wrong. Nope. Dining room. She glanced at the object. "Long Road Home" inscribed on the brass plaque on the front.

Somebody meant to hide the theft of the original.

Carly skimmed through a second inventory done just two years ago for an insurance assessment which listed the value of the original at ten thousand dollars.

Did her friend plan to scam the insurance company? Why would she? She gained no advantage by insuring a fake piece of artwork unless she planned to burn the house down—which she hadn't so far—or she intended to fake a burglary. Again, not so far.

So maybe Anne was right. Gary was stealing from her.

Only now, Carly discovered he was pilfering much more than just money.

She ran her finger down the most recent report and found the listing for the room she and Mike were staying in—the Laramie Room. Four-poster bed. Check. Matching dresser and side tables. Check. Norton.

She didn't think so.

Which is why the ugly print over the bed had struck her earlier as out of place and out of character.

Carly headed up the stairs and tiptoed into the room, not wanting to disturb Mike.

Except he wasn't there.

Well, she'd solve that mystery later.

For now, she wanted to know about the painting.

She climbed up onto the bed and squinted at the signature. Not only wasn't the painting of a western scene, it wasn't signed by anything even vaguely resembling Jim Norton's realism style.

She turned the painting over to reveal the back. Cheap cardboard instead of professional stretchers. She undid the cheap metal clasps and released the painting from the frame.

As she expected, it was a cheap print. On paper.

She'd have her hands full identifying everything he'd stolen.

And when she did, Gary best be watching over his shoulder.

+++++

Mike tossed his pen on the desk and sat back.

He'd spent an hour strolling around the lake, a fishing pole in hand, looking for the perfect spot.

Which he never found.

His body might be out in the beautiful Wyoming countryside, but his mind was still back in his room, tethered to the conundrum of the program like a buoy tossing in a storm.

The only solution was to postpone fishing for a day when his could give it his full attention, instead of worrying about why things still didn't add up with Philip Osgood and Financial Freedom Inc.

He chuckled at the thought. Things not balancing were definitely in Carly's department, not his.

He pulled his assignment folder closer and leafed through the pages. He must have missed something. Misread a spec. Misinterpreted a request.

But no. The words were clear and concise—but the outcome wasn't.

In that case, he must be making the mistake. Something in his coding was initiating an unexpected result.

That was the only answer.

He would find the problem and correct it.

Three hours later, he signed off the server and shut down his computer. He checked the time. Four-thirty Central time.

Osgood should have called him back by now. Well, he'd keep pestering until he got hold of somebody.

He keyed the numbers on his cell phone and waited for the call to connect. An automated voice with a slight Mid-west accent greeted him and invited him to leave a message. He gritted his teeth. As much as he loved programming and technology, he hated answering machines.

Once again, he left his name and phone number, then added for good measure, "I am truly troubled by the inconsistencies I'm seeing in the program results. I have double- and triple-checked my program, so I know the problem isn't there. I'm fairly certain there is a hidden module in the program that has migrated into my test version and is operating independently. Until I have some direction or explanation from you, I cannot move forward with the project. Call me immediately."

He repeated his number again for good measure, then disconnected.

If Philip Osgood didn't understand where Mike stood once he listened to this message, Mike was better off not working for him.

He slid back from the desk, stood, then stretched his arms over his head in a good stretch.

Time to do what he enjoyed third best in the world.

Programming was number two.

Eating—which he planned to do soon—was third.

And Carly was right—when it came to his number one favorite thing in the world, he was incorrigible.

+++++

Carly shook her head when the waiter offered her a second glass of wine, and he moved on to fill Anne's glass—for the fourth time. But who was counting?

Her friend's cheeks were pink, and her eyes shone. Under other circumstances—sans the alcohol—Carly would have considered her beautiful and vivacious. However, the falsely induced camaraderie echoed a mite too hollow for Carly's liking.

She set her napkin on the table and clasped Mike's hand. "So, Anne, I've spent some time today going over your books and statements."

Anne set her wine glass on the table, the base resting precariously on her knife. The red liquid sloshed over the edge, staining the white linen tablecloth. She giggled. "Silly me. Maybe Gary is right. I am such a klutz."

Carly touched the back of her friend's hand. "You are not a klutz. You're a successful businesswoman who has been under a lot of strain lately."

Anne sat back and dropped her hands into her lap. "I wish it was only lately, Carly."

Mike righted the glass. "Why don't you tell us what's going on?"

"Going on?" Anne shrugged. "I'm not sure. Things have gone missing. The

41

business is showing a loss when I know I've made a profit. Gary going on unexplained business trips. Charges on our credit cards. Withdrawals from our bank accounts." She paused and swallowed hard. "You've seen it, haven't you?"

Carly nodded. "I have. And I noticed something strange today."

Mike tipped his head in question. "Don't tell me another mystery?"

She swatted at his hand. "No. But I was going through an inventory you did a while back for insurance purposes. The painting listed as being in our room isn't there."

Anne's brow drew down. "What?"

"I've seen this kind of thing before. People purchase costly assets, do an inventory, increase their insurance coverage, then sell off the assets and claim they were stolen."

"You don't believe I did that, do you?"

"No. Usually when that happens, the theft or the fire happens soon because people like that aren't very patient or very smart. Your inventory was done almost two years ago. Besides, I know you."

Anne's mouth lifted in a half-smile. "I'd never think of doing something like that. It's—it's—"

"Illegal." Carly finished her friend's sentence, just as they used to do in college. "What else?"

Anne's shoulders slumped. "Nothing much."

"You mentioned that Gary said you're clumsy?"

Anne nodded. "Right."

Mike cleared his throat softly. "Excuse me, ladies, for a few minutes. I'll be right back."

Carly tossed him a grateful smile. He'd clued in that maybe Anne needed another girl-talk moment. "Don't get lost."

He planted a kiss on her cheek. "Don't worry about that. I've got a GPS programmed for you, babe."

Carly waved him off then turned back to Anne. "There is nothing to be ashamed about. My first marriage was no picnic. I often ran into doors or tripped on the stairs."

Now her friend's eyes shone from tears as one slipped down her cheek. "But my first was heaven."

"Not always, I suspect. But enough that you thought so." Carly offered her napkin to her friend. "Which can be a problem, too, if you set yourself up for unrealistic expectations."

Anne nodded and swiped at her nose. "That's what I thought at first, too. But then—"

"When did he start hitting you?"

Anne's hand went to her upper arm. "He didn't, at first. About six months after we were married, I said something—I don't even remember what it was—and he took it the wrong way and lost his temper. He pushed me against the wall and raised his fist to me." She pressed her lips together. "I was so scared he was going to hit me. Then he dropped his hand and smiled. Almost as if he wanted that reaction from me."

Carly's dinner soured in her stomach at the thought of what her friend had gone through. She felt as though she were reliving her own disastrous marriage where loathing had replaced love, and fear pervaded. "And he said he was sorry, didn't he?"

"Right. Swore it would never happen again, but I'd made him so mad. That's what he said. Made it my fault." Anne drew a deep, heaving breath. "But it did happen."

"It always does." Carly looked up. Mike peeked into the dining area from the hallway leading to the restrooms. "Would it be okay with you if Mike rejoined us?"

Anne nodded. "Of course. I trust him as much as I trust you."

Carly beckoned to her husband, crooking her finger in his direction. He rejoined them, and reached under the table to clasp her hand.

Carly turned back to Anne. "What happened next?"

"As a pre-marital asset, the house remained in my name. He wanted it put in joint title, but I resisted, which made him angry. But I didn't trust him. I suspected he was gambling or doing something that could jeopardize the title, so I finally agreed to add his name to the business bank account. I figured if he cleaned me out, that's the worst that could happen."

"But he wasn't satisfied with that, was he?"

"No. The abuse got worse. And my shame grew. I couldn't talk to anybody. Or felt I couldn't. He told me repeatedly it was all my fault. That I had no head for business. That he should take over our finances completely. He wanted me to sign a power of attorney, but I'd heard stories of wives being committed to a mental hospital so I didn't sign it. I changed my will to leave the house and my estate to an international ministry I support, and he was livid. Said I was stealing from him."

Carly sipped her water, composing her response in her head. "Because he thought yours was his, and his was his own?"

"He didn't have anything. That's the thing. I had the house and business, and he worked at the railway, when he worked. Which wasn't much." Anne shook her head. "I should have known. He seemed like a charming bad boy who just needed a woman's love to straighten him out. I was so lonely I didn't stop and think why he would want me."

Carly slapped the table. "Don't think that way. You're a beautiful, intelligent woman with a big heart and a great sense of humor. You could have any man."

Anne gestured around the room. "I don't exactly see them beating down my door."

"You would if they knew you were available."

"It's a small town, Carly. What you see is what you get."

Mike chuckled. "Let's get back on topic. You aren't looking for a husband yet. What happened once you gave him access to the bank account?"

"I thought things would change. If he saw I trusted him with the money, maybe he'd become more trustworthy. But that didn't happen. In fact, it got worse. He thought every phone call was a lover calling me. Every time I left the house, he believed I was meeting somebody." Her half-smile didn't fool Carly. "He seemed to think I'm attractive to other men. It became unbearable."

Carly knew how her friend felt. She'd gone through the same things. The two of them should write a book on being the poster children for wives of abusers. "When did you decide to divorce him?"

"When he hit me again. In the past, he took care not to leave marks where someone would see them."

Mike leaned forward. "He hit you more than once?"

Carly laid a hand on her husband's arm to calm his expected response. "Mike."

He glanced at her then back at Anne. "Why would you put up with that?"

Anne's bottom lip trembled.

But Mike pressed in. "You don't need a loser like that."

Carly tried again. She squeezed his arm. "Mike, dial down the intensity a little."

He sat back and took a couple of deep breaths. "I'm sorry. Carly's told me a little about her first husband. It's a good thing he died in that car accident or I'd have killed the creep myself."

Anne swiped at a tear. "I understand, Mike. I can't explain it myself. My father never treated my mother that way. He never lifted a hand in anger toward me, either." She shrugged. "I think abuse starts insidiously. Verbal. Emotional. By the time it escalated to physical, I believed I deserved it. I started it. I didn't understand him."

Mike shook his head. "He'd brainwashed you."

"I couldn't see that at the time."

Carly patted Anne's hand. "So what changed?"

"He left bruises where I couldn't explain them away. Where they were visible. The marks humiliated me. I didn't leave the house for two weeks." She pulled her hair back from her face to expose a yellowing patch on one cheek. "You can't see much now, but you can imagine how it looked. Right down to a blackened eye. I swore he'd never do that again. I went to court and got a temporary restraining order. That took place almost a week ago. He moved out, although I know he comes back when I'm not there."

Carly spluttered. "But you could—"

Anne held up a hand to silence her. "I've changed the locks, but he still manages to get in. I don't know how. I suspect he jimmies a window. Or maybe he comes through the cellar. It's an old house, and not everything is tight. Things go missing. Things are moved. I wonder if he's trying to make me think I'm going crazy."

"Have you called the police?"

"I have, but there's no evidence of forced entry. He doesn't leave fingerprints. All he leaves me is doubt that I am the person he says I am."

"What about a security system?"

Anne shrugged. "Difficult to maintain with guests coming and going. Plus there isn't a local company in Danforth."

Carly stood and went to her friend, pulling her into a hug. "You knew something was wrong a few months ago when you called. Were you already planning to divorce him?"

Anne nodded. "I had the papers served on him, which I think is what escalated the abuse. I thought we could work this out amicably. You know, live in the same house like roommates."

"But that didn't happen. It rarely does." Carly squeezed her again then released her. "We'll get to the bottom of it." She looked to her husband. "Won't we, Mike?"

Mike shrank back. "I don't know, Carly. Sounds like you have your hands full with the financial stuff. I'll be around the house, of course, so if Gary tries to come back in, I'll protect you ladies. But this seems to be a battle best won in divorce and criminal court. If he truly is stealing, and you ladies can produce the evidence, then we'll get him."

For once, Carly agreed. She'd much rather solve the mystery and free her friend of this albatross around her neck. And having Mike around could offer them some protection if things got out of hand—not that she thought they would. Still, men like Gary worked hard to keep the lifestyle he had become accustomed to. Something he could not afford, and didn't want to give up. She smiled at him. "But if we need a knight in shining armor?"

Mike puffed out his chest. "I'm your man."

They stood to go, and Carly wove her arm through Anne's. "How about we have coffee at your place?"

Anne leaned into her. "Sorry. High heels. Not used to them."

Not to mention four—or maybe five—glasses of wine. Carly tugged her close. "Mike, pay the bill, will you? We'll meet you in the car."

Anne protested, but both Mike and Carly overrode her, and the two girls headed for the car, giggling, their heads close together, just as they did in college. The Terrible Twosome, their friends called them. Always up to one set of hijinks or another.

As they slipped into the backseat of Anne's vehicle, Carly turned to her friend. "Did you ever report the abuse to the police?"

Anne shook her head. "It's a small town. Everybody knows everybody. When it started, he had a job, and I feared that if word got out, he'd lose that job. And then later—well, it just seemed by that time I'd waited too long and they wouldn't believe me." A tear slipped down her cheek. "I guess I felt it was better for them not to know than to tell them and they do nothing."

"Understood."

Anne laid her head on Carly's shoulder, and by the time Mike climbed into the driver's seat, her friend's soft whistling snores indicated she'd fallen asleep. Carly patted Anne's arm as Mike backed out of their parking space and headed back to the house.

This might be the most peaceful sleep her friend would get in the coming weeks.

Because one thing was certain: once Carly had her sights on a target, she didn't stop until she'd brought it down.

Giant conglomerate, Midwestern numbered company, cattle rustlers, mobsters—she didn't care who they were.

Which meant that an abusive bully like Gary Torbin would not hold a candle to her.

Chapter 5

Mike's fingers flew over the keyboard as he continued with the program. Now that he knew what he was looking for, he searched for telltale signs of embedded ghost modules and program paths designed to direct the program in a different direction than originally intended.

Occasionally he checked his cell phone to ensure he had adequate coverage should Philip Osgood attempt to contact him.

Four bars out of five.

Should be enough.

One misplaced message he could fathom.

Unlikely the cyberspace swallowed both his messages. And if Osgood was indisposed—ill, for example, or out of the country—somebody monitoring his phone calls would have heard the urgency in Mike's voice on that last message.

Osgood wasn't calling because he didn't want to call.

Mike paused, his fingers poised to strike the next keys. He could stop all work, return the retainer, and enjoy the rest of his vacation.

He shook his head. That wasn't his way of doing business. Even when the client threatened to blackball him in the industry—as his previous client had—Mike kept working. And when that same client ended up dead and Mike was suspected because of their falling-out, that hadn't kept him from the work.

The question was: what to do? He could alter the code and effectively turn off the aspects of the program not on the up and up. But he hadn't been hired to change that part of the code. And although the program might seem to be a tangle of *if this* and *then*, it didn't belong to him. Program code was intellectual property, fiercely guarded and controlled.

He could scrap the original code and start from scratch, but he'd been hired to write but one small part of an upgrade and expansion to the company's program. Writing a new program would take a lot of time—more time than he had—and then he'd have to test it, submit it for beta testing, and get the client's approval to reinstall and hope it worked as expected.

He released his fingers to continue. No, he needed to stick to his work specifications and write the code that directed the program how to calculate and divide income amongst the partners in proportion to their investment, their work product, the profit of their individual divisions, and the overall profit of the company.

Complicated, to say the least, but at least Osgood had provided the calculations. Mike's part entailed writing the code to interact with the various sources of information, compile and tabulate those numbers, and do the actual calculations.

He chuckled. Sounded simple, but it wasn't.

Carly would have had a field day with this project. An old-fashioned paper girl at heart, she'd want to set up columnar-paper spreadsheets, at least forty-eight, he suspected. Maybe more. And then if she needed to add even one more column, the entire program would need revision.

Which was one of the reasons he loved programming. No matter how wide or deep the information, a computer program could handle it. Given enough time, he could probably write a program that would write its own programs.

Hmm. That was a thought. If he—no, he needed to keep his mind on this project. Do what he was hired to do and—wait a minute. He paused again. What was that?

No. It couldn't be.

He copied and pasted the suspect section into a runtime program and set it through its paces. He leaned back in his chair and waited while the code streamed down his screen, scrolling like credits at the end of a B-movie—just fast enough to catch snatches of words and figures, but too fast to read.

After a couple of minutes, a list of numbers and accounts appeared on his screen.

His initial suspicion was correct.

This particular segment of code operated through a convoluted series of processes that initiated the false business identifications and amounts as well as generated account numbers to access, hiding under a shell company name. As the end user of this program, Financial Freedom Inc, a telemarketing company, dealt in thousands of credit card transactions every day.

Which meant the amounts would soon add up.

He returned to the original code to double-check his suspicions. Yep. The scam was limited to credit card transactions, probably on the assumption that folks didn't watch credit card accounts as closely as they did bank accounts. Not to mention that most people he knew checked their bank balances regularly, while these same people tossed their credit card statements into a drawer, trusting the company was processing entries properly.

He copied and pasted the code again and ran it through its paces once more to check. Maybe he was missing something. Maybe there was a check-sum in the code further down that corrected for this anomaly.

Twenty minutes later, Mike sat back, hands clasped behind his neck, his initial findings double- and triple-checked. Same results.

Freedom Financial was only concerned about lining their own pockets with other people's money.

He clicked onto the FBI's website. After scrolling through several layers of information, he found what he was looking for: reporting fraud. Near the bottom of the page, he found the department specially focused on telephone and mail fraud, along with a contact number, which he noted in his file.

Mike checked for a message or missed call from Osgood once more before dialing Financial Freedom's number. He'd give the man one more chance to explain himself before calling the feds. Nothing. He dialed and waited until the same voice prompt came on. He disconnected then dialed the number on the website.

"Federal Bureau of Investigation Telephone and Mail Fraud." The woman on the other end of the line sounded overly chipper for the kind of work she did. "How may I help you?"

"I'd like to file a report of telephone fraud, please."

"One moment."

Musak played in his ear as he waited for the transfer. After a minute or so, he contemplated disconnecting. Maybe he was wrong. And if he was, Osgood had every right to blacken Mike's name throughout the programming community.

But if Mike was right. . .

"Special Agent Walt Jamison." Unlike the woman who answered first, this man sounded tired, like he'd been up all night. Or had done this work for far too long. Seen the seamier side of life and wished he were elsewhere. "You have a telephone fraud to report?"

"Yes."

"How do you think it works?"

"Steals money from people's credit cards. At least, I think that's what it does." Mike wanted to kick himself. How could he make this person believe him if he didn't believe it himself. "What I mean is, it does steal from their credit cards."

A long sigh. "This isn't another one of those alien credit card scams, is it? Because honestly, I've got as many of those as I need right now."

Alien what? "No." Mike sat up. He needed to make this guy understand how serious this scam was. "I'm a computer programmer and—"

"Thanks, but we don't need any more programmers. Got our hands full. And I wouldn't be the one to hire you, anyway. I can give you the number for HR."

Mike exhaled. "I'm not looking for a job. I am a programmer, and I've been hired to write code for a company, and I think I found something hinky in the program they use."

Another long sigh. "Sorry. We get lots of crazies calling here about all sorts of things. Some of them are actually the ones who started the fraud, and now they're hoping we'll give them a job and a front page thank you for solving the problem. I wish they wouldn't publish our direct phone number all over the Internet."

"Well, I'm glad they did. I was surprised at how easy it was to find you. I commend whoever designed your website and—"

"Excuse me." Jamison broke in. "Can we get to the point of your call?"

"Right. Sorry."

Over the next fifteen minutes, Mike explained what he knew, what he didn't know, and what he suspected about Freedom Financial and their financial dealings. Special Agent Jamison stayed quiet most of the time, but apparently his fingers flew almost as fast as Mike's as he took notes on his computer. The man's attention was gratifying, and his ability to understand the complexities of Mike's information encouraged him.

As far as Mike was concerned, having the good guys working for the government was a comfort.

When he ended his recitation of events, Jamison was quiet for so long Mike thought they'd been cut off, except he still heard computer keys tapping on the other end of the call.

After a long moment, Jamison spoke. "I think I have all that. And you're right to question this program. I'll send an agent to meet with you tomorrow. It's a short train ride from DC to Portland, and he can rent a car and be there by noon. Sound okay?"

"Fine. Except I'm not in Bear Cove now, and I won't be there tomorrow, either."

"Right. I should have asked. Just assumed from the area code on the caller ID."

"We're in Wyoming for another week or so."

"Wyoming?"

"Yes."

"Why?"

"My wife is a forensic accountant, and she's helping a friend with her divorce."

"Oh. That changes things. Not much, but a little. Hold on while I check something."

More muzak. Another couple of minutes went by as slow as a turtle in shackles.

Then Jamison came back. "Okay. Just spoke with the Denver Regional Office. They'll send Special Agent Riley Wilcox out tomorrow. He's in the Grand Junction office today, but he should be there by end of day tomorrow. We gave him your cell number so he can call once he's ready to make contact."

"Sounds good." Mike paused. "In the meantime, what do I do if the client calls? I left two messages expressing my concern about the project."

"We don't want them to get suspicious that they're found out, because these kinds of organizations will simply shut their doors and start up somewhere else under a new name, making it difficult for us to connect the dots and link them with this business. If they call, tell them you were an idiot and misread the code, or you mis-keyed something to give a wrong output. Just imply you're continuing with the project."

"Should I call and leave a message to that effect before they call me? If they get spooked, they might skedaddle before your guy gets here."

"Good idea. If you talk to someone, let them know you were wrong, and apologize. Offer them a discount for the aggravation. Whatever it takes to keep them calm and unsuspecting."

"Feels wrong to lie to them. I don't operate that way."

"Then come up with something you're comfortable with."

"Will do."

Mike hung up and contemplated his situation. He was caught between a rock and a hard place, and understood a little better how Carly felt when she got herself in this situation. Which she did. Often. Too often for his liking.

And whenever she did, he always blamed her for jumping in without considering the implications.

But surely this situation was different. He hadn't known that Financial Freedom was crooked before he took the contract. He'd done his due diligence and checked out their website, and they seemed on the up-and-up. Members of the local Better Business Bureau. Several prominent clients and glowing recommendations listed on their site. And they'd contacted him, citing a previous job he'd worked on for another client that was similar to the one they had in mind. And they agreed to his price without hesitation.

He smiled. That should have been the clue.

From now on, he'd price his work high enough so potential clients would want to negotiate. And if they didn't, he'd have enough money to hire a good criminal lawyer for himself if he got into trouble.

He stood and paced the room. No, that wasn't his way, either. And taking that mindset wouldn't set a good example for Carly, either. Because she needed good examples, what with her propensity to get into trouble. Although she'd argue she didn't go looking for trouble—it always seemed to find her.

He sat again to make his phone call. He dialed the number and waited through the voice prompt. "Hi, this is a message for Philip Osgood. Mike Turnquist here. Mr. Osgood, I feel silly making this call. Please disregard my previous message, and I hope there aren't any hard feelings. I overstated the problem, and work is continuing. Must have had a brain lapse or something. I'll get back to you in a couple of days with the first module. Call me at this number if you have any questions."

He disconnected the call and set the phone on the desk. Would Osgood call back? Would Mike lose this very lucrative contract? So far he'd received his retainer, which covered half the job, and he'd done less than twenty percent of the actual code, so he wasn't out money, technically speaking.

He'd keep on as if nothing was wrong.

As if he hadn't just talked with an FBI Special Agent in Washington, DC.

As if he didn't feel like he needed to take a shower every time he thought of Financial Freedom.

+++++

Carly tossed her pencil on the table where it rolled off her notepad and headed toward the edge of the surface.

Carly grabbed the pencil and tucked it behind her ear before turning her attention back to the columnar pad in front of her. If Mike were here, he'd tease her about using paper. But she didn't trust computers. A person could spend hours—years, even—on a project, then poof! Gone in an instant. Or if one simple equation was wrong, incorrect information carried from one sheet to another, and a person might not find the problem unless they checked it the old fashioned way—with a calculator.

No, paper was her fallback, particularly on a project like this that required deliberate thinking. She wasn't simply filling in blanks and balances—she was dealing with her friend's future.

Not to mention she didn't want Gary Torbin getting one penny more than necessary. Although she'd never clapped eyes on the man, she knew him. Or men like him. Who saw a good thing and latched on to it, sucking the life out of the woman, the business, the marriage, the bank accounts, until there was nothing left.

She should know the type.

She'd been married to one many years before.

Carly pulled another packet of papers toward her and leafed through them. Interrogatories from Respondent Counsel, asking for information on all manner of topics, primarily regarding change in net worth. Which was what she'd do in Gary Torbin's place—prove the increase in the value of Anne's assets during the marriage. The law was a funny creature. It didn't care who did the work—the assumption was that any increase in pre-existing assets during the marriage was attributable to the marriage itself, even if one party did all the work and the other party did nothing. Even if one party did everything to spend their way into bankruptcy or insolvency, as it appeared Gary had done.

Net worth at the time of marriage.

Humph. If that were a question on the marriage license, perhaps fewer people would marry these money-grubbers. But it wasn't, and it was up to her to try to determine that for Anne.

Carly flipped over a few more pages. No answers to Anne's interrogatories to Gary. No surprise there. He likely wouldn't file his until after she filed hers, a common ploy used by crooked attorneys to downplay their client's assets and cry "poor me".

She shuffled a couple of boxes of documents aside looking for the tax returns for the B&B for the year before Anne's marriage. That should have a copy of her balance sheet and income statement. Carly pulled out the documents and turned pages until she found what she was looking for. Anne had been in decent shape, showing the house, furnishings, equipment, property, and bank accounts valuing at over a quarter million dollars. Debts, including the mortgage, less than a hundred thousand.

Net worth: a hundred fifty-eight thousand, four hundred twelve dollars and nineteen cents.

Don't forget the nineteen cents.

Next question: list all improvements to the house, their cost, and the value, if known.

She sighed.

It was going to be a long day.

Three hours and six cups of coffee later, and Carly's head pounded. The questions asked by Gary's attorney were intrusive and repetitive, as though he was trying to catch Anne in a lie. Which made sense, since Gary was obviously lying to Anne, and likely to his attorney as well, when it came to his own assets.

What she didn't understand was why Anne's attorney didn't see through this ruse and put a stop to it.

She shoved the documents aside. At least that part was done with.

Until the next round, of course.

And in the process of responding to these questions, Carly got the documentation into order, carefully referencing the question on the respective piece of information, then recording that information on her columnar pad, including amounts. As a result, she now had an up-to-date inventory based on the original one Anne had given her, supplemented by details in the interrogatories.

She chuckled. Gary hadn't been quite so smart as he thought he was. By pointing her in the right direction, asking questions about this asset and that, she now had a list of what he was trying to hide: anything and everything he didn't ask about.

Because it wouldn't make sense for him to ask about the Norton that should be hanging in the room she shared with Mike. No point raising questions about why it wasn't there.

But not asking about it had accomplished almost the same thing.

Perhaps Gary didn't know Anne had that original inventory.

Perhaps he didn't think Anne would hire a professional.

Whatever the reason, Gary's goose was now cooked.

Chapter 6

Carly tucked her arm through Mike's and pressed closer. "I'm so glad we decided to go for a walk."

He responded by releasing her arm and wrapping his around her shoulders. "Me, too. I figured we'd been cooped up inside long enough today. All work and no play and all that."

"And I'm glad we decided to eat out. Anne looked particularly worn out this morning. I think it was a busy day for her. She said another couple is checking in tomorrow, and she was getting their room ready."

"Nothing strange about that. She runs a B&B."

"She said she had a woman who does that for her."

"Maybe the divorce is costing her more than she expected. Maybe she wanted to put a good face on it to you. Maybe Gary took more money than she realized."

"Still, I think it's strange."

"I don't like the sounds of that. Every time you say that, you find a body. Or a killer."

She twisted out of his embrace. "Don't say that, Michael Turnquist. I do not."

He pulled her close and planted a kiss on the top of her head. "Okay. Not every time. Just most of the time."

"That's better. Nothing is always or never."

He bowed from the waist. "I stand corrected." He clasped her hand again. "What's on your schedule for tomorrow?"

"Going through more financial stuff. I discovered something interesting today, though."

"Oh-oh. Strange and interesting. Two words I hate to hear from you."

She mock-punched his arm. "Cut me some slack. Do you want to hear what I found?"

He rubbed where her fist connected, his face contorted. "Took the breath out of me, that did."

"Good. Means you can't talk." She pointed to a bench along the sidewalk. "Let's sit for a minute."

He led the way, then they cuddled on the bench as she filled him in on the pattern she'd discovered regarding Gary ignoring the very same assets Anne suspected he'd taken. "What do you think of that?"

"Sounds like you have a very good case built up. What are you going to do with the information?"

"Encourage her to mention it to her attorney and request supplemental interrogatories." She peered at her husband. Dusk had fallen, creating shadows in the lines on his face. Lines darker than she'd noticed before. Might be the lighting, but—"How about you? What's happening with the program?"

"It's fine."

Oh-oh. What was that clanging noise? A security door slamming shut. What was it about men? Or maybe her husband in particular? When he didn't want to talk about something, that was the time he most needed to open up.

Well, he wasn't going to get away with it. She snuggled closer, pressing into him. "Fine is not an acceptable answer. What's going on?"

He shrugged but didn't break their contact. Which, in her experience, was a good sign. "There were a few things in the program that didn't make sense. Called Osgood, but he's not calling back."

She straightened so she could see his face. "Maybe he's busy. Or out of town."

"Right. Considered that. But the more work I did on the module, the more strange the whole thing seemed." He stared into her eyes. "Ever feel like somebody is setting you up for a fall?" He chuckled. "Ignore that question. You probably think that every day."

"Well, not every day." She rubbed his bicep through his light jacket. "But lots of times. And you usually tell me I'm imagining things. Why would anybody want to set up an accountant from Bear Cove?"

Her husband nodded then pulled her closer, resting his chin on her head. "And I take back every time I ever said or thought that."

"What do you think they're trying to do?"

"Looks like they're in the middle of a huge credit card scam. And since they deal mostly with telemarketing, that means it comes down to phone fraud. Which is a federal offense."

She definitely didn't like the sound of that. She straightened again and clasped his hands in hers. "What does this mean for you?"

"I did the only thing I knew to do. I called the FBI."

"Whoa. That's calling in the big guns. What did they say?"

"They're sending an agent from western Colorado. He should be here by end of day tomorrow."

"How exciting. Working with a secret agent. It's like—"

Mike held up a hand. "Don't say it's just like in a book you're reading. Or a movie you watched. Although I suspect it is."

Carly shivered. "I think it's exciting. But let's head back. I'm getting chilled."

They strolled toward Anne's house, hand in hand, admiring the houses along the way. These western structures had a distinct air about them, as though defying the elements to send their worst. Which the buildings had already survived, no doubt. A century of tornados, snowstorms, torrential rain, drought, blazing sun, and high winds might fade the paint and crackle the woodwork, but Nature couldn't overcome the fine workmanship and attention to detail of the original builders.

Carly drew strength from their solid presence as they neared the B&B. They could take a life lesson from these old houses.

Lights blazed in the main floor windows behind the lace curtains, and despite the chill falling, windows allowed the evening air into the house, cooling the rooms. Mike opened the gate and stepped aside to let her go first, when sounds from the house froze Carly in her tracks.

A man's voice thundered through the open window. "You don't know what you're talking about."

A woman—Anne—responded, her voice shaking with emotion. "I know what's mine. And you're not getting it."

The man replied, his voice lower, cajoling. "Come on, Anne. Let's work this out."

"There's nothing to work out, Gary."

Ah, the soon-to-be ex-husband. Carly's breath caught in her throat, and her feet refused to budge. She might be feisty—okay, she was feisty—but she didn't relish confrontation. Her first husband had taught her quickly—with his fists and his words—that resistance brought only trouble.

"Anne, you don't want to throw away the good years we've had, do you?"

"What good years? Apart from our honeymoon, where you wined and dined me and treated me like a princess, the rest has been misery."

"Not all of it, Annie."

"Don't call me that. Nobody calls me that but my mother."

"Oh, yes, your blessed mother. One of the reasons our marriage never had a chance." A shadow paced back and forth across the window. "She was always meddling."

"Don't say that about her. She's dead and gone and can't defend herself."

"No, but you will, won't you? Always choosing her over me."

"Probably the only good decision I made since I married you. You wanted to stick her in that horrible place."

"It's better than she deserved, the meddling old b—"

Carly jumped at the sound of a hand slapping skin. A feeling she'd been only too accustomed to in her first marriage. Mike gripped her hand, and she squeezed back. "Should we go in?"

Mike shook his head. "Sounds like she slapped him. They need to work out their problems. We'll go in if it sounds like it's getting out of hand."

Gary stood in the window, his silhouette emphasized by the light from within the room and the closed curtain behind him. "I could have you arrested for that."

"Not if you really want to reconcile, you won't."

"Think you've got the upper hand, do you?"

"I hired a professional, and she figured out what you've been up to."

Gary moved away from the window. "Oh, really? And what is that?"

Don't tell him, Anne. Surprise is everything. Keep him guessing.

"You'll soon find out. My lawyer knows everything."

Carly exhaled.

Good girl.

"What do I need to do to convince you that I'm not the bad guy here?"

"Return what you stole."

"Can't steal what's mine."

"The painting in the front bedroom is mine. I bought it before we married."

"But I worked to support you all these years."

Anne laughed, but there was no joy in the sound. "Don't make four years sound like a lifetime. You worked to support your own vices and habits, and little enough at that. You'd have worked less if I let you."

"Now Annie—Anne, I came here tonight to see if we could start over again. Pretend like we just met. Court again. All that stuff. I want this marriage to work."

"I don't think you do, Gary."

"Meet me at the Midway Motel tomorrow at noon so we can talk. Room 8."

"I thought you were staying with a friend."

"I am. I thought some privacy would be better. Let me show you how good I can be to you. I want to make up. Forget this silly court stuff."

Another shadow, smaller this time—Anne?—moved into view, arms folded across her chest. "I already told you my terms. Return what you stole or tell me where you hid it. Some of that has a sentimental value. It's been in my family for years."

"Over my dead body."

Anne turned to the window, and Carly shrank back against the side of the house, Mike plastered to her side. A few minutes later, the back door slammed, footsteps crunched on the gravel drive, and a truck roared to life. Backup lights lit the driveway, and the truck backed onto the street, paused, then squealed its tires down the street toward town.

Carly shrugged to loosen her taut muscles. "I feel like a Peeping Tom."

"I know. We weren't meant to hear that, but I'm glad we did."

"Why?"

Mike pulled her against him, mashing his face into her hair. "Reminds me how lucky we are in our relationship. And if anything happens, we can be a witness to how he treated her."

She pushed away but not out of his embrace. "Oh, Mike, you don't think he'd hurt her, do you?"

"He might. We should stick close to her for the next day or so until he cools down. Once the FBI agent gets here, she should be safe."

"But he's not coming here for her. He's here to investigate your phone fraud."

"But Gary doesn't need to know that, does he? We could let word slip around town that a special agent with the FBI is here to investigate a fraud case. Which is true."

"And if the FBI doesn't want word to get out that he's here?"

"We'll cross that bridge when we get to it. For now, let's go in. You're shivering."

Carly looped an arm around his waist and tucked her hand into his back pocket.

"Not from the cold, though. You're enough to keep me warm."

"I keep telling you I'm hot stuff, baby."

She giggled. He could always lift her out of a funk, soothe her raw nerves, and help her see that things would be okay.

They climbed the three steps to the covered porch that wrapped around the front of the house. Comfortable chairs beckoned, but Carly headed for the door. Maybe tomorrow she could enjoy one of the rockers. Or have morning tea at one of the wrought-iron tables dotting the wide surface.

They entered the house and paused in the foyer. The house was quiet, in stark contrast to just a few minutes before. The scent of cinnamon and sugar wafted through the rooms, and Carly's nose twitched. No, she didn't need anything else to eat tonight, as tempting as the odor was. But she would have a double portion at breakfast.

The other thing she noticed was that only the stairwell light remained on. Anne must have headed upstairs after Gary left.

The angry words of her friend's conversation hung in the air, and Carly was glad Anne wasn't alone in the house.

Leading Mike by the hand, she headed up the stairs to their room. About six steps up, she glanced back at him, and he waggled his eyebrows at her.

She smiled. Her husband was as transparent as a pane of glass.

She touched her index finger to her lips. "Don't want to disturb Anne."

"We won't disturb her. She's at the opposite end of the hall. She won't hear a thing."

Incorrigible, indeed.

They passed an open door on the way to their room, and Carly paused. Anne turned from the dresser she'd been rummaging in, and looked up, surprise evident in her raised brow.

In her hand, she held a handgun. A black revolver.

Anne's gaze went from Carly to the gun and back again. "Hi Carly. I didn't hear you come in."

"We just got here." Not entirely true, but close enough. "Have a good evening?"

"Yes., Quiet. Peaceful. Got the room ready for the couple arriving tomorrow. How about you?"

"Nice dinner. Good to get out for a little walk." Carly quirked her chin toward the gun. "What's with that?"

Anne stared at the weapon as though seeing it for the first time. "This? Oh, it's nothing."

"It's a gun, Anne."

"Everybody carries a gun, Carly. You're in the west now."

"Everybody?"

Anne shrugged. "Well, almost everybody. I was just cleaning out the dresser for my guests and found it here. Belonged to my dad. I didn't think I should leave it here. So I'm moving it to my room. For safekeeping."

Anne's voice raised a notch in tenor with every elaboration.

Carly knew one thing. As dear as she held their friendship, Anne was lying to her.

Leeann Betts

Chapter 7

The next morning, the sun streaming in through the bedroom window woke Carly, and she stretched, arms over her head and toes pointing in the opposite direction. Staying cuddled beneath the satiny duvet was tempting, but she had work to do.

Sighing, she slipped the covers back and sat, tucking her toes into her slippers. A quick trip to the bathroom, and she pulled on her standard work wear: jeans and a shirt. Mike sat at the desk, his back to her, although he mumbled something that she interpreted as "good morning" in response to her greeting.

His fingers flew across the keyboard, and she paused in her travels to look over his shoulder. Screens of gobbledy-gook faced her, filled with partial sentences, letters and numbers and underscores that meant nothing to her. Not to mention all those parentheses.

She massaged his shoulders, and he leaned back into her touch. Wrapping her arms around his neck, she pressed into his bulk and planted kisses behind each ear.

He squirmed. "You're tickling me."

"Too bad. Relax and enjoy the attention."

He spun the chair around and pulled her into his lap. "Say that to my face."

Carly giggled. "Mike, let me go. This chair wasn't meant to hold two."

He waggled his eyebrows. "The bed was. I could meet you there."

She wriggled out of his grasp. "Great idea."

A smile lit his face and he stood.

She ducked out of reach. "In about twelve hours."

Mike clutched a hand to his chest and staggered then slumped into the chair. "Oh, my broken heart."

"Broken, my foot. If I hadn't come over here, you'd have kept working, oblivious to the world."

"True, but milady's touch has awakened this sleeping beast."

"You're confusing your fairy tales." She sat on the bed but thought better of it. No point giving him any more ideas. He already had enough of his own. She moved to the easy chair near the window. "Breakfast should be ready soon. Are you at a good stopping point?"

He snapped the lid on his laptop shut. "Always ready to eat." He held out his arm to her. "Shall we?"

Carly giggled again. "We shall."

They headed down to the dining room, which Carly had cleared of the documents, boxes, and twenty-four-column paper she'd been using for the past three days. No mean feat, given that she liked to spread out in her work area. Still, Anne had assured her the information Carly provided would be invaluable in giving her—and her attorney—the ammunition they needed in the court hearing.

For now, Carly was off duty.

Well, those were Anne's words.

For Carly, her work was just beginning.

She wasn't satisfied to leave sleeping dogs lie, as her father used to say. She would not stop until she located and returned the missing property, because while she'd not met Gary, she knew his type. He wouldn't return Anne's goods just because a judge ordered him to, or because a subpoena was served on him, or even because the divorce proceeding would decide in Anne's favor.

Men like Gary didn't plan and scheme and plot and steal simply to be scared off by a few words on a page or a threat of jail time.

He would do everything he could to keep Anne from recovering her property.

Men like Gary Torbin would keep fresh air from folks if they could.

Voices from the dining room reached her, and she slowed. Mike continued at his previous pace and ended up dragging her along like a puppy on a leash. She disengaged from his grip just before they arrived in the doorway.

He turned to face her. "What's up? Thought you were hungry."

"I am." She quirked her chin toward the dining room. "There's somebody in there."

He shrugged. "So? It's a bed and breakfast. Anne probably has other guests." He studied her for a moment. "Ah. Now I get it. You want to eavesdrop."

"That sounds so crass and uncouth, Mike. I simply want to give them the opportunity to finish their conversation before we barge in on them."

"Right." He dragged the word out into two syllables, an annoying habit of his when he didn't believe her. "Well, I want to get in there before they eat all the bacon and eggs."

"Please wait a moment. And I promise you that if you go in and there isn't any food left, I will take you out for breakfast."

His brow drew down. "I dunno. I think you just want to listen to eavesdrop."

She planted her fists in her hips. "A scientific fact is that simply watching changes the outcome."

"I think they were referring to chemical reactions, not conversations."

"Well, if it's true for scientists, it's probably true for regular people, too."

Mike lifted his nose in the air like a dog following a trail. "I smell toast. And coffee." He peeked around the corner. "Okay, they're done talking. I'm going in."

Carly sighed. Once he had an idea in his head, there was no changing his mind. "Fine. I'm coming with you."

Truth was, now that he mentioned it, she'd die for a cup of coffee.

+++++

The couple in the room didn't look anything like their voices.

At least, nothing like Mike imagined they would.

For example, the guy had one of those high, tinny voices, slightly raspy as though he still had a cold. A voice half an octave above other men, and soft enough that Mike wanted to lean in to hear what they were saying.

Or maybe that was the response men like this one sought.

His dark-rimmed glasses perched on a hooked nose. His white hair, askew in all directions, reminded him of caricatures of Einstein or some other mad scientist in popular culture. His dark suit, complete with elbow patches and a rumpled pocket handkerchief, completed the image of a professor from a less-than-Ivy-League university.

The woman didn't look anything like him, which was probably good, since the man bore a thick, bushy mustache bearing traces of blond, red, and brown hair mixed with grey. In fact, she was his complete opposite. Her hair, a vibrant shade of red never before seen in Nature, matched her lipstick. Her angular frame, loosely covered by some sort of Indian-print fabric, contrasted with his portly shape.

65

The man looked up from the overloaded plate of bacon and eggs—Mike's hopes of a hearty breakfast diminished with every bite the man shoved in his mouth—but their arrival didn't slow his food consumption. Mike stopped and surveyed the room. Three chafing dishes with lit sterno cans heating their contents steamed on the antique sideboard at one end of the room. Perpendicular to the food sat thermal carafes marked COFFEE and HOT WATER, as well as an assortment of juices and one marked MILK.

Carly hovered at his elbow, and he stepped aside to let her pass. She, too, paused and studied the two in the room. "Good morning."

The man looked at his dining companion, and something unspoken passed between them. Mike watched him a moment longer, then followed Carly to the food line and filled his plate.

Thankfully, Mr. Professor hadn't taken all the bacon.

Not taking any chances the man would go back for seconds, Mike took as much as he figured Carly would allow him to eat without embarrassing both of them, including several scoops of eggs and fried potatoes, then set his plate at the end of the table.

The woman scooted her chair a millimeter away, as though politely making room, but her message was clear: we were here first.

Well, these two may have arrived in the dining room before them, but Carly and he had been here several days before.

He filled his coffee cup and returned to the table in time to overhear Carly try again to get these two eating robots to communicate with her.

"I'm Carly, and this is my husband Mike. We're from Bear Cove, Maine."

The woman brightened and set her fork down. "Nancy and George Romer. Small world. We're from Portland."

Carly laid her napkin in her lap. "How fun. Do you travel much?"

"We love Boston. Especially the seafood."

Mike sat and nodded toward George Romer. "Good to meet you."

Romer nodded and sipped his coffee.

But his silence didn't slow his wife.

Mike rolled his eyes toward the man, demonstrating his commiseration with being married to a wife who talked to strangers, but the man either didn't see or didn't understand. His face remained impassive as he forked his breakfast in, hardly giving himself time to chew.

Well, two can play that game.

Nancy Romer picked at her food, pushing it around the plate without ever lifting the fork to eat. Mike tuned out her husband and focused instead on Carly and her new best friend.

"Oh, we love the seafood, but we like to branch out, too. We go to Anthony's a lot. It's Italian. Have you heard of it?"

Nancy Romer shook her head. "No, I don't think so." She turned to her husband. "Sound familiar, Sweetcakes?"

Mike's opinion of the man softened. A husband whose wife called him Sweetcakes in public couldn't be all bad.

The man scowled at her instead of replying then turned his attention back to his food, which he continued devouring.

His wife shrugged. "I guess not. But we love to eat at that new place on the wharf."

Carly's head tipped in question. "The new place on the wharf." She turned to him. "Have we been there?"

Mike emerged from his contemplation of George Romer's table manners. "Don't think so. What do they serve?"

Carly giggled and leaned across the table as though sharing a confidence with Nancy. "Mike can't remember a name, but he never forgets a plate."

Nancy's mouth tipped up in half a smile. "Cute."

When she turned her attention back to her meal, picking up a minuscule tidbit of potato and practically forcing it between her lips, Carly sat back and took a bite of toast. But that didn't satisfy her for long, and when she set her fork on her plate, Mike sighed.

Nancy Romer was in for an interrogation.

"So, what else do you do in Boston? Do you have family there?"

"No family."

Of course, with his mouth full, George managed to make the statement sound like 'no shmamy'.

Mike sipped his coffee. Strange the man would answer a question addressed to his wife, particularly since he hadn't been communicative—at least, not verbally. He'd spoken volumes to both his wife and to Mike without opening his mouth except to fork in more food.

Maybe the man was simply looking for an opportunity. Well, Mike would give him one. "Do you still work?"

George Romer stared at Mike as though he spoke a foreign language. He blinked myopically a couple of times, then returned his gaze to his food.

Dismissed again.

Mike shrugged then stood and did something that gave him great pleasure: he took the last of the bacon.

+++++

Carly wasn't satisfied. And when she wasn't satisfied, she kept digging.

Nancy and George Romer were being less than open with her, and she wanted to know why. Not that she needed to know their whole life story in their first meeting—despite what Mike said, she wasn't *that* nosy. No, she simply liked to know people, ask about their backgrounds, stuff like that. Most people like to talk about themselves, in her experience.

So what were the Romers holding back? And why?

Their vague answers to her questions about Boston were a little unsettling.

Well, if they thought she'd give up, they had another thing coming.

Carly Turnquist never gave up.

Which was another thing Mike often said about her: that she didn't know when to quit.

Maybe not. But was that such a terrible character trait?

She lifted her coffee cup but didn't drink. More of an attention getter, really. "So, Nancy, if you don't have family in Boston, why do you go there?"

Nancy's eyes widened then her face relaxed. "We just like to travel."

Carly quirked her chin toward George. "And eat."

Nancy chuckled. "Yes."

"You know, we'd love to check out that new place on the wharf. Whereabouts is it?"

"Just past the tourist shop. On the same side."

Carly's brow drew down. "I don't recall a tourist shop." Time to ask a trick question. "Is it on the north side or the south side?"

Nancy studied her for a long moment, her fake lashes batting like a moth against a flame. "North or south?"

"Right. On the left or the right as you head down the wharf, going toward the water."

Nancy opened her mouth to answer, but stopped when her husband stood and pushed his chair back so it scraped against the hardwood floor then jerked his head toward the door.

Nancy folded her napkin and set it on her plate. "Sorry, we have to go."

Carly stood and reached her hand out but didn't actually touch the woman. "I hope we get a chance to sit and talk about Maine some more."

"Maine?" George stared hard at her. "We're from Oregon. Portland Oregon."

He gripped his wife's forearm and practically dragged her from the room. Hushed voices accompanied them up the stairs.

Carly waited until they were out of earshot then sat. "Well, that was weird."

Mike shook his head. "You sure know how to clear a room."

"It wasn't my fault."

He swallowed another mouthful of bacon before answering. "No, it wasn't. There was something strange about those two."

"I agree. When I said we were from Maine, she jumped at the idea of talking to someone from the same state. Talked like she knew what we were talking about."

"So what was that question about the wharf? You know it runs east and west."

"Right. Seemed like something was off about them, so I—"

"Tossed in a trick question. Carly, that's so unsporting of you."

"Not really. But I was looking forward to checking out a new restaurant in Boston."

"If they were telling the truth, the next time we go to San Francisco, we'll have dinner there."

"Well, that's fine then, isn't it?"

He lifted an eyebrow in question. "Do I detect a note of sarcasm?"

"Good ear. Yes, you do." She nudged her plate a millimeter. "Why do you think they felt the need to deceive us?"

He shrugged. "Maybe they just misspoke."

"I don't think so. Did you notice how he never said a word, but when you asked about family, he jumped right in. Almost as if he was cutting her off so she wouldn't say something she shouldn't."

"Well, she didn't look like the brightest bulb in the package."

"I won't argue with you there, but why was it important for us to believe they don't have family in Boston?"

"Maybe he meant they don't have family anywhere?"

Carly sat back. "No, I think he was referring specifically to Boston, since I asked her why they go there. And it was important for us to believe that they don't know anybody in Boston. A city they visit often, according to her." She folded her fingers together on the table in front of her. "Interesting."

Mike groaned. "Oh, no. Carly, when you say that, I know trouble is brewing."

She jabbed her chest with a thumb. "*Moi?*"

He clasped her hand and covered it with his like a warm blanket. "Yes, you." He squeezed gently. "Promise you won't get into any trouble."

Did the man think she went out of her way to find situations that weren't always ideal? "Mike, give me some credit."

"I do. Which is why I'm asking you to stay out of it. If they want to mislead—"

"Lie to us."

He released his grip on her and held one hand in the air in surrender. "Fine, lie to us, they have every right. Freedom of speech and all that."

"Just because they can stand on their Constitutional right to free speech doesn't mean they should."

He patted her hand. "I know it offends your sensibilities when people do that. It doesn't mean they're up to something."

"Remember those people in Raven Valley?" Mike and Carly had gone to Arizona for his twenty-fifth college reunion, and she'd met a couple in the elevator who turned out to be connected to the mob. "An innocent old couple, you said. What could they get up to, you asked. Well, we soon found out, didn't we?"

The couple were connected with a murder and a bombing. Old perhaps. Innocent, not.

Mike drained the rest of his coffee and stood, holding out a hand to her. "Shall we get on with our day?"

"Now that you've consumed half a hog, sure." She smiled at him. "Thought I wouldn't notice, didn't you?"

He rubbed his stomach. "Nothing like starting the day with a full tummy."

She accepted his hand and headed for the stairs, stopping when Anne met them in the doorway. "Good morning."

Dark circles ringed Anne's eyes. "Enjoy your breakfast?"

Carly smiled. "Mike singlehandedly decimated the local pig population."

"Hey, not by myself. George Romer did a pretty good job at eating, too."

Anne shifted an overloaded purse to the other shoulder and stepped aside as Carly and Mike paused in the foyer. "I see you met the other couple."

Since her friend opened the door, Carly was going to step through it. "Have they been here before?"

"No. In fact, they were a last-minute booking."

Interesting. "Really?"

"Yes. They called the day you arrived and asked for a room. Didn't know how long they'd be staying, but they were desperate. Not much else available in town beside the motel. I don't usually open this early in the year, but my June bookings are down, so I jumped at the chance to make a few extra dollars. Hoping they stay on for more than just one or two nights."

As Alice in Wonderland would say, 'curiouser and curiouser'. "Seems strange they don't know how long they'll be here."

Mike wrapped an arm around her shoulders. "Not everybody plans their vacations or their business trips down to the minute."

Sometimes his logic could be so irritating. "Still."

He pulled her close. "You're just irritated that you misunderstood which coast they live on."

She shrugged off his touch and gave him The Look. "I was not mistaken. You thought they lived in Maine, too. Because she practically said they did."

"Right. And then you have to go and spoil a perfectly polite breakfast by confusing them about which direction the wharf runs."

Anne laughed and held her hands up in surrender. "Whoa, guys. I wish I'd been a fly on the wall this morning. All this talk has me curious."

Carly smiled. "Mike thinks I go looking for trouble. But I really don't."

He gripped her hand. "She just doesn't know when to stop asking questions."

Tired of the topic, Carly wanted to know more about a previous statement Anne had made. "Why is business slow?"

Her friend shrugged. "Not sure. Gary says I have no head for business."

Carly's gaze traveled over the foyer and up to the second floor landing. "I think you've done a great job of turning this house into a wonderful B&B. And you seem to have thrived here in the middle of nowhere. Maybe people aren't traveling as much."

"Maybe. Folks seem to be looking for more amenities, like a pool, a business center. More things to do in town."

"But lots of travelers like the quiet and the slower pace. Maybe you need to talk up those amenities more in your ads."

Anne shrugged again, but this time her shoulders slumped. "Maybe. I don't know. Maybe Gary is right."

Carly patted her friend's arm. "The only thing Gary is right about is his valuation of the assets he's stealing from you."

Anne set her purse on the floor near the door. A dull thud echoed off the floors. She smiled. "Sounds like I'm carrying bricks in that thing."

Probably not bricks, but something heavy. Carly smiled. "I can't carry a big purse. If I do, I end up overloading it. Give me something big enough for my billfold, keys, and cell phone."

Anne smiled and headed into the dining room, while Carly and Mike went upstairs to freshen up before beginning their workday. Carly pondered her friend's statements. According to Anne's financial records, she'd managed to run the business on her own quite profitably until Gary showed up on the scene.

Seemed he was the one with no head for business.

Unless it was a head for the business of stealing her friend blind.

Chapter 8

If there had been a worse day in her life so far, Anne didn't remember it. Maybe that's what a massive shock did to the memory—made a person forget.

Although she doubted she'd ever forget the sight before her.

Her husband—no, now her former husband—and didn't that roll off the tongue way too easily—lay flat on his back, a surprised look on his face as though caught completely off guard. Which he probably had, judging by the dark hole, roughly circular, about the diameter of her little finger, in the middle of his forehead.

A puddle of almost-black liquid oozed from behind his head near his left shoulder.

And a gun tossed on the floor like so much garbage.

She paused in the doorway of the Midway Motel, a sleazy place no bigger than a turnaround in the highway where Gary asked to meet her. Her perfume clashed with the cloying metallic odor of blood, reminding her once more of her foolishness—she'd thought maybe he suggested a motel because he had hopes of them getting back together again. And she'd fallen for her girlish dreams that perhaps she could salvage her marriage by spraying on some of the scent he gave her for Christmas a year ago.

Bile rose in her throat at the reminder of how much had changed in such a short time. In her. Not in Gary, of course. A year ago, he was already three years into stealing from her, which Carly's investigation confirmed. She didn't really needed to bring her college friend to Wyoming to confirm her suspicions, but simply wanted another set of eyes, just in case she was wrong.

It was one thing for the wife to suspect the husband, another completely for a professional to prove it.

Without proof, her case sounded a lot like he said, she said.

And now Gary wouldn't be able to say one more thing in his own defense.

She studied the room. No footprints on the cheap carpet. She shuddered as she envisioned the feet and the circumstances this dingy shag had witnessed over the past forty years, because it had been there that long if it had been there a day. She glanced at the walls. No, she'd not want to be a fly. . .

What seemed out of place was Gary in this setting. He wouldn't choose such a cheap rendezvous location, no matter how hard up he was. And he wasn't without resources—he'd stolen more than a quarter of a million dollars of cash, bearer bonds, and assets such as coins and artwork from her. Not to mention the money he'd claimed was his as half of the profits of her hard work.

No, if Gary was here, it was because somebody else insisted on this location.

If that were the case, why would he ask her to meet him here? She thought back to the text message he'd sent last evening. Nothing fancy. Just the address, the time, and MEET ME. PLEASE. No signature. No x's and o's, as he'd have done a few years ago.

He knew it was over, and he knew she knew it was over.

No need to play coy or try to change things.

Which made the perfume she'd donned even more ridiculous.

Her breath caught in her throat as she caught a glint of gold on his left hand. He still wore his wedding band. Despite all the bitter words that had passed between them, in spite of his declaration that he would return her belongings "over my dead body'—

She took a single step back and checked the covered walkway that provided access to the rooms. Nobody in sight except an older woman at the far end pushing a housekeeping cart. Anne turned her face away from the woman. Her name wasn't on the room. She wasn't supposed to be here. She doubted the woman could describe her or her car, even if she remembered her.

And then the housekeeper turned toward her and looked directly at her, her head tipped as though in question.

Anne stepped into the room and closed the door behind her, leaning against the hollow wooden structure as though doing so would keep out the big bad world that suddenly seemed intent on pushing its way into her presence.

Practically a prisoner, Anne stifled a grin. How many bad movies had she watched over the years where the criminal tried to escape through a tiny bathroom window in cheap motels just like this one?

And how many had succeeded?

Most of them.

Stepping over Gary's body, she crossed the ten feet of room into the dank bathroom. The smell of mold and sour mops hit her as soon as she entered, and her nose wrinkled. She couldn't imagine coming in here to wash her hands, let alone to sit on the stool or disrobe for the shower.

But the window wasn't the minuscule transom-style she'd imagined.

Rather, an old-fashioned frame window that raised using good old brute strength and lead weights inside the sash greeted her, its paint peeling like a bad sunburn. If needed, she could get out through here.

If needed.

Unable to bear the smell another minute, she returned to the main room. Unfortunately, Gary was still there. As was the hole in his forehead, the pool of blood under his head, and the gun near the door.

She stood over the gun and studied it. A revolver, just like hers. Small nick in the barrel, just like hers. She'd dropped her weapon the first time she fired it, like a rookie, which she wasn't by any means. Even at the ripe old age of twelve. The wooden handle, carved by her grandfather, its patina showing its age and reminding her of the passing years.

And her initials. AM. Anne Matthews. Her birth name. No first husband. No second husband. No history at all. Just Anne Matthews.

How she longed for those days. The innocence.

But those days were gone forever.

And her gun was laying on the floor beside her dead husband's body.

But it couldn't be hers. Her gun was nestled safely in the glove box of her pickup.

At least, that's where she'd stowed it this morning. Before she left the house to run a few errands. Not intending to keep this appointment with Gary.

But the pleading in his text message played on her mind.

She had no intention of reconciling, but she could at least ask him for her belongings back one more time.

She picked up the weapon and backed up to wall beside the door, where her knees suddenly threatened to give out beneath her. She slid down the wall until her backside hit the dingy green carpet. She rested her elbows on her knees, the gun dangling in her hands, its metal cold to the touch, Gary's body slightly out of focus just beyond the toes of her best cowboy boots.

As cold as Gary was right now, she suspected.

Tears blurred her vision as a weight sat on her chest, threatening to choke her, to cut off her next breath, much as a bullet had done to Gary.

No matter how much she hated what he'd done, he didn't deserve to die this way. No matter how much she wanted to see him punished for his callous treatment of her and her belongings, she never wanted him dead.

And despite his response to her the last time she saw him, she doubted he intended to end his life this way. No, this wasn't suicide. The hole in the forehead. The gun near the door.

Not to mention that Gary would have gone out in style, in much nicer surroundings. Leaving the bill unpaid would have been right up his alley.

She could see the newspaper headlines already, assuming the story even made its way to the first page of the local newspaper. More likely his demise would be relegated to page seven, the second-to-last page of the small weekly periodical.

That would tick him off to no end, not to be on the front page.

Anne drew a deep breath to steady her nerves.

She sniffed the end of the barrel after making certain the safety was on. Recently fired.

Well, she did not intend to be here when the cops arrived, because surely they would soon arrive. Somebody must have heard the shot. Even in this near-rural setting on the outskirts of town, folks weren't so accustomed to the sound of guns firing that they'd overlook a single gunshot in the middle of the day. More likely, they'd have called the police immediately. She wouldn't be surprised to learn that this particular no-tell motel was a regular stop for the local cops.

She stood and stuck the gun into the small of her back then pulled the door open. Before stepping out, she checked in both directions. Nothing moved. She closed the door behind her and strode to her car as though leaving her room for the day. When she slid behind the wheel, she leaned her head back on the rest and exhaled before slipping the key into the ignition, starting the engine, and backing out of the lot.

Gritting her teeth in frustration at the snail's pace she forced herself to move, she headed for the highway, paused at the edge of the asphalt, and looked both ways for traffic. No point in getting into an accident so close to freedom.

She turned left, accelerated to the speed limit, and headed for home. As she rounded the next bend, sirens filled her car. Her breath caught again and her chest threatened to explode until two cruisers screamed around the corner ahead of her. She eased off the gas and pulled toward the side of the road to give them plenty of room to pass.

The second car flashed its headlights at her. Did he want her to pull over? She kept her eyes straight ahead, and the driver tossed her a wave of thanks as he went past. Once again, she let out a pent-in breath.

She was free.

Except she would never be free of the image of the body in that rundown fleabag in the middle of nowhere.

And her gun, one of her most treasured possessions, lying beside her dead husband.

Was someone trying to pin his murder on her?

If so, why?

+++++

Carly glanced at the boxes stacked on the floor and sighed. Mike had hauled them up here for her earlier this morning. She wanted to be certain she hadn't missed anything, and since he was still busy with his program, she could keep working, too. She still had three boxes left to go through. Good thing they'd planned a two-week trip, with ten days specifically set aside for staying with Anne. Still, she felt like time was running out faster than sand in a three-minute egg timer. Already most of the day was gone. Next on the agenda: dinner. Maybe a change of position would help.

About an hour later, the back door banged open. Carly sat at a comfy window seat, enjoying the late afternoon sun that warmed her toes while she reviewed more papers, putting her in the perfect position to peek out. Anne's truck sat in the drive, which meant her friend must be home, since it hadn't been in the yard for hours. She'd left shortly after breakfast, simply saying she had errands to run.

But Carly knew there was more to it than that. She'd overheard the conversation between Anne and Gary the previous evening.

When Carly asked if she wanted company, Anne shook her head. "Thanks, but no. This is something I have to do by myself."

If Anne had said she was going for a root canal, Carly would have believed it. Whatever her friend had to do—or wherever she had to go—she wasn't particularly happy.

Then again, Anne had her own life, and if she didn't want someone tagging along, so be it. Not like Carly didn't have enough to do here.

She expected Anne to stick her head in the door and say hi, but a few minutes later, the truck pulled out of the drive. Carly turned to Mike, who lay on his back on the bed. Programming, he said. Snoring, she said. But by that time there was nothing much to say. Anne likely forgot something.

A simple explanation, she was certain.

When they headed down the stairs to dinner, the Romers were huddled together at the top of the basement stairs. Whispering. And looking around as if to ensure nobody could overhear them.

What are they up to?

As a chief practitioner of hiding furtive activities, Carly knew without a doubt they were up to their necks in something. Their conspicuous absences from the table ever since she and Mike had asked a few simple questions. Not to mention catching them in a lie. Mike might think they'd simply misspoken, but she knew better. Not a huge fan of fibs, Carly generally tried to couch answers to questions she didn't want to answer in ambiguous terms. Once in a while, she'd respond with a question herself.

Most people were easily diverted. Most people fell for this trick.

But not Mike.

So why he would think these people were simply a dotty couple who couldn't keep straight which coast they lived on was absurd.

They might be dotty, but they also had a secret.

When they saw her, they closed the door and scuttled off toward the front door, their heads bent together, fingers twisted into knots—a telltale sign of nervousness—and headed outside.

Carly didn't know where they were eating, but it wasn't here.

Which was another strange thing. Their room included breakfast and dinner—a real steal—and they'd missed breakfast, and now seemed intent on skipping dinner, too. The couple didn't strike her as wealthy or frivolous, so why weren't they taking advantage of the bonus meals and eating here?

Carly paused on the second step down as she pondered these questions, and Mike exhaled loudly behind her. She turned to face him—or rather, the third button down on his shirt. "I feel a hot southerly wind on the back of my neck."

His mouth lifted in a slow smile, the kind that sent her pulse racing. Which he well knew. He quirked his chin behind him. "I think that's westerly, not southerly. You've got your directions all messed up. Again."

She jabbed a finger into that third button. "If you're referring to my discussion with the Romers about the Boston wharf, as I said last night, I was not confused."

He wrapped his hand around her finger. "I know. You were trying to trip them up."

"Not trip them up. Exactly." She paused to consider her words. "I was trying to get them to admit they knew nothing about Boston."

"And that was important to you why?"

"Because I—"

"Was trying to trip them up. Point made." He lifted her hand and kissed her palm. "Hungry?"

"Always." She chuckled. "I can't get much past you, can I?"

"Not much. Which is good for both of us."

She turned and continued down the stairs. "Why is that?"

"Because I'm smart. And I know you."

At the bottom of the stairs, she held her hand toward him. "No. I mean, why is that good for both of us?"

"Because it means you can't pull the wool over my eyes."

They passed the television room, where a Midwestern-accented reporter droned on about flooded washes and crop prices, before moving on to a local story.

This story just in. The body of an as-yet unidentified male has been found in a motel along the interstate. Police say foul play has been suspected, but no weapon has been found. An autopsy will be conducted tomorrow.

Carly glanced at the image on the screen.

She knew that man.

She stopped in her tracks, feet frozen to the floor.

Mike, unaware, continued walking until he came to the end of their tether of hands, and, like a puppy on a short leash, jerked to a halt. He turned, his brow pulled down. "Hey, I thought you were hungry. Don't get sidetracked just because they're talking about sugar beets and hog bellies. Dinner is this way."

She couldn't move, and even his words didn't draw a response.

The man on the train.

The one who had fought with the other guy.

Then tossed that hapless victim off.

Likely to his death.

Was now dead.

Her breath caught in her throat.

This day was getting curiouser and curiouser, as Alice in Wonderland would say.

+++++

Mike sat at his desk and stared at the computer screen. Nothing was adding up.

Not Carly's preoccupation with the Romers. Not her sudden headache that kept

79

her from eating dinner—nothing came between Carly and her food. Except a mystery. That was about the only thing he'd ever seen distract her. From everything, not just mealtime.

But this was different.

All was fine until she saw that news story. And then the color drained from her face, and her knees seemed certain to give way beneath her.

But she wouldn't tell him what was going on.

Because although he knew little else, something was going on.

And what was it with her and Anne's other guests? Maybe they simply didn't want to tell her their life story. Not that Carly could believe that folks might not want to share with her. Like that couple in Raven Valley.

Then again, not the best example, because they *were* up to something.

Just not what she'd thought.

He smiled, his reflection in the screen confirming his expression wasn't one of joy, but rather of wry amusement.

If not for jumping to conclusions, Carly wouldn't get any exercise at all.

He glanced at his wife asleep in bed. After the news article, she'd turned around, a hand to her head, and begged off. "Sorry, Mike. I suddenly have a headache. Go eat. I'm going up to lie down."

She wasn't telling him the whole truth, but it was as much as he would get from her right now. Better to let her tell him in her own time and her own way.

So he ate dinner on his own—maybe she was on to something when she talked about the Romers, since they didn't show up to eat—so he took his coffee and rhubarb pie to their room, thinking maybe she'd join him, but her slow, even breathing indicated she'd fallen asleep.

However, she'd stayed up long enough to make some notes. A pen and pad of paper sat on the bedside table, covered in scribbles and question marks and exclamation points. None of which made any sense to him.

He enjoyed his treat and turned back to his computer. Strange the FBI agent hadn't arrived yet. Mike glanced out the window at the green landscape beyond. The fine weather here indicated no reason for delay. Of course, he had no idea about Colorado weather. Could be a late-season snow, he supposed.

He picked up his cell phone and called Walt Jamieson in the DC office. "Hi, Walt. Mike Turnquist here. Wondering if you sent that agent to look into the situation here?"

"Mike. Good to hear from you. Let me look that up." Papers rustled. Computer keys tapped. After a long pause, Jamison returned to the phone. He cleared his throat softly. "The paperwork isn't making any sense to me. How big is this Danforth place?"

"I dunno. A few thousand people, maybe."

"That's what I thought. Which is what makes this strange."

Mike straightened. Strange? Strange was being married to an accountant who stumbled on dead bodies wherever they went. Strange was having a wife who asked probing questions folks didn't want to answer. "What's going on?"

"Seems we had an anonymous call about a week ago from somebody in your town."

"Not my town, Walt. I'm just visiting."

"You get my meaning. Something about counterfeit money and perhaps a drug connection. Wilcox took the assignment six days ago. He should have arrived there at least five days ago. I don't know why we haven't been able to get in touch with him. Seems we tried to call. His cell goes to voice mail. We left him a couple of messages. I'll check and call you back when I know more."

Walt Jamison was right. An agent out of touch with his home office drew attention. "Can you email me a picture so I can keep an eye out? Maybe he was in an accident. Amnesia, or something."

Jamison chuckled. "That only happens in movies."

"I know I'm grasping at straws. Just trying to make sense of it."

"No problem. Everything else okay there?"

"Yes." Mike chuckled. "One mystery is enough for a town this size."

"Oh? Sounds like you think there might be more than one."

"Just trying to understand my wife."

Now it was Jamison's turn to laugh. "Good luck on that one. Been married nearly forty years and still haven't figured mine out."

The man's words didn't settle Mike's anxiety, however. Forty years was a long time. If Jamison couldn't decipher the mystery of a woman's mind in that length of time, how could he ever hope to? "Thanks. Look forward to either seeing your agent or hearing back from you."

"Could take me a day or so. Sometimes phone contact in the mountains and the open plains is spotty at best."

"Gotcha."

Mike disconnected the call and set the phone on the desk beside his laptop. He had plenty to occupy his time. He didn't need to look for any more mysteries or unanswered questions.

Carly was busy enough doing that for both of them.

He needed a way to keep her on track, without her knowing he was.
Without her knowing what he was up to.
Two could play that game.

Chapter 9

When his cell phone rang early the next morning, Mike checked caller ID before answering. *Philip Osgood.* He punched the ANSWER button. "Mike Turnquist here."

"Mike, Mike. What's the problem, buddy?"

Mike gritted his teeth. He'd never noticed the smarmy tone to the man's voice before. Carly would have picked up on that right away. And advised him to stay clear. Not that his wife's judgment of people was always spot-on, but in this case. . . "Thanks for calling back."

"You sounded a little harried on the first couple of messages. But this last one gave me hope that we'd see this thing through. More like the man I'd heard about."

The hair on the back of Mike's neck bristled. "What have you heard?"

"Just that you do good work and you don't mind a challenge."

Mike settled into the chair overlooking the back yard and drive. Carly strolled through the kitchen garden, touching a plant here, sniffing a bloom there. He'd much rather be with her than having this conversation. Still, he refused to let the man's nice words deter him.

"I guess I made a mistake on keying in a function or something." He tossed in a wry chuckle for good measure. "Thought I was looking at something illegal."

A long pause filled the airspace before Osgood responded. "And now?"

"Realized I goofed up. The project is on schedule."

"Good to hear. Hopefully you trust us enough to know we wouldn't ask you to do something like that. Glad to know you're up to a challenge."

"Don't mind a challenge. It's a prison sentence I wasn't looking forward to."

"Tsk-tsk. You haven't gone and done anything illegal, have you?"

Gone and done anything—the nerve of the man! But he had to play along until Wilcox could take a look at the program. Still, he couldn't resist a return jab. "Interesting things you learn about companies by looking at their computer programs."

"Really? How so?"

"You find out what's important to them. Learn their business secrets."

Another long pause. "What have you learned about us?"

"That you want your employee owners to be happy, so you pay them well. Very well, I might add."

Osgood's chair creaked on the other end of the call. "Glad to know there isn't a problem. We didn't expect one. When we hired—and, I might add, paid you handsomely—to reconstruct an existing program to meet some specific needs pertaining to upcoming developments within the structure of our company, we believed we were getting the best man out there."

"So my initial test that indicated your company is stealing from people would be because?"

"Like you said. You entered something wrong. A bug in the program. Mike, I don't know what you saw or think you saw within the code we provided, but we operate everything legally and aboveboard."

"That's good." Mike wasn't certain how far out on this limb he should go. Or if he should even venture there. If Osgood thought he was on them, they might do exactly what Jamison warned him about. Still. . . "So there is no ghost module testing credit card accounts and charging small amounts using an identifier similar to an existing retailer?"

Osgood laughed. "That is some vivid imagination you have." His voice lowered in tenor. "You'd best not try spreading something like that around. You might find yourself sued for slander."

Well, that's exactly what was there. He'd stumbled upon it, and when he ran a test, saw that it mirrored an account that puts the money into a long-term asset account that wouldn't appear in Financial Freedom's income statement. "Like I said, my mistake. Sorry to take up your time."

"I can check with the Development Team boys and see what's going on, if that will set your mind at ease."

"Don't worry about it."

"Good deal. Glad to hear you'll keep working on the project. How are things going besides this little, uh, hiccup?"

Mike relaxed his jaw muscles. At this rate, he'd have a headache and broken teeth to boot. "Fine."

"Good. Like I said, I'll check with Development. See if they've ever heard of this sort of think happening before. I should have an answer for you within twenty-four hours. But keep plugging on. In fact, why don't you send me a quick report by email of your status?"

"Can do. I'll get that out by end of business today."

"And Mike, if it turns out there is something wrong with the code—which I'm absolutely not expecting, we'll make sure to increase your original estimate by whatever amount you say to cover your time to get rid of the problem."

Now Mike knew for certain Osgood was stringing him along. No client worth keeping gave a blanket overage approval. Over the phone. "Sounds like a plan."

Again the chair creaked. Papers rustled. "And I appreciate your professionalism in this. Coming to me directly."

"Understood."

"You have kept yourself to yourself, right?"

Mike forced another chuckle. "What did you think I might do? Call the FBI or something?"

A dry chuckle, devoid of any humor, met his ear. "Right. Because the last contractor who crossed us is now greeting customers at his local WalMart. He couldn't get a job in his industry if he paid for it."

That sounded like a not-so-veiled threat. "No worries there."

Osgood continued. "So just stay on the job. You don't want to be pegged as much of a loony as that wife of yours."

It was one thing to threaten him, quite another to bring Carly into the mix. "I beg your pardon. What does my wife have to do with this?"

"Oh, nothing. It's simply good business practice to check our contractors out thoroughly. And we saw that fiasco where she thought she saw a bank robbery in your little Podunk town. Bean Cove, is it? When the press got wind of that, they really made her look like a fool."

Mike's jaw ached once more. "And if your investigator was worth his salt, you'd know she was vindicated."

"Hmm. The media didn't print much about that. Not quite as interesting a story, is it? But if you say so, I believe you."

"Appreciate it."

Another humorless chuckle. "At any rate, the FBI is much too busy these days. And you have no proof. You said yourself, keyboard error."

Maybe Osgood was right. Why would the FBI care about this? It wasn't like people were getting hurt.

No, people were getting hurt. There was no such thing as a victimless crime. The man in the motel was hurt. The man who got tossed from the train was hurt. Anne was hurt. The credit card holders were hurt, as were the finance companies that backed those cards.

True, he hadn't heard back from Jamison yet. And Wilcox hadn't shown up. Jamison said the agent left six days prior. He could have practically walked here in that time. "The job is going ahead. No worries."

"Good to hear."

"I expect to hear from you within twenty-four hours, as you promised."

"And I'll expect your report. Within the same timeframe should be sufficient. As you promised."

Mike pressed the END button and set the phone on the desk. He hated this part of working for himself. Somehow when he decided to go independent, he pictured himself sitting at his computer for hours every day, running and testing code, sending the module off to a satisfied client, and starting on the next project.

In reality, he spent a lot of time talking to clients who didn't really know what they wanted or how they wanted to get there.

He felt a lot like old Chris Columbus.

At least he wasn't doing it on borrowed money.

+++++

Carly strolled around the corner of the house from the kitchen garden. She'd enjoyed this time outside, getting some fresh air, absorbing the sunshine. A chance to think. About the man's picture on the television last night. She watched the morning news, but there was still no identification. Not even a 'pending notification of next of kin' statement that police agencies often used.

A chill ran up her arms, and she rubbed her hands up and down her skin to warm her, except this cold was coming from inside. And no amount of friction would help.

The memory of the police officers at her front door all those years ago resurfaced.

The rain fell in torrents, the drops caught in the glow from her porch light. Their black slickers and clear plastic hat protectors repelling water like off a duck's back. Their mouths drawn down. The police cruiser parked at the curb.

All to tell her that her first husband, an abusive alcoholic, had just wrapped his car around a tree after losing control on the slick roads.

He was dead.

At the time, all she'd been able to think was how relieved she was not to be in the car with him. But after that came feelings of shame and sorrow. Shame that he was still her husband, that she hadn't had the courage to leave. Sorrow she was widow to a man who beat her whenever the urge hit him, but limited in her opportunities to speak the truth about him now that he was dead.

Glad he was out of her life forever. Angry he'd died before she could grow a backbone and leave.

She paused and leaned against the house, taking comfort in its solid brick construction, pressing her shoulder blades into the rough surface until it hurt. Sometimes it felt good to alleviate the pain of her younger self through something as minor—in comparison—as pressure-induced pain, or pinching the skin on the back of her hand, or biting down a little harder on her bottom lip. Something—anything—to remind herself she was alive.

She sighed and pushed away from the house. Maybe she'd made a mistake coming here to help Anne. Not the help itself, but the circumstances of the situation. The nasty divorce and the abuse brought back a lot of memories.

How did folks fall in and out of love so easily? Certainly, Anne loved Gary when she married him. Still did to some degree, Carly supposed. But the man's lying and stealing managed to erode any tender feelings and replaced them with mistrust, anger, and hurt.

Carly continued around to the rear of the house, and stopped short. The scene looked much the same as the first day they'd arrived, with chickens pecking, goats nibbling. But today, the double doors to the cellar were propped open. Which was unusual. So far as she knew, access to the cellar was always through the basement stairs inside.

Carly crept up to the doors and looked inside. She couldn't see anybody, but definitely heard voices. A man's and a woman's.

The Romers.

Whatever those two were up to, it wasn't good. Of that she was certain.

First, they lied about being from Portland, Maine and knowing Boston, then when caught in that lie, made themselves scarce. Probably so she couldn't ask more questions.

It's what she'd do in the same circumstance.

Although why anybody would lie about where they lived was beyond her. Didn't make any sense.

Unless—unless they were in the witness protection program and got their stories mixed up. Like maybe they really were from Maine, but forgot that wasn't their new cover story.

Carly's pulse quickened. This was so exciting. She'd heard about the Program, as it was called in law enforcement—hadn't everybody?—but she'd never met anybody in it.

Then again, maybe she had but didn't know it. Which just went to show it really did work.

Maybe she could get them to admit they were in the Program. Could give her some tips, in case she and Mike ever needed to enter. Not that they lived *that* kind of life, of course. But truly innocent people did end up in precarious situations. Like the guy on that reality television program who saw a murder, and when he came forward, somebody tried to kill him. So he had to go into the Program through no fault of his own, until he testified in court. And then they had to move him all over again when his young daughter got upset at preschool because some other kids were teasing her and blurted out that she was special because she had two names. The one they knew her by, and the one her parents used to call her but they changed because the bad man was looking for them.

The voices from the cellar grew louder, accompanied by approaching footsteps. Carly would soon get her questions answered.

If she didn't scare them off first.

George's head appeared first, and when his eyes locked with Carly's, she knew she was right.

Abject fear mixed with dismay reflected in his expression.

She put on her biggest smile. "Relax. I know all about you."

Nancy's head appeared over George's shoulder. "You do?"

"Sure." Carly gestured to them. "Come on up. I have about a hundred questions."

George's brow drew down. "Questions? You said you know all about us. What questions?"

Carly waved off his words like an annoying fly. "I may have exaggerated when I said I knew all about you. Maybe not all. But I have a pretty good idea what you are up to."

George clambered through the opening and up the steps to ground level. He reached down and helped his wife.

If she really is his wife. Maybe that's part of their cover.

Going into the Witness Protection Program would probably be hard. She couldn't imagine going through the rest of her life not being able to contact Tom, Sarah, and Bradley. Or Denise and the grandkids. No, that definitely wouldn't be fun. Exciting, perhaps. But not fun.

And Mike would kill her for getting herself—and him—into such a situation.

She giggled. Which was worse? Some mobster gunning her down on the street, or Mike killing her for sticking her nose where it didn't belong?

George and Nancy stood before her, their faces smudged with dirt, and something looking suspiciously like a cobweb in Nancy's hair.

Yuck.

Cobwebs meant only one thing.

Spiders.

She gestured to a bench and a couple of chairs on a concrete slab nearby. "Let's sit and chat."

George and Nancy exchanged a look—similar to the one that passed between them at their first—and last—meal together. Nancy nodded and the two led the way to the conversation nook. They sat side by side on the bench, leaving Carly her choice of two identical chairs.

Carly glanced at the sky to check the position of the sun, and chose the one that let her sit with her back to the orb. No point in having to squint.

Once they settled in, Carly waited. When they seemed hesitant to do open up to her, she plunged in. "Why were you in the cellar?"

"Mice."

From George.

"Spiders."

From Nancy, accompanied by a shudder.

Carly knew how the woman felt. Mice were a lot more manageable than those creepy-crawly insects. And mice were less likely to come into her house in Bear Cove than spiders, thanks to Doc the cat.

But their differing answers only confirmed what she thought was really going on.

She nodded, peering at each in turn. "Why were you really in the cellar?"

George laid his hand on Nancy's forearm. "Mice."

"Then why did she say spiders?"

George leaned back in the bench and looped his arm over the back, near his wife's shoulders, as though they were on a date at the movies and he was getting ready to cuddle with her. His fingers tapped the wooden bench in time with a melody only he could hear. "We saw spiders down there while looking for mice."

Carly brushed at her hair and quirked her chin toward Nancy. "I see you found evidence of spiders."

Nancy picked at the strands of spider silk, her nose wrinkled in distaste. "Yes. That's right. We found spiders."

"So why didn't you go down through the basement stairs?"

George glanced up as though hoping a contrail or alphabet-shaped clouds spelled out the answer. Carly followed his gaze, but saw nothing that answered the question.

He looked back at her then at Nancy. "I don't know, Sweetums. Why didn't we go through the house?"

Nancy swallowed hard, her eyes wide. "We were outside for a walk when we saw that big black mouse scurry down the steps. Remember?"

He stared at her overlong then realization lit his face. "Right. And so down we went. We didn't think anybody would mind."

Carly knew the old make-it-up-and-follow-along canoodle when she saw it. She was an expert. Mike, not so much. He was so honest and candid he couldn't follow her story long enough to convince anybody of anything. Which made her stories even more outlandish than they need be.

"Did you find anything else?"

Nancy's head snapped around. "Like what?"

Carly shrugged. "I don't know. Like a body, maybe?"

Nancy's head rotated like she was watching a tennis match—from Carly to George and back again. Her mouth opened a couple of times as though she was going to speak, but no sound came out.

Why a silly question like that—because she'd meant it as a joke, of course—should generate such a bizarre and panicked response was beyond Carly.

Unless they really were looking for a body.

Or hiding one.

Carly scooted to the edge of her chair. This was really getting interesting. The only reason to explain this couple's bizarre behavior she came up with was the Witness Protection Program. Maybe this was much more nefarious. Maybe they were murderers, trying to dispose of a body. Or undercover cops, trying to find a body.

Like the one that was thrown off the train.

The question was: did they throw, or were they looking?

She sat back. No, that didn't make sense. The man on the television was the one who tossed a man off the train.

Which only left undercover cops as the explanation for who George and Nancy Romer really were.

She scooted forward again and tapped an index finger alongside her nose. "I know who you really are, and why you're here." She sat back again. "But rest assured, I won't tell a soul. Your secret is safe with me."

George blinked several times. "Our secret?"

"Sure." She repeated the gesture for sharing a confidence. "Say no more."

Nancy opened her mouth again, but George silenced her with a quick shake of his head. "Glad we can keep it between us. We'd best be going."

He grasped his wife's hand and pulled her from the bench, and the two scurried off around the house.

Carly relaxed into her chair. It felt good to share a secret with somebody. Like she held something valuable. Something fragile. Something shared.

Of course, she also held a basket of questions that they hadn't answered. Like which agency they worked for. If they truly were husband and wife. Who they thought the body was. Was it the body from the train?

Because two things she knew for certain.

They weren't telling her everything. Few people ever did.

And if they were looking for the body thrown from the train by the unidentified dead man, how did the rumors about bodies in the basement of Anne's house get started?

She made a mental note to ask Anne about that.

While rumors about such things in old houses weren't always true, most times they grew from some nugget of fact.

Chapter 10

Carly pushed her plate away at breakfast the next morning. "I feel like I've gained five pounds from all this good food."

Across the table, Mike chuckled. "Me, too. Maybe we should go for a walk after breakfast?"

"Sounds like a plan. Let me finish this last sweet roll first, though."

Mike rolled his eyes at her. "Waste not, waist not."

She giggled at his play on words, one they'd spotted on a bumper sticker.

The words described her perfectly, as though written for her.

Or about her.

Not desiring to be the poster child for that particular motto, she left two bites of Anne's delectable cinnamon roll crusted with honey pecans and a touch of nutmeg on her plate.

She could always have another with coffee later on.

Because while Anne and the Romers were conspicuously absent, the baked items and full-course meals were not.

She and Mike pulled on their light jackets to brave the cool morning. Since coming to Danforth, apart from walking around the garden, she'd not managed to enjoy the outdoors. A brisk walk—or a gentle stroll, preferably—sounded like a good intro into her day.

She clasped Mike's hand and together they went down the front steps, along the walkway, and turned left at the gate. "How is your work going?"

Despite usually working from home—and now from Anne's home—they didn't get as much time to talk as most people thought. Part of that was their different work styles—Carly preferred to plunge in and get through the material, while Mike liked to ponder and think and program in his head—or his sleep.

He sidestepped a stone on the concrete. "Okay, I guess."

She paused, forcing him to stop. "Just okay? Doesn't sound like you. You're either so hyped about a project that you don't stop talking about it. Which is not the case here. Or else you're bothered by something and you never mention it."

"I think I've stumbled upon something illegal, and I'm not certain what to do about it."

She stared at him. Mike, the ultra-conservative man who wouldn't even drive five over the speed limit, didn't know what to do? "Tell me what's going on."

He walked on, and she fell into step by his side. "Not really sure."

A glance at his profile confirmed the tension he was under. Creases around his eyes and mouth. The hint of shadows under his eyes.

Had she been so preoccupied with her own work she'd missed this?

A pang of guilt flashed through her. She looped her arm through his and snuggled closer as they continued their walk. "I'm sorry, Mike. I should have picked up on it sooner that something was bothering you."

He shrugged. "I guess it didn't really come to a head until yesterday."

She gripped his arm. "Right. And you didn't want to bother me."

"I didn't want to bother you."

"Because you knew I had my own concerns with Anne."

"You had your hands full with your friend."

She stopped again, and waited until he looked at her before continuing. "But you're my husband, and my chief concern should be you."

"I hoped I was wrong. I thought maybe I was blowing it all out of proportion."

Carly knew how that was. How many times had she recalled the scene on the train and hoped she'd misinterpreted what she thought she saw? Too many times to count. But no matter how she tried to spin it, she still came to the same conclusion: the unidentified man whose body was found in the motel had pushed another man off the train.

She stretched up on her tiptoes to plant a kiss on Mike's mouth then turned to walk on. "So what changed that?"

"Philip Osgood, the owner of Financial Freedom, finally returned my call."

"Finally?"

"I left two messages over the past two days. Which was strange in and of itself, since every time before when I called, he answered right away. Even if he was in a meeting. It was like the program was a top priority with him, and now it isn't."

"Or he's trying to avoid you."

Mike shook his head. "I don't think that's it."

Carly released her grip on his arm and instead allowed him to envelop her hand in his. "It's what I do when I don't want to explain myself."

He grinned. "Is that why you don't answer your phone when I call?"

"Sometimes." She returned his smile. "But seriously, if he's not trying to avoid you, maybe the project isn't so important."

"Maybe. But he threatened me in a backhanded way. And he offered me carte blanche on my billing. Both of which are not best business practices."

She paused again. They were never going to get their walk done if he kept dropping bombshells like this. "So how did it end?"

"I told you I called the FBI in DC. Talked to Special Agent Jamison. Told him I'd left a couple of messages for Osgood about a problem. Jamison suggested I leave another telling him I made a mistake and everything was fine."

"Why would he want you to do that?"

"So they could close in on Financial Freedom before they close up and move somewhere else under a new name but the old scam. So I did. I think I convinced Osgood I'd overreacted. But he still warned me about not going to the Feds."

"Did he say anything else?"

Something passed across her husband's face—if she didn't know him better, she'd say he was hiding something from her.

But that was like him.

He shook his head. "Not much. I think he's okay. Wants me to send a report. Said he'd check with his Development Team and get back to me."

She continued walking. "Sounds like everything is okay then."

He shook his head. "I'm not so certain. There was something about his voice and his careful choice of words." He shrugged. "I don't know. Maybe I'm just hanging around you too much."

"Never. I'm a good influence on you. Getting you to be more spontaneous."

He laughed, and the sound lifted her spirit. "Coming from the woman who needs advance notice to be spontaneous, that's a good one."

She hated when he started quoting her words back to her. A good comeback required quick thinking. But apparently she'd consumed the proper combination of coffee and sweet rolls this morning—how many of each *had* she consumed?—because a sharp response sprang to mind. "Spontaneity is good for the soul. Planned spontaneity is good for the mind."

He chuckled but continued on, turning right at the next corner. "Good one."

"So what are you going to do?"

"I told him I would keep working. Send him the report. He said he would check with Development. Right now, I'd say it's a stalemate. We're both holding the other to the fire, so to speak. The good news is I'm about three days ahead of schedule, so I can wait him out."

"He claimed not to know about the problem?"

"Right."

"Do you believe him?"

"Not sure."

Another left turn took them through a small park with a set of swings and other outdoor play equipment for kids. Set apart in one corner was a bench that looked inviting.

She quirked her chin toward it. "Let's sit for a few minutes. The sun feels nice."

"Okay."

They settled within minutes, Carly snuggling against Mike's arm, her head on his shoulder. "So what does this mystery program do? Or is that a mystery, too?"

"No mystery there. It charges credit cards small amounts using a name similar to a recurring entry, and always right before the statement closes for the month."

Carly the accountant stared at him. "What good would that do? Once people get their statements, they'd find it and report it. Try to track down the company. Or contest it with their credit card company."

He pressed her head back onto his shoulder. "You'd be surprised how many people don't reconcile their bank accounts or credit card statements on a regular basis."

She raised her head again. Had the world gone mad? "I do, every month, down to the penny."

He returned her to her original position. "But not everybody is like you. If a person looked at the statement and saw the charge, they'd think their recurring charge came out a day or so early. They'd make a mental note to check the next statement. But by the time a month rolls by, they forget about it."

"But what about those people who do report it to their credit card company?"

"It gets reversed. The program is designed to check the next month's statement for that. If that happened, it waits six months and then chooses another recurring payment or a frequented retailer, and mimics the account information."

"How do they make money if people get the charge reversed?"

"They are accessing millions of credit card accounts monthly, and even if the charge was just for one dollar, and fifty percent of the charges were reversed, that would be half a million dollars of pure profit per month."

"Where do they get that information?"

He shrugged. "Not sure. That might be something you'd know more about than me."

She mock-punched his arm. "Why? Because basically at heart I'm a nefarious criminal?"

"No, silly. Because this kind of thing is right up your alley. Hidden assets and all that."

"That's better." She pondered the situation as a couple of toddlers and their mother played on the swings. "I have to go to the bank today to ask about some accounts for Anne. I could probably ask there."

"Sounds like a plan." Mike stood and pulled her to her feet. "Time to head back. I need to check some other things I've already done in case I continue. But I'm hoping the FBI agent gets here first. Which I almost forgot to tell you. He was assigned to come here before I called."

"What?"

"Seems there was an anonymous tip about counterfeit money and a possible drug ring. And he's not been heard of since leaving somewhere called the Western Slope in Colorado."

"Where's that?"

He shrugged. "Don't know. We can look it up when we get back to the house."

"It galls me to think he'll take your work and have somebody else build on it, and you won't get the credit. In fact, Osgood will likely get a bonus for saving the company money."

"It's his company, Carly. He probably gives himself bonuses all the time."

She laughed. "We work for ourselves. We should give ourselves a bonus once in a while."

"We do. We come on these extravagant vacations to out-of-the-way places. Not to mention all the adventures you get us tangled up with."

"No fair. You're neck-deep in one of your own."

"Yes, but you're the pro at ferreting out mysteries, aren't you?"

Mike knew her too well.

But still he loved her.

+++++

Shortly after Carly left to visit the bank, his cell phone rang.

Walt Jamison.

He answered. "Mike Turnquist here."

"Glad I caught you. Any sign of our missing friend?"

"Nothing yet. I was hoping maybe you had news."

"Well, I have some new information. Seems there was a massive late-winter storm in Colorado. Most of the agents went home and hunkered down for the duration. Which is why my calls to the office weren't being returned."

"Would have been nice if somebody was checking the voice message."

"Phone service was down, too, so no go on that. But I did get through today through a series of relays. And here is what I learned. Riley Wilcox took the train to Danforth because a landslide blocked the highway. He got out of the Western Slopes, whatever those are, and managed to get to Denver, where he boarded the train. That was six days ago."

"Assuming the rails between Denver were open—"

"And they were."

"Then he should have been here by now, even if he took the milk run."

"The milk run?"

Mike chuckled despite the seriousness of the situation. A missing FBI agent was no laughing matter. "That's what we call those routes that stop at everybody's back door. Like the milkman's route."

"Gotcha."

"Did you get that picture?"

"Did. What's your fax number?"

Mike rattled off his online fax service number that appeared like a regular fax number to the sender but came through his business email. "Once I get that, I'll print out a copy for me and one for Carly so she can keep an eye out for him. I tease her that she always gets her man. I hope it's true in this case, too."

Jamison's dry laugh communicated his concern over the missing Wilcox. "Anyway, we received confirmation that he boarded the train in Denver."

"Did he have a suitcase?"

"Funny you should ask. He did, and it's still sitting in the station in Danforth. It got off, but he hasn't claimed it yet."

"Maybe I could pick it up so it doesn't go missing."

"Good idea. If—or maybe I should say when—he shows up, he'll likely be ready for a change of shirt."

Mike's mind cast back to the time he was trapped in his car in the forest. A clean shirt was the last thing on his mind. "I'll probably need authorization for that."

"I'll call them and find out what they need when we hang up, then I'll send you an email."

"Sounds good. What train was he on?"

"The westbound 857."

Something niggled at Mike's mind. That sounded familiar. But the train he and Carly arrived on was called the Pacific Prince. Couldn't be the same one.

Even for Carly, that would be too great a coincidence.

+++++

Carly's cell phone rang as she strolled toward the downtown area. Anne Torbin. She answered the call. "Anne, so good to hear from you. How are you?"

"Sorry I haven't been a very good hostess. Or a very good friend."

"Nonsense." While not entirely true—Carly had thought her friend's absence a little strange—she understood some of what Anne was going through. "Are you okay?"

Anne sniffled. "Sure. It's just been hard, you know?"

"I do know, Anne. I've gone through much of what you're facing. Except my husband was killed before I had the chance to divorce him."

A sharp intake of breath filled the line. More sniffling.

Something serious *was* going on.

"Anne, listen. I was on my way to the bank to check on some things, but I could meet you wherever you like. The bank can wait."

"No, it really can't. That's the reason I was calling. I just got a returned check notice. Checks I wrote to vendors and utilities. I don't understand what's going on, Carly."

"Did Gary have signing authority on the account?"

"Yes. But why would he try to destroy the business? It just doesn't make any sense. He was trying to claim half of the B&B as marital assets. If I have to close the doors because he's taken the money, that doesn't benefit him in any way."

What her friend said made sense. But then again, desperate people didn't always make rational decisions. "Maybe he thought he'd cut and run instead of taking his chances with the divorce court."

"Maybe. But I don't think so. He wasn't staying—"

Carly paused and turned her back into the chill wind whipping down the street. "Have you seen him?"

"No. I—I—"

Carly had never known her friend to stutter or stammer. Anne was always cool and calm, poised and professional. So unlike Carly in so many ways. She'd been envious of her friend's ability to fit into almost every situation.

In fact, the only other time she'd known Anne to lose her composure was when she was caught in a lie about sneaking out after curfew to spend some time with the boy who would become her first husband.

Which meant—no, why would Anne lie to her?

"Anne, you haven't been around for a day or so. You're hiding something from me now. I can help if I know what's going on."

A low moan like an animal in pain was her only answer.

"Anne, tell me where you are. I'll come to you."

More sniffling. "I can't, Carly. I'm in so much trouble. I don't want to involve you."

"You've already involved me simply by being my friend. I want to help. But I need your help, too."

"My—my help?"

"Can you call the bank and the insurance agent and give them authorization to give me information?"

"I'll do that as soon as we hang up. Thanks for all you're doing for me."

Carly's mind raced. Could she convince the police to put a tracer on Anne's cell phone? Could they even do that? Find where she was hiding out? Maybe, if she could convince them her friend was going to do something drastic. Like take her own life.

Or somebody else's.

"Anne, is this abut Gary? Has he hurt you?"

"No more than usual." Muffled voices in the background. "I've got to go now. I'll call again. Or I'll see you at the house."

"Wait a minute. Tell me—"

But the line went dead.

Carly pressed the REDIAL button and listened to the ringtone indicating the call had gone through, but after about twenty rings, she hung up. Wherever Anne was and whatever she was doing, she didn't want to be contacted.

Or talked out of it.

+++++

Mike's hand paused on the keys to Anne's guest vehicle hanging from the rack near the back door. Their host hadn't been around at all today, so he couldn't ask permission. Still, she said they could borrow the pickup anytime.

This was an anytime. He wanted to go to the station to ask questions about the Westbound 857. Carly was headed downtown. Maybe she'd appreciate a ride back, too. It wasn't like the town was very big, so her journey wouldn't take her long. But he had too much on his mind to spend ten minutes walking to the railway station when he could drive in two. Perhaps he could kill two birds with one stone. Get some information and collect his wife.

And speaking of killing, the missing agent caused him more worry by the minute. An ordinary person might get lost or sidetracked along the way. Somebody like Carly would find a dozen reasons to divert from the main path and explore something else of interest.

But not a trained professional.

Particularly not one sent to investigate a case.

Which was something Mike hadn't thought too much about until now.

He exited the house, crossed the yard, and headed toward town.

Comparable in size to Bear Cove, at a population of about four hundred souls, Danforth nestled in a small valley between two rocky formations the locals called palisades. He squinted at the formation closest to the road into town. Standing about two hundred feet above the valley floor, these palisades did look something like the walls of a fortress from which they drew their name. Piles of soil, resembling flowing folds of a royal cape, billowed at the foot of the cliffs. Small trees and bushes struggled to find foothold in the nooks and crannies, but the bare granite peaks pushed through as though reaching for the skies.

And while some might feel penned in by the rocks, Mike drew comfort from their stalwart presence. No doubt they held back harsh winds and storms and had done so for years. Perhaps that's why the soil fell to the valley floor, nourishing and replenishing the pastures and farmland, drawing more people to live in their shadows.

He smiled at his personification of the range. Carly would take one look at them and wonder if there were any bodies hidden within the crevices. She'd probably say they were the perfect place to conceal a murder or a stolen treasure.

Mike left the palisades behind and pulled into the train station perched on the outskirts of town. The depot building, a one-story affair that looked like it had stepped right out of the pages of an old western movie, sat on the southern side of the rails, with an expanse of about fifty feet of boardwalk separating the station from the trains. Stacked alongside the building were crates and boxes destined for local businesses, private residences, and trucks bound for routes not so fortunate as to border the rail line.

A uniformed man, hunched over a lectern to one side of the doorway, studied papers on a clipboard. Mike parked the car and walked toward him. The porter looked up and tipped the brim of his silver-braided hat, the buttons of his uniform glinting in the midday sun.

Mike nodded in return. "Hi. Are you in charge here?"

The man smiled, revealing tobacco-stained teeth. "Not sure what you mean by in charge. But I guess I'm as in charge as anybody else."

Mike held out a hand. "My name is Mike."

"Brian." He pointed to his nametag, a confusing jumble of consonants with only one vowel. "Don't try to figure out the last name. Just call me Brian."

Brian it was. "I wanted to ask about a train."

"Then you've come to the right place. We got trains."

Mike smiled. Perhaps this was the old man's way of making sure he others treated him with a modicum of respect. Maybe it was a Wyoming thing. He wasn't certain, but he was willing to play the game. "And I expect you know everything there is to know."

The porter smiled, turned his head, and spat tobacco juice toward a beetle scurrying across the boardwalk. He missed. "Everything worth knowing."

"My wife and I arrived on the Pacific Prince a few days back."

Brian nodded. "I recall you. Had some kind of trouble back the line, didn't you?"

"That's us."

The man leaned closer. "I think your woman looks for trouble, doesn't she?"

Defense for Carly screamed to be spoken aloud, but Mike suspected he'd get more from the man if he kept playing his game. "Sometimes."

"My first wife was just like that. Always asking questions folks didn't want to answer." He peered at Mike. "She like that?"

"Sometimes."

"I heard she saw someone thrown from the train. Is that right?"

"Yes."

His one-word responses seemed to satisfy the man, who launched another wad of 'baccy juice, this time at no particular target. Which is exactly what it hit—nothing.

Instead, it splatted on the edge of the boardwalk near the rails.

Mike swallowed hard. "Does every train have a specific name?"

"Yep."

"So if I gave you the name of a train, you could tell me when it would come through?"

"Theoretically."

"Theoretically?"

"Well, they don't always run on time, you know. People hold up the trains. Cargo holds 'em up. Sometimes the weather sends them off schedule." Brian leaned one elbow against the lectern. "Why, one time I recollect a storm that lasted for four days. Snow up to the windows. That was a bad one. Trains stuck all along the track. Folks going hungry. They ran out of fuel to keep the engines running so people were getting cold. One man got frostbit when he left the train to go for help. Lost two toes, I think."

Glad that his own train experience wasn't nearly so dramatic, Mike nodded. When the man finished talking, Mike tried to pull him back on topic. "So, for example, the westbound 857? When does that come through?"

Brian stared at him for a long time, one eye slightly off center. "Are you pulling my leg?"

"No, sir. I really want to know."

The porter looked around. "No you're not. Where's the hidden camera? Am I going to be on one of those reality programs where they trick folks into looking silly?" He peered at Mike. "Not trying to make this old country bumpkin look dumb, are you?"

Mike took a step back, hands up in a gesture of surrender. "No, sir, Brian. I wouldn't do that."

The old man stared at him again, and Mike wondered if he'd misunderstood the rules of this game and offended the man in some way. Was he not going to learn what he needed to know? Or was the man pulling his leg?

After a long minute, Brian laughed and smacked Mike's back in a congenial old-boys' gesture. "No, I guess you're not. Forgive this old fool. Been watching too many movies, I guess."

Mike smiled. "So the westbound 857?"

"Why, that's the same train your missus saw somebody tossed off. Or says she did. Course, they haven't found a body yet." Brian mimicked holding a glass, waggling his hand as though he was intoxicated. "Then again, maybe she had too much drink with dinner, hey?" He leaned closer again. "Come on, you can tell me."

Mike shook his head. "She didn't have any alcohol that night. She saw what she saw."

"You always believe your wife?"

Mike hesitated. True, he'd given her the fifth degree when she told him, but he was convinced—despite evidence to the contrary—that she saw two men struggling. Whether one actually ended up off the train, he wasn't certain.

But she was.

And that was good enough for him.

"My wife is a trained investigator with very good observation skills. She knows what she saw."

The old man studied him for several heartbeats then nodded slowly. "Good answer. A man who won't stand up for his wife isn't a man I would trust. No matter how batty the wife is, I stand up for her."

Carly batty? Never. Headstrong, yes. Nosey, absolutely. Good at finding mysteries and bodies? An expert. But no matter how wild or extreme her theories, she was rarely wrong when she said something was wrong.

Driving away from the station, Mike considered the possibilities.

Either Carly was way off—which she had been once or twice in the past, although something was always going on, just not what she thought.

Or she was right.

Somebody had been thrown from the train.

And that thought chilled him to the bone.

Because at this point, the only person he knew on the missing list was an FBI agent named Riley Wilcox.

Mike was not looking forward to telling Carly.

She would take this and run with it.

And he'd be lucky if he stayed on for the ride.

Chapter 11

Carly headed for the only company in town that sold life insurance policies, a well-known national company with a large client base in agricultural communities. There was something about dealing with a business that targeted farmers and ranchers that felt down to earth, grassroots friendly. Like John Deere tractors. Or buying organic milk or cage free eggs.

Somehow, it automatically felt like these people would treat their customers right.

And while not strictly a customer, Carly hoped the town was small enough and perhaps the staff innocent enough to give her the information she needed.

That is, if Anne hadn't followed through and given them authorization to answer her questions.

She pushed through the old-fashioned door with a bell that announced her presence. A woman at a desk facing the door looked up from her computer. "Hi. I'm Velma, the office manager and chief cook and bottle washer. Can I help you?"

Carly introduced herself and her reason for being there. "Anne Torbin, my client, said she would—"

At the mention of Anne's name, the woman's smile melted away like an ice cube in July. "Of course. I talked to Anne earlier this morning. She said she was fine, but she didn't sound like it?"

The question hung in the air between them, begging a response. Carly bit her bottom lip to keep from replying. If Anne wanted this woman to know what was going on, she would have told her.

Thirty seconds passed, and Velma's brow rose millimeter by millimeter until Carly was certain it would stick near the back of her neck. Finally, the woman gave up and gestured to the chair opposite her. "Take a seat and let's see what we can do for you."

These words, spoken in a tone about twenty degrees cooler than her welcome, communicated the woman's displeasure at not being included in juicy information she'd no doubt pass along the gossip grapevine before the door closed behind Carly. Carly liked tidbits and details as much as anybody.

Just not at her friend's expense.

"Anne probably told you why I'm here."

Velma shrugged. "Something about helping with her divorce." She clasped and unclasped her fingers on her desk. "Although why she feels it necessary to divorce such a hunk as that Gary Torbin is beside me. Not like there's too many other choices in a small town like this."

Carly knew exactly why Anne was divorcing Gary, but once again, if Anne wanted the town to know, she'd have made her reasons public. "We don't know what goes on behind closed doors, do we?"

The woman blinked a couple of times as she pondered the statement. "Oh, I don't think they had any troubles in that area. At least, not according to Gary." She leaned forward as though sharing a confidence. "He says they enjoyed each other that way. A lot." A wink sealed her statement. "If you get my drift."

Carly got the woman's meaning, loud and clear. If this was the kind of talk Velma enjoyed, Carly wanted none of it. She'd stick to the facts, thank you, ma'am. "Do you have a copy of their policies? Anne couldn't locate the file."

Velma turned to a large four-drawer cabinet lining the wall beside her desk. "Got it right here." Her fingers walked across the tops of file folders in the S through Z drawer, finally lighting on the one she sought. "Doesn't surprise me about Anne losing the policy, though. Gary says she can't keep two dollars in her wallet but she loses one of them."

"Sounds like you and Gary are old friends."

"Not really." The woman slid the folder across the desk. "We play darts down at the club. A bunch of us get together to unwind." She flicked a tendril of hair from her forehead. "Not much to do for fun in a small town, you know."

Right. Except tear somebody's reputation to pieces.

Carly flipped open the folder. The top page was a copy of Gary's life insurance police. A large red CANCELLED across the top indicated its status. "When did he cancel this?"

Velma tapped some keys on her computer keyboard then peered at the screen. "Two weeks ago."

Carly turned the page and stared.

He'd doubled Anne's policy the same day.

Five hundred thousand dollars.

She looked up. "Does Anne's policy have an increase rider?"

"There's nothing illegal about what Gary did." The agent's hands trembled where they lay on the desk. "Anne granted him ownership of the policy a couple of years ago."

I didn't say anything about illegal. Funny she should jump right to that.

"She didn't say anything about that to me."

"Gary says she has a memory like a sieve."

"Did he say why he was canceling his policy?"

Velma snickered. "Guess he wasn't planning on dying anytime soon."

"Did he say why he thought it necessary to increase hers?"

Velma studied her lacquered nails. "You sound like you know what you're talking about, so let's cut to the chase. When she granted him ownership of the policy, all he had to do was wait for the next rider increase date. That just happened because she turned forty-five." She leaned back. "Nothing illegal. Nothing immoral. Just good sense."

"So he did say why the increase?"

"Maybe he was concerned the amount wouldn't cover his needs in the case of her death." Velma pushed a strand of hair off her forehead. "I barely remember breakfast, let alone a conversation I had two weeks ago."

"Didn't you think it strange he canceled his own and increased hers?"

"I'm just his agent, not his marriage counselor or financial advisor."

"Did you serve Gary the day he came in?"

"I did." A slow smile spread over Velma's face as though relishing a delectable dessert, savoring its flavors. "I helped him with the paperwork." The woman pulled the folder toward her out of Carly's grasp. "Now, if you don't mind, I've told you all I know. I have a lot of work to do."

All she knew, perhaps. But not all she suspected.

"Do you think Gary was planning to leave town?"

Velma tapped the folder on the desk. "Not that he told me."

"But you heard something through the grapevine?"

"I don't listen to gossip."

No, but she enjoyed generating it.

"Have you seen him around town?"

Velma tapped her index finger against her chin. "Now that you mention it, not for a day or so."

Carly thanked her and left the office, anxious to get home and share her news with Mike. As she walked, she pieced together what she knew and what she suspected. One man disappeared from a moving train. One soon-to-be-ex-husband not seen for a few days. Money and paintings missing. Bank accounts closed. Insurance coverage doubled.

None of which solved Anne's immediate problems.

That would be next on her list to work on.

+++++

Mike's email program pinged to tell him he had a new email. He clicked on the mailbox.

Walt Jamison.

He clicked on the attachment, and Riley Wilcox's face slowly appeared on his screen, beginning with the top of his head, working its way down to his chin. Intelligent eyes. Short-cropped hair. Serious smile.

Even if Mike didn't know it, he'd say this man was law enforcement. Career stuff.

He printed two copies, fingernails tapping on the desk as his portable printer ground out the images. When the first one finished, while he waited for the second, he studied the picture again. He hadn't seen the agent around town. Not on the train, either.

"Oh, no. Not again!"

Mike whirled in his chair at his wife's anguished cry. "What?"

"I know that man, too."

"What?" She was right. Oh, no, not again. "How can you know him?"

Carly crossed the room and took the sheet of paper from his hand. "Well, I don't mean that I *know* know him. But I've seen him before."

"Where?"

"He's the man the dead man on TV threw off the train."

"Are you sure?"

She planted her fists on her hips. "Am I sure? After all we've been through over the last week, and you have the nerve to ask me that?"

He stepped back. Out of striking range. Even her mock punches could raise a bruise. "Sorry. I didn't mean to sound like that. But he has a fairly ordinary face. And it was at night."

"The landing they stood on was lit. Our train was stopped. And since I don't see two men fighting every day, I paid close attention. They twisted and turned to avoid each other, circling like two dogs in a fight. I saw him. I recognize him. Just like I recognized the man they found in the motel room."

Mike tapped the second sheet from the printer. "This is the missing FBI agent. Riley Wilcox."

Carly sank into the other chair in their room and stared at the image. "Oh, that's terrible." She looked up. "Do you think he's dead?"

"Since there was no body, I guess we can hope he wasn't badly injured and was able to get away."

"Then why hasn't he checked in with his office? Or gone to the local police?"

"Amnesia?"

She shook her head. "You don't believe that any more than I do. That's only in the movies. And sappy mysteries."

"And this is no sappy mystery."

She hung her head. "No, this is real life."

"Let's not mourn for him until we know for certain one way or the other. I talked with a man down at the railway station today. The train that the agent was booked on was the one that passed us that night. So it's looking more and more like he's either the man who was thrown from the train, or the man who did the throwing."

"That's important information." His wife's bottom lip jutted out. "No, he's definitely the one who fell. The question now is: who is the killer?"

"Any suspects?" He groaned. What was he doing, asking her if she had any suspects. Of course she did. "Good thing I was on the train so you can rule me out."

A hint of a smile tickled her lips. "We weren't together at the time so you could have had time to jump off our stopped train, run down the tracks, jump on the moving train, get into a fight with a complete stranger, push him off, and return to our train before it started up again."

"And I might have done, except for one thing."

"What's that?"

He held out his arms to her and waited until she crossed the room and sat in his lap. "You always get your man. I wouldn't be foolish enough to try to outwit you."

+++++

She liked that.

You always get your man.

She had the only man she truly wanted.

Carly leaned her head against his chest and sighed. "You're right. But that kind of sweet talkin' doesn't bring us any closer to a solution."

"You've been out for a while. What have you learned?"

She straightened but remained sitting on his lap. "The bank said Anne's accounts were closed by Gary about five days ago. He took out every red cent, not even leaving enough money to cover the checks she'd written recently for vendors and utilities."

"Sounds like the man was getting ready to leave and didn't care how much of a disaster he left behind."

"That's what I thought, too. But then I visited the insurance agent where they held their life insurance policies." She filled him in on what she'd learned there, including her take on Velma's proclivity for gossip. "So I think he wanted to make certain Anne was left high and dry if anything happened to him."

Mike rubbed his hand up and down her back, and she relaxed into his touch. "Do you think he was planning to kill her for the insurance?"

"I don't think so. But then again, I'm not sure. I'll have to ask her what she thinks." She straightened again. "I asked the woman at the bank about credit card scams, and she confirmed the kind you told me about is pretty common. There have been a number of reported instances of work laptops being stolen or compromised. Big retailers are scurrying around trying to close the barn door after the horse got out, so to speak. She suspects there are many more instances of lost or stolen credit card information that are never reported to either the cardholder or the general public. In fact, she has a list of retailers where she said she'll never use her credit card again."

"In a strange way, that makes me feel better. It was such a bizarre plan, I was starting to doubt myself as to whether somebody would actually try to pull it off."

Carly settled back again. "And this woman told me only about twenty percent of cardholders check their statements on a regular basis, which means that more like seventy percent or more of these charges are slipping through every month."

"Wow, that could be a lot of money."

"Which explains why Osgood wants you to keep quiet."

Mike's chin on her head bobbed. "He said he hoped I wasn't foolish enough to involve law enforcement. Said he didn't think they could do much."

"Businesses like this simply close shop, change their name, and move somewhere else. But since everything is on the Internet now, they can operate anywhere."

"Sounds like those numbered companies you once got involved with."

Carly harrumphed. "I didn't get involved with them. But they did threaten me. Much like Osgood tried to bully you." She looked up at him. "Nobody's tried to run you off the road, have they?"

"No. Been spared that, at least."

"Good."

"Don't want to lose me just yet?"

She recognized the playful tone in his otherwise serious question. "It's not that."

"Oh? What is it then?"

"I just want the chance to increase your life insurance if anybody is seriously thinking about offing you."

"Offing me? What kind of language is that?"

He tickled her ribs, and she squirmed to release his grip on her.

"Mike, stop. You know how much that tickles me."

But he didn't listen.

He rarely did.

Which was okay with her.

+++++

An hour and a nap to recover from the tickles later, Carly and Mike headed downstairs for a quick snack before returning to work. Although she'd not seen Anne in recent hours, Carly knew her friend—or someone working on her behalf—had been there. The dining room table—off limits for her to use as a work surface since the Romers arrived—was laden with an assortment of cold cuts, cheeses, condiments, and bread choices.

Their quick snack turned into a leisurely lunch, however. Mike was waiting to hear from the FBI about Riley Wilcox's whereabouts, and from Philip Osgood about his company's understanding of the ghost module. Carly hoped Anne might show up, in which case she planned to grill her on what was going on and why Gary was on the MIA list.

She swiped a napkin across her mouth and sat back. "That was good, even if it was only supposed to be a light meal."

Mike chuckled. "The only way we could eat a light meal would be to consume helium-filled balloons."

"Well said." Another sip of iced tea. "What next?"

He waggled his eyebrows at her. "Seriously?"

"No way. Let's sit on the patio in the sun for a bit."

He groaned. "We went for a walk this morning. And then you walked downtown. Haven't you had enough walking?"

"You never seem to have enough of the eyebrow-waggling."

"That's completely different."

She stood and pushed her chair back. "I don't think so. But that's okay. I'd like to relax in the sun."

He sighed. "Come on. Let's go. Might as well. Things are pretty quiet in here."

Within just a minute or so, they settled onto the bench and leaned their heads back against the plump cushions. The sun, while not overly hot, warmed Carly's skin, giving her images of Vitamin D production in overdrive without the concern of sunburn or skin cancer. Wyoming weather—despite the heavy winds—was delightful.

She sniffed. Green stuff. Like leaves. And grass.

She breathed deep and her nose wrinkled.

Chickens. Goats.

Nope, she wouldn't want to live here full-time.

She missed the salt water. The humidity that plumped out her skin, although Mike would likely imply the second dessert was probably the culprit.

She opened one eye and risked a glance in his direction. His eyes were closed, his face relaxed, and his mouth slightly open. Any second now and she'd hear that soft grumbling breath of his, even though he insisted he didn't snore.

Right. How many times had she threatened to set up a recording device to prove him wrong?

She smiled, glad he decided to join her. He worked hard, sometimes too hard in her estimation, and he deserved a working vacation that was more rest and less work.

And she wasn't complaining, either.

A cloud covered the sun briefly, and a light breeze picked up, carrying a sound from around the other side of the house.

What the—?

Easing out of her chair so she didn't wake Mike, she crept to the corner. Probably the meter reader. Or the milkman. She'd feel silly if she jumped out and confronted either of them. And scared them to death. Anne would never forgive her.

She peeked around the brick to the side yard. A fence ran down the perimeter of the property, with a plant bed filled with a lush lilac hedge trimmed back to contain the branches.

And right there, not ten feet away, the Romers crouched in front of a basement window.

That it was the Romers was indisputable. Carly noted his flyaway Albert Einstein hair and plump hips that strained at the seams of his hips, causing the pants pockets to bulge in a most unbecoming way.

She had a cloth of some kind in her hand, and she rubbed at the pane of glass as though cleaning it.

For a second, Carly thought about stepping forward and hiring them to come to her house. Washing windows was something she didn't like and rarely did. It would be nice to be able to see out through her basement windows.

But she held herself back. They were up to something. She'd known it the first time she met them. She'd known it when she saw them huddled by the basement stairs and when they came out of the cellar.

They were not being completely honest with her—not that they had any requirement to do so, but still it seemed strange that they manufactured a new story every time she confronted them. And each iteration was more bizarre than the last, taking on a life of its own, it seemed.

What next? That they were hunting for aliens? Buried treasure? Or maybe they were trying to hide a treasure.

Or a body.

A shiver ran through Carly as she debated whether to step forward or stay put. If she interrupted them, they'd make up another tale or scurry off before she could talk to them. If she stayed where she was, perhaps she'd be able to figure out what they were about.

She glanced back at Mike. If he saw her, he'd come over, loud and questioning, and for certain the Romers would get away.

Not that she had any authority to hold them here or question them. Oh, where was a police officer when she needed one?

Then again, the cops would likely arrest her instead. If the Romers told them how many times Carly had snuck up on them—their words, she was certain, not hers—the police would probably arrest her for stalking. Or harassment. Or both.

She surely didn't need that on her file.

She'd had enough trouble with the law in the past—and not because she was a criminal, either.

Despite what Mike said, it wasn't her fault she kept tripping over dead bodies or stumbling into mysteries.

She turned to study the couple again. Now George Romer stepped into the small window well and pressed something against the pane. A diamond-edged glass cutter? That didn't make sense. If they wanted to get into the basement, all they had to do was open the door and go down. It wasn't like there was a huge crowd of people around who would ask them what they were doing.

Just a small crowd of one. Her. And they could time their excursion for when she was upstairs or out of the house.

No, they didn't want to be seen. And didn't trust that she wouldn't stumble upon them.

Either that, or the room they were trying to get into was locked from inside the basement.

Which would mean they'd already been downstairs, which of course they had—the day they said they were looking for mice. Or spiders. Depending on whose story she believed.

Which was neither.

Click. Flash. Click. Flash. Click. Flash.

They weren't trying to break in—they were taking pictures. Pressing the lens against the glass and using the flash allowed the camera to light up the room and remove the reflection in the glass, a trick Carly thought she invented when visiting museums. There were few things as frustrating as taking a bunch of pictures where the reflection of the flash obliterated the crucial information. There were special lenses that compensated for this effect, but her point-and-shoot camera was the limit of her photographic knowledge.

Click. Flash. Click. Flash. Click. Flash.

Carly held her breath as the pair straightened, whispered, then moved on to the next window, about five feet from her location. She stepped back and pressed her cheek to the cool brick, breathing slowly out through her nose, hoping it didn't choose this moment to whistle. So far, so good.

She inched forward, her right eye closed, her left eye positioned so she could peek out using the mortar line as her spyhole. Appeared they were repeating the process they'd used before. She cleaned the window, he took the pictures with some direction from her as to angle.

When they straightened again, panic rose in Carly's stomach. Did they plan to come back here? If so, they'd see her and figure maybe she'd been spying on them. She was such a lousy liar. Mike saw through her every time, which was good between husband and wife, not so good when she was trying to cover her tracks with others.

What to do? What to do?

If she rushed back to the bench, she'd be out of breath. Maybe she'd wake Mike and he'd ask questions. When he saw the Romers, he'd know she was up to something. And he wasn't very good at following her stories—as she called them. Lies, according to him.

So she'd have to be upfront with everybody if she hoped to get out of this in one piece.

She pasted on a smile. "Mike, I'm going to check the mail for Anne. Coming with me?"

"Huh?"

She stepped around the corner and ran smack dab into Nancy. "Oh, sorry. Didn't see you there."

Nancy stepped back and stuck the hand holding the camera behind her back. "No worries."

"Out for a walk?"

"Yes." This from George, who grabbed Nancy's hand and pulled her toward the street. "See you later."

Carly grabbed Nancy's other hand—the one holding the camera—forcing the pair to stop. "We've missed you at meals. Seems a shame to miss such good food. Especially when it's included in the room price."

George scowled. "We have to be careful about what we eat."

Carly rubbed her stomach. "Me, too. I can't pass up dessert. Will we see you at dinner?"

Nancy pulled her hand from Carly's and tossed her a lopsided smile. "Maybe."

"Don't wait for us." This from her husband. "Let's go for our walk."

"What's going on?" Mike appeared beside Carly, his hair mussed from his nap. "Oh, hello. Nice to see you again."

Great. Now she'd never have the chance to ask them questions. Mike would be all nicey-nice, and they'd get away again.

Sure enough, George nodded to Mike—as though they'd preplanned this—and he and Nancy trotted—yes, they didn't walk or stroll, like they would if going for a *walk*—they trotted, scurried, hurried toward the street, down the walkway, through the gate, and turned left before vanishing from their view.

Carly turned to Mike, her brow pulled down. "I was just getting ready to ask questions, and you let them off the hook."

"Off the hook? What are you talking about?"

"They were acting suspiciously again."

"I could see that. They were holding hands and going for a walk." He smacked his forehead. "Wait a minute. They're a married couple. Holding hands. Call the cops."

"That's not what I mean. They were taking pictures through the basement windows."

"Oh, that explains it. Very suspicious."

"Well, why didn't they take the pictures from inside the house?"

He shrugged. "Maybe they're trying out a new camera to see how it works. Maybe they learned a new technique in photography class and wanted to practice."

She grinned. "See, you're almost as bad as me."

He stepped back, his eyebrows raised. "I sincerely hope not. Why would you say such a horrid thing to me?"

His smile belied the mock seriousness of his words.

"Without any prompting, you came up with two reasons why they would take pictures through the basement window of a house they don't own."

"But that makes me only almost as bad as you why?" He pulled her close. "Oh, I get it. You would have come up with more nefarious reasons."

"Right." She held up one hand and checked each off on a finger. "They're getting ready to break in and steal something. Maybe not here, but they want to practice taking pictures through glass to aid in that plan. Or they're trying to find something they can't see from inside the house. Maybe they're measuring the room size to see if there are hidden walls or secret compartments where money or bodies are hidden. Or they want to hide something in the basement. Or the room they took a picture of is locked from the basement side and they want to case the joint before robbing it. Or—"

Mike clasped her hands in his. "You have run out of fingers. And your ideas are getting more and more silly. They are just a nice old couple who like to take photos. Nothing more than that."

"Sure, a nice old couple who can't remember which coast they live on."

"Sometimes you badger me so much with your questions that I don't remember which *country* I live in." He planted a quick kiss on her mouth. "Have we done enough to warrant dinner?"

She shook her head. "I don't think so. We had lunch only about an hour ago." She glanced at the street. "I wish—"

"I know."

She looked up at him, her tall and rugged husband who could read her like a book.

Which sometimes was good, and sometimes wasn't.

"You do?"

"Yes."

"Okay, what was I going to say?"

"You wish you knew where they were going."

Close, but not quite. Still, she didn't have to let him know that. "Right."

He tipped his head in question, as though he didn't quite believe her, but he didn't press the matter. "Let's go to our room and review what we know about our various projects. I might make a few more phone calls to some guys in the industry, see if anybody knows anything about Financial Freedom."

She took his hand. "Okay. I'd like to check out local news and see if the man from the motel has been identified. You'd think there's been enough time to notify next of kin by now."

"Sometimes that can be a tedious process. Folks travel. They don't always leave a good itinerary. And maybe the dead man didn't include a list of his emergency contact in his papers."

"Or maybe he's estranged from his family." She turned to him. "Imagine if something happened to Jerry before he reconciled with you. What would have happened to Bradley?" An ache filled her throat at the thought of her young nephew alone out there in the world. "He'd have ended up in foster care, and we might never have known about him."

"But he didn't. And he has a great home with Tom and Sarah."

She smiled. "The Big Guy Upstairs must have been looking out for him that day."

Mike looped his arm over her shoulders as they headed inside. "Guardian angels. And you work yours overtime."

Not entirely true, but she wouldn't argue with him.

This time.

Chapter 12

For Mike, dinner the night before had been a quiet affair with only the two of them in attendance again. In fact, the whole reason for staying at a B&B was lost on him. Friends of theirs often talked animatedly about their experiences, particularly the people they met. One couple stayed at a B&B run by ranchers in the middle of Montana and met a man bicycling from Anchorage Alaska to Ohio for his 50th high school reunion. Another friend stayed with a couple from San Jose California who wined and dined him every night of his stay.

He smiled. All-inclusive took on a new meaning for some people.

But so far, their stay here—apart from fraud and murder, had been quiet.

Then again, maybe not.

He needed to redefine 'quiet'.

Apart from Carly seeing a man thrown off a train, recognizing another dead man as the one who did the throwing, and then him being threatened to keep working or else face ruin, this had been a fairly quiet trip.

Nothing nearly as exciting as being held up at gunpoint or seeing a murder on an airplane.

He sighed.

Maybe quiet was good.

He sat on the bed and towel-dried his hair, then combed it into place. Another day in quiet Danforth Wyoming. He didn't have anything specific on his plate except to eat breakfast—he chuckled at his own pun—and then maybe check in with Jamison at the FBI again.

Carly emerged from the bathroom, her skin still pink from her shower, a plastic shower cap keeping her hair dry, a large bath towel wrapped around her. Even after four years, she was still modest around him.

For some strange reason, that was such a turn-on.

As she passed him, he reached over and tugged at the towel. Caught off guard, her fingers grasped at the thick terry material but missed. He pulled her toward him onto the bed.

She struggled just a second or two, then smiled at him. "You're going to mess up your hair."

He laughed at her mock warning. "Won't take me but a minute to fix it."

"We'll be late for breakfast."

He glanced at the digital clock beside the bed. "We have fifteen minutes."

A mischievous look glinted in her eyes. "And what are you going to do with the other twelve minutes?"

They both chucked at a line from a sit-com about a home improvement cable show host and his foxy wife. That couple was the exact opposite of Carly and him. In that program, the husband was always getting himself into trouble because he tried to improve every piece of equipment and system in his house, usually failing miserable. His wife, the sensible one, tended to get him out of a pickle.

He pressed his lips to Carly's mouth, and she responded.

Breakfast could wait.

+++++

Thankfully, the serving dishes were covered so that when Mike led the way downstairs almost thirty minutes later, the food was still hot. He planted a kiss on the back of Carly's neck as he pushed her chair in, and she responded with a giggle, which resulted in another kiss. And another giggle.

When he went back for thirds, she ducked out of reach. "If you don't sit down, we'll never get through this meal."

He rounded the table to his usual seat, then removed the covers of the dishes and scooped out fluffy scrambled eggs, pan-fried potatoes, and slices of ham, passing the dishes across the table to Carly when done. He lifted a forkful of eggs to his mouth while she poured coffee for them, nodding his appreciation.

He sipped the java. "I know we talked about this last night, but I don't really want you investigating by yourself."

"You don't think I'm in danger, do you?" She chewed and swallowed some potato. "This isn't New York City."

"Understood, but I know you well enough that you can find danger anywhere. You found it before in Bear Cove. I know you could find it here."

She drew a small circle in the air with her fork. "Danger is everywhere."

He rolled his eyes. "Don't remind me."

"I'll be very careful."

"You always say that."

"You could come with."

"I would if you'd postpone until tomorrow. Today I need to be here in case I hear from Osgood. Time is running out for him to convince me to continue the work. I was ahead, but the last couple of days mean I'm back at par again. If I'm satisfied, I need to start work again right away. He won't extend the contract simply because I wasn't comfortable with the program."

"And if you miss the deadline?"

"I forfeit the remainder of the fee—which is fifty percent of a large number—and I'll have to pay additional hefty fines."

"Doesn't seem fair when he's the one who wouldn't answer your calls or emails. And now he's making you wait an additional two days. Feels like he wants you to miss the deadline."

Mike shrugged. He'd wondered the same thing. "Don't want to accuse him—even in our minds—until we know the full picture."

She sipped her coffee. "Good thing I'm not the one working for him. I'd tell him to take a flying leap."

He smiled. "Good thing it is. He'd blackball you in the industry and you'd never work again. Probably have to get a job as a greeter at a big department store."

Her mouth turned down. "Then I'd have to move out of Bear Cove since the closest mega-store is in Portland."

"And since we don't want that, I'll deal with Osgood."

She straightened. "Which means you're okay with me going to Gary's apartment?"

"And where did you find the address?"

"In Anne's files."

"Does she know you're going there?"

His wife held her arms at her sides, palms up. "I haven't seen her to tell her, have

I?"

He sighed. "Make certain your cell phone is with you. Fully charged and on. And promise to check in with me every hour on the hour."

Her shoulders slumped. "Mike, that's going overboard with the caution."

"Okay. Cell phone with, charged and on. And promise to answer my calls."

She smiled. "That will work."

For some reason, her easy acquiescence didn't quiet his concerns. But he wouldn't tell her that.

Sometimes keeping Carly in the dark was the only way to stay one step ahead of her.

He quirked his chin toward her plate. "Then let's finish breakfast so we can get on with our day."

+++++

Twenty minutes later, Carly headed out the door with nothing more than a slip of a plan in her mind. She hoped to find Gary Torbin's roommate at home. And then convince him to let her into Gary's room.

Her only problem—okay, maybe not her *only* problem, but for sure the chief one—was to convince him why he should let her in. It wasn't like she was Gary's wife—then again, maybe he'd never met Anne. That could work in her favor. Of course, she wouldn't come right out and say she was Anne Torbin, but if she alluded to it, maybe, just maybe—

If he knew Anne or at least what she looked like—well, she'd cross that bridge when she came to it.

The address a block off the main throughway was easy to find, and Carly checked out each house in the quiet neighborhood. Since most driveways were empty, she assumed this was a working-class area and folks were gone for the day. Which didn't bode well for her to find Gary's roommate at home.

But when she reached number 63 Applewood Way, for once luck was on her side. A newer looking two-door sedan sat in the drive and the inside front door was open. As she neared the house, the unmistakable sound of a vacuum cleaner came from within.

She rang the cracked doorbell, pleased to hear the chimes sounding. A couple of seconds passed before the vacuum noise ended and footsteps neared from the rear of the house.

A man in his mid-thirties, a shock of red hair hanging low over one eye, came to the screen door. "Yes?"

Carly smiled at him. "Is Gary in?"

The man shook his head. "Who are you?"

She'd always found the easiest way to not tell a lie was to answer a question with a question. "When do you expect him?"

He shrugged. "We're roommates. Don't know." He peered at her. "I know you."

Carly's heart sank. Oh, no. She'd been found out.

Wait a second. How could he possibly know her? She'd only been in town a few days. Hadn't gotten her face on the news or in the paper once—which was probably a record.

Maybe she should use that tidbit of information the next time Mike accused her of always getting into trouble.

Then again, probably not.

She swallowed hard. So much for her slip of a plan. "You do?"

"Sure. Gary told me all about you." He eyed her up and down. "Though I must say I thought you'd be taller."

"Taller?"

Was the man high on something?

He opened the door. "I don't think Gary would mind you coming in. He's said some nice things about you. Like how glad he is that he married you. How much in love you used to be."

She stepped inside. This bozo had mistaken her for Anne. All on his own. Well, she wasn't about to set him straight. While Mike might argue this was the same as a lie, it was for a good cause. Helping Anne.

Not to mention satisfying her curiosity.

But really, her chief goal was to help Anne by finding out where Gary hid her money and her stuff.

The bungalow, reminiscent of the craftsmen houses built after the Second World War, was neat and tidy, surprising given there were two bachelors living here.

Carly paused. Maybe she was making a huge mistake here. After all, she was alone in a house with a man she didn't know. Who could have been Gary Torbin himself, out to do her harm. Truth was, she wouldn't know the man from Adam, Anne having already ridded the house of all pictures of him.

She shoved her hand in her pocket, the solid feel of her cell phone a comfort. She wouldn't set another foot deeper into the house until she knew who this guy was. "Gary didn't say he had such a nice place. I assumed he'd be living in a fleabag motel."

The young man grinned. "I know Gary through a friend of a friend. I needed a roommate, and there he was." His brow drew down. "Did I introduce myself?" He stuck out a hand large enough to wrap around her throat twice. At least. "Zach."

She shook his hand, noting how hers disappeared into his. "Which room is Gary's?"

"The first one on the left. Was there something you needed?"

Indeed there was. Like Gary's location. Where he hid the stuff he stole. The answers to many questions.

Instead, she nodded. "He has some papers for me."

True, if he had the money.

Zach waved her through. "I'll keep cleaning, if you don't mind. I hate it, and if I don't finish it now, it won't get done for another week."

"Go right ahead. Don't worry about me."

Zach followed on her heels, and she ducked into the first room, closed the door, then leaned against it and listened. The vacuum turned on again—although that could be a ruse—she'd used that one herself in the past—and the swishing sounds of the carpet brush filtered through from the room next to Gary's.

She pulled her phone from her pocket and made a quick call to Mike. He didn't answer so she left a message. "Mike, I'm at Gary's. Zach let me in to look around Gary's room." No need to mention he thought she was Anne. "I should be leaving here in about ten minutes. I'll call you then."

And if Zach came in and killed her before then, at least Mike would have a starting place to search for her body and a prime suspect.

Not that either of those bits of information would be much consolation to him.

Or her.

She riffled through a stack of papers on the dresser, peered beneath the bed, and checked the pockets of his pants and a couple of sports jackets hanging in the closet. The dresser drawers were mostly empty. Just the top one held socks and underwear. Nothing of interest there, apart from the fact Gary wore boxers. Not that that would interest her, of course.

She was about to give up when a last search of the closet revealed a small box in a corner, pushed as far back on the shelf as possible. Standing on tiptoes and using a hanger, she was able to pull the box far enough forward that it dropped into her hands.

Perching on the edge of the bed, she opened the hinged lid, thankful there was no lock. Old bank statements from before he moved to Danforth. A couple of expired lottery tickets. A postcard from Hawaii from a friend.

Nothing much of interest until the last two items.

No, three.

Carly's breath caught in her throat. One was a US passport with a picture and a train ticket from two weeks before. From Danforth to Haglen Nebraska. The other was another US passport, same photo, different name.

She studied the photo. The man looked familiar.

She opened the first passport. Gary Eugene Torbin.

She studied the pictures.

Same guy in both.

Two different names.

Why would Gary go to Haglen Nebraska?

And better yet, why would he end up dead in a motel in Danforth?

Because without a doubt, this was definitely the picture from the TV.

+++++

Mike's fingers itched to answer his ringing cell phone, but he had an ache in his gut that told him he wasn't going to like that Osgood had to say.

Still, he'd never know for certain if he didn't talk to the man.

He pressed ANSWER. "Mike Turnquist here."

"I was expecting a report from you yesterday."

"Good day to you, too."

"No time for niceties. We aren't dating. Where's my report?"

Mike sighed. He should have sent the man a brief summary of what he'd done. But he wasn't certain how much to tell the man. "I know. I should have sent it."

" I have shareholders screaming down my neck. I have a Development Team in an uproar because of your allegations."

"I didn't make any allegations." Mike gritted his teeth. Talk about a tempest in a teacup. "I merely drew your attention to—"

"To nothing. They don't know anything about it. Are you a man of your word or not?"

"I am. I will send the report. Today."

"You have a contract to fulfill. We expect you to be a man of your word on this contract. And if you don't—"

Mike didn't hear the rest of the man's threat because he pressed the END button and set the phone on the desk. His head pounded, and he rubbed his eyes in hopes of easing the ache deep behind. He sat back in his chair and looped his fingers behind his head, his eyes closed. Sometimes Carly had the easier job. She dealt with numbers.

And according to her, she liked it that way. Numbers didn't change.

Implying, of course, that people did.

And not always for the better.

The alarm on his email program pinged to alert him to a new message. He exhaled and sat forward, scrolling through his inbox.

Osgood.

Mike clicked on the message and read the words instructing him to click on a link.

He did, expecting to see a copy of his original contract with them.

Which was just like Osgood to adopt a bullying attitude and remind him of his obligation to the company.

He was wrong.

This was bullying of another kind.

He squinted at the screen.

What the—?

He leaned in closer. Must be time to get glasses.

There's no way Philip Osgood would say what he thought he'd just read.

But no, Osgood had said it.

An outright threat.

> Complete the contract or I will personally see that you never work again. Not only will I blackball you in the telemarketing community, I will blacken your name everywhere. What I say about you won't even have to be true. If you try to pin this illegal module on me or my company, I will say you wrote that program and tried to hold the company ransom. And don't worry—there is no trace of the ghost module anywhere except on your computer, and we'll say you wrote that code. Don't even think that making a copy of this communication or the link will prove your case—by clicking on the link, you activated a self-destruct mechanism within the message. In the time it takes you to read this twice, this message will be deleted. Do the work—or else.

As he hit the CTRL P keys, the text on the screen faded to grey then disappeared completely.

As though it was never there.

But he knew it was.

The words were burned into his memory.

He tapped out two words—five letters—hit SEND, and waited for a reply.

Apparently the words—I QUIT—had their intended effect.

Osgood didn't call, and he didn't respond to the email.

Ten minutes passed and still he stared at the screen, willing the words of the message to reappear.

When they didn't, he returned to the original email and clicked on the link.

ERROR 404 FILE NOT FOUND.

He sighed. Osgood was as good as his word.

He spent a few more minutes typing up and sending the promised report. He was a man of his word, and he would do what he said he would do. It was only right.

But when his phone rang again just two minutes later, he snatched it up and answered it in one swift movement. "Osgood—"

"Sorry, Mike, it's Walt Jamison." The FBI agent's chuckle, like a burbling creek, released some of the tension in Mike's shoulders. "Don't know what's going on, but I'm glad I'm not this Osgood fellow."

"I think I just burned my last bridge with him."

"Tell me what happened."

Mike sat back and shrugged the kinks out of his neck. "I did as you suggested and played along with him. Left a message saying to forget the previous messages. I'd made a mistake. He finally called. I think he knew I wasn't being completely honest with him."

"Why? What did he say?"

Mike quickly recapped their conversation, his promise to send the report, and Osgood's offer to check with the Development Team. "But when he called back today, he was singing a different tune. Demanding the report. Demanding I finish the work. And when I hesitated, he sent me an email with a self-destructing link that threatened to turn this around and accuse me of holding his company ransom." He drew a calming breath. "I'm sorry. I probably messed up your investigation."

"Don't beat yourself up. You did your best."

"What's new with you?"

"Still no word from Wilcox. He isn't checking in with his Grand Junction office, he isn't answering his cell phone which, by the way, is likely out of power since it goes right to voice mail. We sent a couple of emails, but nothing there, either. We're going to contact local law enforcement, which will be the Highway Patrol, and get them going. We're also releasing his picture to the media in hopes somebody has seen him."

"I did tell you Carly thinks he's the man she saw thrown off the train, didn't I?"

"Right. But you didn't sound too certain of her identification. And we thought we'd have found him by now."

"Has anybody beside the railway police gone back and checked the area?"

"I don't think so. I'll mention it to Highway Patrol. They might come around and ask both of you some questions."

Mike exhaled loudly. "I don't know anything. I was in our sleeper car, wondering where my wife had gotten lost. She was supposed to go to the gift shop and pick up a mystery novel."

Jamison chuckled. "Tell them what you know. Don't let her embellish."

Sounded like Walt Jamison knew Carly. "Now why would you think she might do that?"

"Let's see." Mike envisioned the man checking his responses off on his fingers in much the same way he'd seen Carly do. Perhaps Jamison and Carly were more alike than either knew. "She has been trained to investigate. She likes to read mysteries. She likes to ask questions. She has a tendency to find bodies. And get into trouble."

"Fine, fine. I see you've read her email."

"Always like to know who we're dealing with. When we cleared you, her name came up. Along with about a dozen newspaper articles about her antics."

Mike groaned. "Only a dozen? Don't let her know. She'll be disappointed."

The men agreed to touch base the next day, and Mike disconnected the call.

Some working vacation.

He'd just gotten fired.

And now the cops were coming to talk to him.

+++++

Carly was pleased to see Anne in the dining room when she and Mike came downstairs for dinner. The house had been much too quiet over the past few days, and she had questions to ask. Mike was asleep on the bed when she came back from her afternoon visit, so she'd let him be and instead sat at the window overlooking the back yard, compiling a list of the things she knew and the things she wanted to know.

As usual, the second list was much longer than the first.

For once, Carly was glad the Romers were not in attendance, although she hadn't really expected them, given the number of times she'd caught them in places and situations they had no good reason to be—at least, none that placated her, the queen of unbelievable excuses.

Between the main course and dessert, while Anne poured coffee after serving a delicious-looking blueberry pie, Carly decided to talk about the elephant in the room. "You know Gary is dead, don't you?"

Her friend's hands trembled, and she set the coffee pot on the table, her gaze on her hands in her lap. "Yes."

Mike leaned forward. "What? Gary is dead? How do you know that?"

Carly laid a hand on her husband's arm. "I saw his picture on the news a couple of days ago. He's the man who was fighting with the guy who fell off the train. And I saw it again today on his passport."

Anne raised her eyes. "Gary wouldn't do that."

Carly snorted. Not very ladylike, she knew, but the only response she could ever come up with when somebody—usually a family member—tried to protest their loved one's innocence.

Or, in Anne's case, a not-so-loved one.

Mike pulled his arm from Carly's touch. "What's this about Gary being dead?" He looked at Carly. "How long have you known this?"

"I just figured it out today when I visited Gary's apartment."

Anne's brow drew down. "Why were you there?"

"I was hoping to find your money and belongings, or at least find a clue to lead us to them."

Anne didn't look happy. "Did you break in?"

Carly waved away her friend's words. "Of course I didn't."

Mike leaned closer. "How did you get in?" He studied her for a moment. "Carly, you didn't tell him you were Anne, did you?"

"Of course not." Carly crossed her arms over her chest, righteous indignation rising in her. Not that the thought hadn't crossed her mind, but she was such a terrible liar. . . "But what his roommate chose to believe was his business."

"And you didn't set him straight? When you knew he thought you were Anne?"

Mike wasn't going to let this one go.

"No. I was there on a mission."

"And the mission trumps the truth?"

"Sometimes." She sat back in her chair and glanced from Mike to Anne and back. "Are you both going to gang up on me?"

Anne's shoulders slumped. "No. I'm glad it's out in the open. I've been so afraid for the past few days. Sure that every knock on the door would be the police coming to arrest me."

Carly sipped her coffee, keeping her eyes locked on her friend over the rim. "Is that why you haven't been around much?"

Anne nodded. "I snuck in and did the rooms, then hid out at a motel up the highway." She shuddered. "Not the one he was killed in, of course. But there are several better quality places where nobody asks questions."

"What did you find?" Mike stared at her. "All of it. I'll know if you're holding out on me."

She sighed. He was right. She couldn't hide anything from him, unless he was asleep or working. "Well, Gary's roommate is a nice guy. Zach. He didn't know much about Gary except as a friend of a friend. He needed a roommate, Gary needed a place. Simple as that. They didn't hang out. He didn't seem overly concerned that Gary hadn't been around for a few days."

"Did you tell him Gary was dead?"

What was it with Mike? She was the one who was supposed to be asking questions and getting holes in her information filled in.

"Of course I didn't. But I saw a photo of Anne and him on a dresser, and I saw the passport pictures, and I put two and two together and—"

"And came up with four. This time." Mike's tight mouth and furrowed brow attempted to communicate his displeasure at her antics. But she knew better. "Which is a miracle."

"Untrue. Anyway, Zach let me in to Gary's room—"

"Because he thought you were Anne."

"And I looked for the missing money and stuff."

Anne set her cup down. "And?"

Carly sighed. "Nothing. Not even a stray penny in his room."

Mike squinted at her. "But you found something."

"Right. Two passports. One looked legitimate, the other had his picture but another man's name." Carly turned to Anne. "Any reason you know that he might have two passports under different names?"

Anne's mouth turned down. "No. What do you think?"

Mike held a hand up for Carly to pause. "Don't ask her that question. She's had a couple of hours to come up with at least five good reasons why Gary would have two passports. And they'll all involve either being a spy, being a government agent, or being a crook. Or all of the above." He turned to Carly. "Had the passports been stamped?"

She shook her head. "But that doesn't mean they weren't used. Only a few countries use the old-fashioned ink stamps on passports anymore. The US only uses it if you ask them, kind of like a souvenir."

Anne pushed her slice of pie away, her appetite seemingly sated. "Anything else?"

"I also found a used train ticket tucked into one of the passports. It was for a couple of weeks ago, to Haglen Nebraska. Know where that is?"

"Western Nebraska. About twenty miles over the border. It's in the middle of nowhere. You'd have come through on your way out here, but if you weren't watching for it, you'd have missed it. Not much more than a dot on the map."

This tidbit of information interested Mike, because he perked up. "Does he have family or friends living there?"

Anne shrugged. "I don't think so. I don't know why he'd go there. Or why he'd keep the ticket stub."

Carly looked to Mike. "So, do you have any thoughts about what's going on? Or anything new to add?"

"Been talking to the FBI, and they say the agent they sent here has disappeared."

Carly lifted one shoulder. "Of course he has. I told you he was the man Gary threw off the train before I ever knew it was Gary on the train." She faced Anne. "Which is strange, don't you think? That he went to Haglen two weeks ago, and then just six days ago he went there again. I mean, if the town is as small and insignificant as you say, why would he need to go there twice in two weeks?"

"Good question." Anne offered the coffee pot around, but Carly declined. "Maybe he has a girlfriend there."

Of course! She should have asked Zach about any romantic entanglements in which Gary may have been involved. She made a mental note to ask him.

"Possibly," Carly conceded. "But I didn't see any evidence of that in his room. No cards. No teddy bears."

Mike tipped his head to one side in question. "Why would Gary have cards or stuffed animals in his room?"

She giggled. "New love, Mike. You remember. Any excuse for a card or a gift."

The doorbell interrupted their discussion of how individuals celebrated new relationships. Anne's eyes widened at the sound and the color drained from her face. She looked from Carly to the door and back again.

Carly took the hint. "You stay here. I'll go see who it is."

She crossed to the front door and peered through the lace curtain covering the stained glass window.

A uniformed man in the easily recognizable Stetson-style hat of the Highway Patrol faced her. Behind him stood two other officers, and at the curb, three police cruisers.

These guys meant business.

She glanced back at the dining room. Mike's voice rumbled toward her, although she couldn't make out the words. Probably trying to distract Anne's attention.

Carly opened the door. "Yes?"

"Mrs. Anne Torbin?" He flashed a badge in a leather holder. "Can we come in?"

"I'm not Anne. But she is here." Carly stepped back and opened the door wider. "Come in."

The three men entered, filling the foyer with their bulk.

Anne stepped through the dining room doorway, pulled back her shoulders, and gestured to the front room. "This way, gentlemen."

The three went first, then Anne, followed by Carly and Mike.

A macabre parade, to say the least.

The officers settled on the oversized sofa, filling the length, then waited, their hats in their hands. Anne sat in a wing chair opposite them. Mike sat in its twin, and Carly perched on the arm of his chair.

The room was deathly—no, she shouldn't think in terms like that. The room was quiet. The cold air carried in by the officers also brought with it a hint of fresh soil and newly mowed grass. Had one of the officers been called in on his off day? She sniffed. Had he showered first?

She shook her head at her foolish thoughts.

Anne's future—indeed, her very life—could be on the line.

She needed to stay focused so she could help her friend in every way.

The lead officer began. "I'm Ed Markwood, Special Investigator, and these are Troopers Hayes and Foote."

Each man nodded in turn then sat back, arms crossed over their chests, hat dangling from their fingers.

Anne turned to Mike and Carly and introduced them before turning back to SI Markwood. "You wanted to talk to me?"

Markwood nodded. He glanced at Carly and Mike. "Perhaps you'd feel more comfortable if we talked privately?"

Anne shook her head. "Carly and Mike are close personal friends. They can hear whatever you have to say."

"We're here to take you into custody on suspicion of murder."

Anne's sharp intake of breath telegraphed her surprise. "I didn't kill Gary."

A slow smile spread across the detective's face. "I didn't mention your husband's name. Why do you think it's about him?"

Carly leaned forward, elbows on her thighs. "It's a small town. His face has been all over the news."

The detective stared at her a long moment then checked a notebook he pulled from a jacket pocket. "Right. I have some notes here. Saw a body on the tracks. Reported same to railway police." He eyed her again. "Always in the middle of the action, aren't you?'

She held her hands up in surrender. "I suppose you checked into us."

"No."

She exhaled. At least he didn't know about her proclivity for finding bodies.

"I checked into you."

She straightened and pulled back her shoulders, her chin held high. "I didn't kill Gary, either. And neither did my husband. In fact, I could probably provide you with the names of almost everybody in town. Because I don't think any of them killed him, either."

At least she hoped not. Otherwise, she was rattling a hornet's nest while blindfolded.

"Almost everybody?" He smiled at her. "Know everybody in town, do you? And their motives—or lack of—for killing Gary Torbin?" He checked his notebook again. "From what I've heard, he wasn't well-liked."

She threw her hands into the air. "Well, that's the answer then. If everybody who isn't well liked ended up dead, then we'd have nobody left to investigate."

Markwood blinked several times before his mouth lifted in half a smile. "I like your sense of humor."

She folded her arms over her chest again and pulled down her brow. "I wasn't joking."

"Sounds like you have a tiger on your side, Anne." Another glance at the notebook. "So, let's see what we have here." He looked up. "Do you own a gun?"

Oh, no. Not the gun. The weapon she'd seen in Anne's hand. The weapon Anne declared everybody in Wyoming carried.

She'd not seen the revolver since.

Of course, she'd not seen Anne since, either.

She patted her friend's shoulder. "Go ahead, Anne. Give him the gun. Prove you didn't kill Gary."

Anne turned to look at her. Her eyes glistened with unshed tears, and her lips trembled. Where before her face had been white, now two round red spots accented her cheeks. "My gun killed Gary." She faced the officers. "But I didn't kill him."

The two officers at the far end of the sofa tensed as though ready to spring into action. Markwood cast a glance at them, and they settled back, but their hands clenched and unclenched as though anxious to grab some perp and wrestle him—or her—to the ground.

Markwood held Anne's gaze. "Where is the gun?"

She glanced at the unlit fireplace. Markwood quirked his head to the officer nearest him—Hayes?—and the man trotted across the room, bent over, and poked around the unburned logs with a poker. He reached in and moved a log, then straightened and pulled a pair of latex gloves from a vest pocket.

Carly, fascinated, leaned over to get a better view, and nearly fell from the chair. "I thought they only did that on TV."

Markwood's brow drew down in question.

"Carry disposable gloves."

Markwood exhaled, his patience with her clearly worn thin. "What have you got?"

Hayes straightened and turned around, a revolver hanging from his index finger by the trigger guard. "A revolver. Looks like the same caliber as the bullet that killed our vic." He sniffed the barrel. "Recently fired." Next he spun the cylinder. "One shot missing."

Markwood turned back to Anne. "Sounds exactly like the weapon we're looking for. We'll test it, of course, to confirm it fired the kill shot."

Carly wasn't about to give up this easily. "Anybody could have planted that there."

"But she knew exactly where it was, didn't she? She looked directly at it when I asked her about it."

"That's not enough to convict, and you know it."

Markwood read from his notes. "Gary's attorney Loyola Lockert says you threatened your husband."

"That's not true." A tear slipped down Anne's cheek. "I've never even met the man."

"He said you'd say that. Says you confronted Gary in a bar. He was there."

Carly waggled her head from side to side. "Well, wasn't that convenient. His lawyer there with him when his soon-to-be ex-wife supposedly threatens him. If you put that in a book, people wouldn't believe the coincidence."

He turned his attention to Anne once more. "Would you submit to a gunshot residue test?"

Anne looked to Carly. "Should I?"

"You don't have anything to hide. Prove to him he's got the wrong person."

That would be a most satisfying moment, when the test came back negative for GSR. That would wipe the smirk off the detective's face.

Of course, she could have been wearing gloves. . .

No. Anne did not kill her husband.

Anne nodded to the detective, who nodded to Foote, who pulled a small kit from his vest pocket. "This is just a presumptive field test kit, ma'am. Depending on the results, we may do a forensic test at the station."

Within a few minutes, the agent swiped her friend's fingers, palms, and forearms with a pad, which he extracted from a small foil packet that reminded her of a finger wipe napkin favored by barbeque places. Then he sprayed the pad and waited.

What looked like a perfectly clean swab gradually morphed into blue with dark blue specs.

Carly stared at the small round disk of cotton that screamed gunshot residue. "She could have gotten that just from holding the gun."

The detective's mouth lifted in another half-smile. "So you acknowledge she handled the gun?"

"I'm not acknowledging anything. But it's her gun. And everybody in Wyoming owns a gun."

"You've been here what? Three days? Four?"

Mike laid a hand on her arm. Their signal for her to stay quiet a moment. He turned to the detective. "This is our sixth day."

"Plenty of time to see her and her ex in action?"

"No, detective, we didn't."

"Did you hear them?"

Mike hesitated.

Carly screamed in her mind for him not to answer that question.

But he didn't—or couldn't—hear. "We heard them."

"How were they getting along?"

"Detective, they are a couple in the midst of an ugly divorce. He stole from her. How do you think they got along?"

"When was this?"

Mike shrugged. "I don't recall exactly. The third day we were here?"

He looked to her for confirmation.

Ah, now he wanted her input? After he'd all but hung her friend?

Well, she'd set them both straight. "Gary came here and when Anne confronted him with his theft, he laughed at her. But then he had the nerve to say he wanted them to get back together."

"And what did she say?"

"She'd said he needed to tell her where her things were."

"And he said?"

"He said 'over my dead—'" She clamped her lips shut. "I mean—"

Anne stood and held her hands in front of her. "Arrest me. It's what you came here for. He said 'over my dead body'. Then we arranged to meet the next day."

Carly laid a hand on her friend's shoulder. "You don't need to say anything else, Anne. We'll get you a lawyer."

Anne nodded. "Thanks for all your help. And for all you tried to do. I'll be fine."

How she could say that, Carly didn't know. She hadn't done anything except seal the detective's case with her diarrhea mouth. In her rush to prove her friend innocent, she'd as well as locked her up and thrown away the key. So long as they had Anne, they wouldn't look for the real killer.

Because if Carly knew one thing for certain, Anne was innocent.

Hayes slipped a pair of handcuffs on Anne's wrists, double-locked them, and checked them for fit. Then he led Anne toward the front door. Foote and the detective followed close behind, Foote donning his hat at the doorstep.

Markwood turned to face Carly and Mike, who hovered near her elbow. "I'm sorry things didn't turn out the way you'd hoped."

Had he read her mind? Her desire to show him how wrong he was?

She really needed to work on her facial expressions.

It was one thing to lose.

It was another to look like a loser.

Chapter 13

Whistling woke Mike, and he opened his eyes and reached for Carly.

But she wasn't there.

He lifted his head and peered through sleep-filled eyes. What was she up to? Not trying to sneak out, apparently, since her off-key and out-of-tempo rendition of *Raindrops Keep Fallin' on My Head* would have woken all but the most hard of hearing. "Carly?"

She poked her head out of the bathroom, a toothbrush foaming in her mouth. "Yesh?"

He smiled. If only he had a camera handy. Wait, he did. On his phone. He stretched his hand toward it, but she shook her head and ducked back into the bathroom. A quick run of the tap, and the evidence was down the drain.

She emerged a moment later, mouth lifted in a smile, no telltale white on her lips. "You called?"

"Wondered what you were doing."

"If I were you, I could claim I was programming."

He flung off the covering and slipped into the pants he'd hung on the bedpost the night before. "Which means you're devising a sneaky scheme to get yourself into trouble without me knowing about it."

"Not so sneaky if I was whistling."

"True." He planted a kiss on her lips. "But you're not denying the sneaky scheme part."

She stepped back out of reach. "Ugh. Morning breath." She stabbed a finger toward the bathroom. "Off with ye, I say, into yon bath chamber to brush your teeth."

He nodded. "Yes, milady. At once, milady."

A few minutes later he emerged, teeth cleaned, face washed, a razor passed over his stubble, and his hair combed. He donned a polo shirt and socks, then turned to his wife. "What's next?"

She stood at the window overlooking the back yard. "We need to help Anne."

"Okay. I have some free time today until I hear back from the FBI. What do you want to do?"

"I'm kind of hoping we can kill two birds with one stone. How about a walk to the train station after breakfast?"

"I have no idea what you're up to, but I'm game."

He looped his arm around her waist and they set off downstairs. At the bottom, he led her to the dining room, where a sumptuous but not so extravagant breakfast awaited them. Quiche, fruit, and coffee this morning. But that was okay. Eating a huge breakfast every day could pack on the pounds.

He pushed her chair in for her. "I don't mind lighter meals."

"Me either." She surveyed the table. "But I did enjoy her cinnamon rolls."

He shrugged. "Oh, well." He served her a slab of quiche, the cheese oozing onto the plate. "I'm just glad I don't have to cook."

Carly nodded. "Me, too." She looked around the room, her gaze lingering on the furniture and artwork. "What do you think about—"

"Absolutely not."

Her bottom lip jutted out. "But I didn't even finish my sentence."

"I know you well enough. You like this place. You think it would be great to run a B&B of our own."

"Well, I wasn't going to go that far. Maybe not a real B&B. But what about if we rented—"

"No."

"But—"

He shook his head. "Nope. We're not renting out Tom's old room. We're not renting out Denise's old room. We'd have to build an addition to make room for the stuff in those bedrooms. No way. Forget it."

They ate in relative silence, with Carly opening her mouth a couple of times, but snapping it shut when he shook his head.

They lingered over coffee, and Mike rose to refill his cup. "So, what's your plan?"

"Let's go to the train station."

"What are the two birds you want to kill?"

"I thought we could ask about Riley Wilcox, and I could go to Haglen and look around there."

He sat. "I like the idea of asking about the agent. Jamison was supposed to call in an authorization for me to pick up his suitcase. I could bring it back here and look at its contents to see if Riley had any notes or anything that will help with figuring out where he is."

"That all sounds good except for one thing."

"And what's that?"

She stared at him over the rim of her cup. "The part about you bringing the suitcase back here to look in it."

"What didn't you like?" He studied her a moment then snapped his fingers. "Got it. You want to be there when I open the suitcase."

"Of course I would. Wouldn't you, if the roles were reversed?"

"They could be reversed. We could bring the suitcase back here and you could look inside it, and I could take the train to Haglen."

She shook her head. "Don't like that plan at all."

"We could both go to Haglen, and pick up the suitcase on our way home after."

"Nope. There could be important information that will sit another day without being acted on."

He set his cup down. "What difference does that make? It's already sat there for a week."

"True. But now it could be critical to finding Agent Wilcox."

Mike hated what he was thinking, but it seemed best to get it out there in the open where they could deal with it. "He's probably dead, isn't he?"

She nodded, her eyes wet. "I think so. If he was alive, he'd have been found by now."

"When I was missing, did you think maybe I was dead?"

She shook her head. "Never. The sheriff tried to prepare me, but I wasn't listening to him. Even when the state patrol guy insisted you had taken our money and run off to a desert island, I said that wasn't possible."

"You were that sure of my loyalty to you?"

A hint of a smile tickled her mouth. "You'd never run off to a desert island. You hate sand. It would be like sentencing yourself to hell."

Well, two could play that game. "When you were missing in the snowstorm, I figured you were holed up somewhere warm, toasting s'mores, enjoying the company of a couple of friendly ranch hands."

Her eyes widened and her mouth formed that cute little "o" he adored. "You didn't."

"No. But I love your reaction."

She shook her head and laughed. "Got me." She sobered. "But the thing is, although it makes for a good story in a movie, amnesia from an accident is rare. And with today's technology, they could run his fingerprints and get his identity. So unless he's being held in a cabin in the woods, he's probably dead."

"My thinking, too." He stood. "Okay. Let's head for the train station, and then we'll figure out what we're going to do from there."

She folded her napkin and set it on her plate, then followed him to the foyer. After donning their jackets, they headed for the back door. Since one—or both—of them would bring the agent's suitcase back to the house, they decided to borrow Anne's old pickup.

Mike grabbed the keys from the rack near the back door and stepped out into the brisk morning. The sun shone but didn't lend much heat, and a light coating of frost decorated the truck windows. Carly paused as she passed Anne's pickup, and Mike waited for her to catch up.

When she slid into the passenger seat, he reached over and covered her hand with his. "What are you thinking?"

"It's hard to believe she's in jail. Facing a murder charge. I know she didn't do it."

He patted her hand. "You haven't seen her for many years. People change."

"Not that much."

He straightened and started the engine, letting the motor idle. "That's what everybody says who lives next door to the latest serial killer. How nice the guy is. How he went to church. Never beat his dog or his wife."

She folded her arms across her chest and stuck out her bottom jaw. "But this is different. I know Anne."

"Correction, you *knew* her. Thirty years ago. How many times have you heard from her since?"

She shrugged. "Christmas and birthday cards every year. And maybe a note once or twice a year in between."

"Not really heart-felt communication, would you agree?"

"I get your point." She sat up. "Do we have some heat yet or are we going to have to scrape the windshield?"

He blasted the defroster, the fan motor squealing in protest, effectively cutting off all other talk.

Which seemed fine with Carly.

+++++

The station was quiet at this time of day.

Quiet as a grave.

She really needed to stop thinking in such macabre tones.

Carly rubbed her hands up and down her arms. Despite the heat in the truck and her jacket, she was cold.

But not from the outside.

From the inside.

And that was a cold that wouldn't go away with a blast of warmth or a hot shower.

The agent's disappearance was troubling. If someone would harm a law enforcement officer, they would harm anybody.

Unless they didn't know he was a LEO. Which was a possibility. Unlike local police agencies, FBI didn't wear a uniform or display their badge unless they were on official business. Perhaps Wilcox and Gary Torbin got into an argument over something trivial, like an unintended bump in the aisle or a tiff over their political views. From what she knew of Torbin through Anne, he had a short temper and a shorter fuse. And he was no stranger to violence.

That didn't explain why the altercation would have moved out into the open. Had Wilcox sensed the situation escalating beyond simple disgruntlement, surely he'd pull his badge and make Gary back down.

As Mike pulled into the parking spot closest to the depot, she turned in her seat to face him. "Was Wilcox an experienced agent?"

He put the vehicle in park and rested his forearms on the steering wheel. "I think so. Walt Jamison said their office had already dispatched him here to look into a fraud case, so that seemed right up his alley."

She stared through the windshield, already beginning to fog with the engine off. Her decreasing visibility mirrored what she understood—or thought she understood—about this case.

It simply wasn't making sense.

If Wilcox really was here to investigate Gary, then Torbin must have known that the agent's disappearance would only cause more agents to flood the area looking for their colleague, a murderer, and to solve the original case.

Not that Gary Torbin could be called sensible.

A hothead, yes.

A bully, definitely.

She shrugged. "What kind of fraud case?"

"Don't know. Jamison never said. Ready?"

"As I'll ever be."

She slid out of the truck and joined Mike at the bottom of the steps leading into the station, holding his hand more for comfort than because she needed assistance. His hands were warm, firm, sure.

He steadied her in so many ways.

Inside the depot, the smell of coffee and old paper greeted them. While fluorescent lights overhead and a computer on the single desk bespoke progress, much of the original station from more than a hundred years before remained the same. Many shoes of different sizes and styles had walked the scarred wide-plank flooring, worn low in some places, still showing original finish in the corners. And the large counter, separated by fancy wickets with brass bars, reminded her that rail travel wasn't always as homogenous as it was today.

The proverbial clerk with a green visor and steel elastic armbands looked up from the newspaper spread on the counter and peered at them over his eyeglasses. "You folks are out early this morning."

Mike stepped forward, releasing her hand. "Mike Turnquist. I believe you're holding a suitcase here for me?"

The clerk nodded. "Got that right here. Give me one minute."

Carly sidled over next to her husband. "Is it cold here, or is it just me?"

"It's a little chilly."

The man returned with a small carry-on suitcase on wheels. "Here it is. If you could show me some ID and sign for it."

Mike fished out his wallet and extracted his driver's license. The clerk glanced at Mike then the photo, nodded, and handed it back. He shoved a register book across the counter and jabbed an index finger at a line. "Put your John Hancock there."

Mike chuckled. "Has anybody ever taken you literally on that?"

The clerk's head snapped up. "Huh?"

"And signed *John Hancock*?"

When the man's brow drew down in question, Mike shook his head. "Never mind."

Carly stepped up to the window. "I'd like to buy a ticket to Haglen."

The man's head tipped to one side. "Nebraska?"

A moment of panic rose in her. "Is there any other?"

"Not that I know of."

She heaved a sigh of relief. "Then Haglen Nebraska it is, please."

"When?"

"The first train going there today."

"You could take the 9:01 and get there at 10:00, or take the—"

"I'll take the 9:01."

"Okay. She arrives in about six minutes and leaves at—"

"9:01. Got it." She dug into her wallet. "How much?" She paid for and received her ticket, tucking it into her back pocket, then turned to Mike. "Let's take the suitcase to the truck."

He peered at her. "I could just take it back to Anne's and look at it later." He glanced at the oversized station clock on the wall to their right. "You've got ten minutes until your train leaves. Don't want to make you late."

"How long can it take to go through one suitcase?" She studied him a moment. "You're teasing me."

His smile slipped. "I also don't know what we might find. I don't want to upset you."

"I don't think anybody has stuffed—" She paused and glanced at the clerk who'd turned sideways to listen in on their conversation. Carly looped her arm through Mike's and pasted on a smile. "Let's go to the parking lot where I can give you a proper good-bye kiss."

Mike wasn't catching on. "Huh?"

She nodded toward the truck twice. "Let's go to the *parking lot*." When he didn't move, she tried again. "With the suitcase."

Understanding dawned and his face lit up. "Gotcha." He nodded toward the railway clerk. "Thanks for your help."

"No problem."

Carly smiled her thanks and led the way back to the pickup.

Despite his words, the clerk was sorry not to be part of their discovery of the contents of the suitcase.

Mike lowered the tailgate and placed the case on the scratched bed of the truck, then unzipped the bag. He checked the inside cover pocket. Nothing.

On top of the agent's neatly packed clothes lay a file, which Mike opened. "Case notes. A picture." He showed it to Carly. "Recognize him?"

"No. Who is he?"

Mike flipped over the photo. "No name." He continued leafing through the pages. "Seems Jamison was right. Wilcox was responding to an allegation of mail and telephone fraud."

"I knew it. And Gary threw him off the train to keep it quiet."

Mike shook his head. "Had nothing to do with Gary or Anne. Had to do with a woman who was scammed out of her life savings. Says here she was too embarrassed to go to local police, and because it involved telephone and mail fraud, she went to the Feds." He flipped another page. "Well, that makes sense."

"What?"

"Danforth seems like too small a town to actually have two instances of fraud happening at the same time. He was actually coming here on the train to transfer to another line. The case is about a hundred miles north of here. Martinville."

"Never heard of it." Carly, who'd been standing on her tip-toes to see into the suitcase, settled back into a more comfortable stance. "So do you think Wilcox was just in the wrong place at the wrong time?"

"Maybe. It happens."

Tears welled. "That makes what happened even more sad."

Mike laid a hand on her arm. "We don't know for certain he's dead."

She looked up at him, a lump forming in her throat. "But it seems more and more likely he is."

A train pulled into the station and came to a stop, wheels screeching.

Mike glanced over her shoulder. "Your train is here."

She nodded. "Then I'd best get going." She swallowed hard. "But not without a kiss."

He complied and held her an extra-long moment, then patted her back and released her. "I'll get back to Anne's, then call Walt Jamison and let him know what we found."

"Sounds like a plan. I should be back around suppertime, I guess, so don't make plans before you check in with me. I'll probably want a ride home when I get back."

He pecked her on the cheek again then steered her toward the train. "You'd better get going. It won't wait for you."

She sighed but walked up the steps, across the platform, and handed her ticket to the same man who'd sold it to her not twenty minutes before.

He nodded and handed her back her stub. "Enjoy the trip."

"Thanks."

She climbed up the steps of the combination passenger and cargo train, and sat in the first vacant seat, settled in, and, using her jacket like a blanket, closed her eyes. A little nap would do her a world of good, and maybe by the time she arrived in Haglen, her entire outlook would be different.

Right now she felt like she was going to a funeral.

An hour later, Carly awoke as the train jerked to a halt. Through bleary eyes, she read the station name: HAGLEN. She shrugged into her jacket, made certain she had her purse, and followed the short line of three other passengers getting off.

The nap definitely helped, or perhaps it was the sunshine and clear sky. Whatever the reason, she stepped onto the station platform feeling that today she would get some real answers to the huge questions of this case.

She stepped inside the depot and headed for a man in an official-looking uniform. "Sir, are you in charge here?"

He tipped his hat. "Yes, ma'am. I'm the station master. But you can call me Ian."

"I'm wondering if you might remember a man who came through here a couple of weeks ago? And maybe more recently." She showed him a copy of the picture from Gary's passport she'd made before leaving the house. "You probably see a lot of people go through here."

Ian chuckled. "Not so many as you might thing. And most of them live here or are visiting here, so I get to know them." He studied the picture. "Can't say as I recall seeing him. But I'm rarely out here among the people. Usually in my office up to my eyebrows in paperwork. Your best bet would be Ken, the porter. He remembers everybody."

Carly followed Ian's directions and found Ken helping an older woman with her suitcase.

She waited until he was free before approaching him. "Excuse me, Ken. Ian said you might be able to help me."

Ian nodded. "I surely will if I can."

She showed him the picture. "Do you remember this man? He came through about two weeks ago?"

"Yes, ma'am, he surely did. And several times before that. And once since."

"Why do you remember him so well?"

"Every time he came here, he was carrying several packages. He always gave me a generous tip for helping him. The first time, I handed it back because I thought he'd made a mistake. But he said no, he meant to give me a twenty for helping him, and there would be even more in the future. So I always made sure to help him after that."

Gary with money. Throwing it around as if he was Rockefeller. Interesting.

She folded the paper and stuck it in her purse. "Any idea where he went?"

"He rented a car."

Carly glanced around. Haglen didn't look like the kind of town that had car rentals. "Where?"

"He went to the last taxi in line, talked to him, and made a deal to rent his car for the day."

"Do you remember which driver?"

"Sure." Ken pointed to the line of three taxis waiting at the curb. "He's the second one."

Carly pulled a five-dollar bill from her purse. "Thanks for your help."

He tucked the bill into his pocket and nodded. "Anything else, you come find me. I'm here most of the time."

The first cab pulled away with a passenger, and the driver she needed to talk with pulled into the first position. She hurried over to catch him before he got another customer. She rounded the car and knocked on the window, which he rolled down.

"Yes?"

Carly pulled out the picture and asked much the same questions she'd asked Ken. The driver confirmed what the porter told her.

Gary rented his car for the whole day several times, offering much more than he could have expected to make ordinarily. But there was one condition: Gary drove. The first time, the cabbie was a little reluctant to let a stranger go off with his car, but Gary gave him five hundred dollars for a deposit, and he agreed to pay by the mile.

The driver didn't remember much about the first couple of times, but the last time—a week ago—Gary returned the car about four hours later, the gas tank full, and fifty miles additional on the odometer.

+++++

Back in Danforth, Mike headed back toward town. After dropping Carly at the train station, he returned the suitcase to the B&B, hiding it in the deep recesses of the closet in their bedroom.

Minus the file.

This he pored over for about an hour, looking for more clues as to what Wilcox was working on when he disappeared. According to the information, the woman who'd been scammed gave him the name of a company, but that was all the information she could provide. Traumatized, embarrassed, humiliated, her elderly mind couldn't recall the name the man used—not that it was likely to be his real name. She'd waited several months before calling the FBI, and then only because her children learned of the crime. In many states, defrauding the elderly rated the crime as elder abuse and carried a heavier prison sentence if convicted and the courts determined there was a vulnerable victim enhancement.

After doing some internet research that landed him little to no new information, Mike made a call to Gary Torbin's attorney and secured an appointment. He pulled into an angle parking spot on the main street in front of a two-story brick building that looked like it was one of the town's original structures. Over the front door, griffins guarded the entry, and the '1876' carved into the granite archway in the brickwork confirmed the building's longevity.

Mike checked the directory and located Lockert's office number—201. He pushed through the brass-festooned oak door and climbed the wide stairway to the second floor. If Carly were with him, she'd no doubt have commented on the plasterwork on the ceiling, the intricate spindles supporting the handrail, and the shine on the original hardwood floors.

Mike chuckled to himself. Even when she wasn't here, he noticed these favorite details of hers just in case she asked about them.

At the top of the stairs, which divided the building approximately in half, he followed an engraved brass sign to the left to Lockert's office at the far end. All of the offices, which housed various businesses including an accountant firm, an optometrist, a travel agency, and a cleaning service, boasted a similar oak door with a frosted glass window bearing the name of the business inside. In over 125 years, this building had likely seen many people through the halls and inside the offices.

Loyola Lockert PC occupied the last two offices, and Mike stepped inside. A soft chime sounded when he opened the door, and a woman at a desk in the first office looked up.

She smiled at him. "Can I help you?"

"I have an appointment with Mr. Lockert."

She frowned and clicked a couple of times on a keyboard on her desk, and stared at the screen. Then her expression relaxed. "You must have made your appointment directly with Mr. Lockert."

"Yes, I called earlier before your office opened."

The receptionist gestured to several chairs lined against a wall. "Take a seat. He'll be right with you."

Mike sat and crossed one leg over the other. The waiting area, outfitted with a coffee table littered with large photograph-heavy books and popular magazines, including *American Lawyer* and *The Legal Journal* seemed designed to occupy clients for a long time. He sighed and hoped he was wrong. Framed newspaper articles dotted the walls, demonstrating the lawyer's apparent friendships with well-known celebrities and big-case attorneys.

Mike snorted. He'd been to that kind of conference, too, where the keynote speaker had photo sessions with everybody in attendance—for a fee.

The door opposite the waiting area opened, and a short man in an expensive suit stepped through. He glanced at the receptionist who nodded in Mike's direction.

Mike stood and crossed the space then introduced himself. Feeling like a lamb shuttled off for slaughter, he preceded the attorney into the next office.

Loyola Lockert edged him toward a chair grouping. "Have a seat, Mike."

Mike sat and waited, elbows resting easily on the arms of the wingback chair.

Lockert rested his elbows on the desk and stroked his well-groomed goatee. "What can I do for you today?"

"I'd like information on a client of yours. Gary Torbin."

Lockert tilted his head to one side and peered at him. "A client of mine, you say?"

"Right."

"And why should I tell you anything about a client?"

"The man is dead." Mike studied him, watching for body language to reveal the attorney's thoughts. "I presume you knew that?"

"I watch the news."

This was like pulling teeth.

Time to go in for the kill.

As Carly would say.

Mike leaned forward, elbows on his thighs. "They haven't released his name yet. How did you know?"

Lockert shrugged. "Small town. Could have been the coffee shop. Could have been another client."

He wasn't going to give out even a crumb of extra information.

Then again, if Mike were in his shoes, would he?

But that never stopped Carly from asking more questions. She thrived on extracting information from people. Particularly when they didn't want to tell her anything.

Not that she ever noticed their hesitancy.

"So you admit he was a client?"

"Not admitting anything. I knew him, of course, from around town. Like I said, it's a—"

"I know. A small town." Mike did know. Bear Cove Maine had 400 souls at the height of lobster season. But that was beside the point. "Were you representing him in his divorce?"

Lockert peered at him. "I think you know the answer to that. You and your wife are friends of the petitioner in the case."

"Who believes your client stole assets in an attempt to hide them from the divorce court."

"I don't know what you think I can tell you, Mark."

"Mike."

An insincere half-smile lifted one side of the attorney's mouth. "Mike. My apologies. But surely you understand that if—" He leaned forward. "And I emphasize if—Gary Torbin was my client, I couldn't tell you anything. Attorney-client confidentiality, you know."

Now it was Mike's turn to smile. "And you and I both know that privilege extends only to discussions about the case you're working on for him."

"Really? Are you an attorney now, Mike?"

"No. But I know enough about the system to know the difference."

"So enlighten me as to what you think doesn't constitute the privilege."

Mike's mind raced to come up with an example. "If you're representing him on the divorce, and he says he hired a contract killer to get rid of his wife, that wouldn't fall under the confidentiality provision."

Lockert nodded, his lips pursed. "Good example. And you're right. I could divulge that piece of information. But Torbin didn't say anything like that to me."

"Well, that's good to hear. I'm sure Anne will rest easier tonight know that."

The attorney's wry chuckle chilled Mike. "I'm sure she will. In jail."

Word did indeed get around in this small town.

"Did Gary pay his bill before he topped it?"

Lockert's fingers splayed and twitched. "Let's just say he paid all my fees. Money never seemed to be a problem."

"That's a relief."

"It does help me sleep better."

"Gary wasn't working. Any idea where he got the money?"

Lockert shrugged. "No. I don't think he robbed a bank or anything like that. And if I knew the money was the result of ill-gotten gain, I wouldn't have cared. So long as he didn't involve me, that is."

"Where do you think he got it?"

Lockert leaned back and checked his watch, a gold and stainless glob of metal big enough to choke a horse. "I'm not in the conjecture business. I deal with the absolutes of the law. And now I have several important clients who are probably already waiting. I did tell you when you called I could give you five minutes. Busy, busy, and all that." He stood. "If you'll excuse me."

Since the man left no other option, Mike stood and exited the office through the reception area.

The empty reception area.

Not a waiting client in sight.

Mike went down the stairs and out onto the street. A deli-coffee shop occupied the space on the ground floor, and Mike's stomach growled. Breakfast was a long while past, and a snack would hold him until dinner when Carly returned. Coffee and a pastry—or maybe a sandwich—sounded good.

He opened the door and stepped inside, pausing to inhale the delightful odors of fresh-roasted coffee, warm pastry, and quality deli meats.

A man wearing an apron beamed at him across the cheese case. "Can I get you something?"

"A roast beef on rye and a large coffee."

"Coming right up."

Several empty tables lined one wall, and the checkered cloths created a fun atmosphere. Mike followed the man's progress down the sandwich line as he built a sandwich Mike wasn't certain he'd get into his mouth. At the register, the deli man loaded a tray with the food, the coffee, and a bag of potato chips.

Mike pulled out his wallet. "You don't find many of the personal service delis these days."

The man nodded. "Know what you mean. Disappearing faster than the dinosaurs." He held a hand toward Mike. "Name's Paul."

"Mike." He shook the man's hand. "You work here long?"

"Since I was about three. My parents owned it, and their parents before them. Course, back then, it was a diner. Then a pizza parlor. Won't make me rich, but I get to do what I love. Not many people can say that about their job."

Once again, Mike appreciated his own line of work. Most of the time, he thrived when he was programming.

Not so much on this job for Financial Freedom.

Although having quit did give him a certain sense of freedom.

"You passing through town?"

The man's question pulled Mike back. "Not really. We're friends with Anne Torbin. Do you know her?"

Paul nodded. "I do. Nice lady. Tough what's going on between her and her old man."

"You know about that?"

"Just that they're having trouble. And I heard a rumor he stole from her. Not that it surprises me."

Mike leaned closer. "No?"

"Never liked him. And then I hear he's in cahoots with that crooked lawyer."

"Which one?"

Paul laughed. "Loyola Lockert. He owes me money. Has me deliver lunch there and never has petty cash." He swiped at the counter with a damp rag. "He says."

Mike picked up his tray. "Got time to come sit a minute?"

Paul glanced around the empty shop. "Might as well take a load off. Let me grab myself a cup of joe."

Mike chose a table away from the door and set his food down. Paul joined him a moment later with a coffee big enough to bathe a baby. They sat in companionable silence for a couple of minutes, long enough for Mike to relish the delicious sandwich and half of his coffee.

Paul toyed with the saltshaker. "Lockert owes other guys too."

"Such as?"

"Heard he's overdrawn at the bank. Runs a credit with the grocer. Still owes money for car repairs to the garage."

Mike swallowed his last potato chip. "A lot of money?"

Paul shook his head. "A few hundred here, a few hundred there. But it all adds up. Makes it harder on us small guys who run a cash business. Bank can carry him better. I suggested he take out a bank loan to pay us little bills off, but I get the feeling he can't borrow more money."

"That's strange. I just talked to him, and he said Gary Torbin paid his bills. That should have brought in a chunk of change for him."

"Dunno. All I do know is what I hear."

"Maybe I misunderstood."

"Maybe."

Mike stood. "Thanks for the great food. I'll mention this place to my wife. She'd love it."

"She's the lady who finds missing money, right?"

Mike chuckled. "You're right. It is a small town."

Paul stood and gathered Mike's tray and empty dishes. "Maybe she can find the money Lockert owes me."

"I'll mention it to her."

Mike exited the deli and headed back up the stairs. He was certain he hadn't misunderstood the attorney when he claimed to have been paid, but Carly would surely ask him to clarify. He strode down the hallway, meeting only one person coming from the opposite direction, who had just exited from the optometrist's office.

He turned the knob to the attorney's office and pushed, fully expecting the door to open.

But it didn't budge.

Strange. Maybe he misremembered and the door pulled out.

Nope.

He knocked. Nothing.

Then he pressed his ear to the glass. Quiet.

And when he tried to see inside, noted it was dark.

Several waiting clients indeed.

He headed back the hallway and downstairs. Now what?

A man in a suit walked toward him and headed for the deli shop.

Mike nodded at him. "Excuse me. Do you know Loyola Lockert?"

"The attorney?" The man paused. "I do. You looking for him?"

"Yes."

The stranger pointed down the street. "That's him. Or rather, I should say that's his SUV. The navy blue one. Only one in town like it."

Mike thanked the man then trotted to Anne's pickup, climbed in, and started the engine, but by the time he backed out of the parking spot, the attorney's vehicle had disappeared.

He drove to the next intersection, then the next, and the next, looking in all directions for the unique car. By that time, he'd reached the outskirts of town, and he turned back—empty-handed as it were—to retrace his steps.

How was he going to explain that he'd lost both the man and his vehicle in such a small town?

Better yet, why would Lockert avoid him?

Chapter 14

After asking directions at the diner in the rail depot, Carly wandered around Haglen, ducking in and out of a couple of tourist-oriented boutiques, resisting the urge to buy anything.

No point in spending money she wasn't going to charge, especially now that Anne was in jail. Her friend would need every penny for legal fees.

Her objective was to talk with someone in the real estate office, but a visit there proved fruitless since the business didn't open until 11:00. So she checked out a coffee shop, indulging in a dark roast Americano and a bagel.

The appointed time finally rolled around so she dusted the crumbs from her shirt and headed that direction. The sign in the front window read OPEN and lights were on inside.

Carly pushed through the door and stepped out of the chill mid-morning breeze that had battled her all the way up the street. She paused to catch her breath and straighten her hair before making eye contact with the man behind the first desk.

The only other person there, as it happened.

Three more desks, empty, their banker's lights off, dotted the office.

Business must be slow.

She crossed the hardwood floor and plopped into the chair opposite the agent.

"Hi. I'm wondering if you can help me."

The man—identified as Robb Parker by the nameplate on his desk—assuming he was sitting at his own desk, of course.

Perhaps she'd wait until he introduced himself.

He held out a hand. "Robb Parker. And you are?"

A full-time job. At least according to Mike.

But that was another story.

"Carly. I'm visiting from Danforth Wyoming."

"Thinking of moving here?"

Carly held her face impassive. At least, she hoped it was. Live here? Away from the ocean? In the middle of nowhere? She didn't think so.

But the man, who'd obviously chosen to live and work here for reasons of his own—maybe he was in the witness protection plan and didn't have a choice—wouldn't see it the same way. Maybe he loved living here. Although, for the life of her, she couldn't think why. "No."

He settled back into his chair, the smile melting away like snow under a July sun. "Do you own property and want to sell?" He picked up a pencil and tapped it, eraser down, on the desk. "Although I thought I knew all the owners around here."

"Nope. Don't own property."

"Then how can I help you?"

"I was hoping you helped a friend of mine. Gary Torbin."

"In what way?"

"Maybe he wanted to buy property? Or rent it?" No, that didn't make sense. He wouldn't want to take a chance on a landlord coming into the property and discovering what he was up to. Whatever that was. She shook her head. "No, he probably wanted to buy."

Robb Parker tipped his head to one side and jabbed at his chin with the eraser on the pencil. "Don't recognize the name."

"Could you check your records?"

When the man didn't move, she tried an often-successful tactic.

She begged.

"Please? This is really important?"

Parker studied her like an insect under a microscope for several heartbeats before tossing the pencil on the desk. He turned his swivel chair ninety degrees to his right and pulled out the second drawer of a file cabinet. His fingers walked through the files, then he nodded. "Thought so."

"You found something?"

"No." He turned to face her again. "Like I said, nothing in our files."

Carly pulled the picture of Gary from her pocket and unfolded the paper. "Do you know this man?"

Parker sighed then glanced at the picture. His face brightened. "Sure, I know him. Ted Grover."

Carly held back a snort. Figures that someone as dumb as Gary Torbin would come up with a pseudonym using his initials in reverse order.

She tapped the paper. "You're sure it's the same guy?"

Parker squinted then nodded. "Sure." He turned back to the cabinet and pulled out the top drawer then selected a folder. "Ted Grover. He first came in—" He clutched the file to his chest. "Why do you want to know?"

"I'm a forensic accountant, and I've been hired to find assets this man may have attempted to hide from his ex-wife."

Parker's eyes widened until she worried his eyeballs would pop out. "Forensic, like those shows on TV?"

"Well, I don't deal with bodies and stuff." Carly suppressed a chuckle. Let people hear the forensic word, and they typically forgot everything else she said. "I look for hidden assets. Go through accounting records. Stolen money. That kind of thing."

He set the file on the desk. "So not like on TV?" He glanced around. "Am I being filmed?"

"No, Mr. Parker, you're not." She quirked her chin toward the folder. "So, did he buy?"

The agent's shoulders slumped. "Not right away. He came in here looking for property. Said money was no option, but he wanted something remote. I showed him a couple of places, but he didn't buy. Something about wanting water access and a dock."

"But eventually?"

"Yes. A property came on the market." He reached for a brochure. "We have great fishing and hunting in the county, lots of water, lots of woods. People come here from all around the country to buy recreational property. He chose this smaller one. Said he didn't need a lot of house. Just wanted some place where people wouldn't stumble on him." He chuckled. "That's the term he used. Stumble on. Like people were out there wandering around. I explained that's not how we operate here. It's all private property. Nobody wandering around without permission." He leaned forward. "A person could get shot that way."

"Understood. How far out was this place?"

"About seven miles one way. I can give you directions."

"Thanks." Not far enough to account for the distance on the rental car. Unless he made several trips. "Did you see him around town?"

"Nope. Just when he came here to get a listing. Then a few weeks later when he came back to sign at closing. He always rented a car from one of the cabbies. Different one every time. Then he'd take off. Come back later that day or a couple of days later." He clasped his hands on the desk. "He didn't do something illegal, did he?"

"Not sure yet. I'll let you know if I find out. Directions?"

"Oh, yes."

Parker drew a rough map on the back of her photocopy of Gary's passport picture, then ran a finger along the lines as he explained the directions. Carly folded the paper and took her leave.

Next would be to rent a car and follow the yellow brick road to Gary's secret hideaway.

But first, she had to make a phone call.

+++++

When Mike saw Carly's name on the caller ID, he groaned. It was too early for her to call for a ride back from the train station.

Which meant something was wrong.

Although why he thought he could send her off on her own and not expect her to get into trouble, he couldn't explain.

Just once it would be nice.

But apparently not this time.

He pressed the ANSWER button. "Hello Carly. What jail are you in this time, and how big is the fine?"

When she didn't respond right away, he waited.

She was trying to come up with a good story.

The more time he gave her, the better her tale.

And he wasn't disappointed.

"Hi Mike. How are you doing?"

The too-happy lilt in her voice was a dead giveaway.

She was up to something.

"Fine."

He would brook her no quarter. No giving her a lifeline to grasp onto.

He waited.

"Get anything from the lawyer?"

"Yes. And we can talk about it when you get home." He paused again. "You are coming home, right?"

"Of course I am. Um, just not tonight."

"What jail, Carly?"

"No jail, Mike. What kind of trouble do you think I'm getting in here? I haven't landed in jail in a long time."

He chuckled. What she said was true. It had been a few years.

But not that long since she'd had law enforcement look at her askance.

"Is there no train coming west tonight?"

A heavy sigh. "I detect a note of sarcasm in your question."

"More than a note, I hope. A healthy slathering. What's going on?"

"Nothing. But I have a great lead and I want to follow it up, but I don't want to go wandering alone in the woods when it will be dark in a few hours and you know my sense of direction and I don't want to get lost and—"

"Hold up, Carly. I know you're spinning a yarn when you start stringing your sentences together. Take a breath."

"No yarn, Mike. Just telling you what's happening. I've been trying to call you for about an hour, and either I'm not getting a good signal or you aren't. I couldn't even leave a voice message. I did send a text, but that probably didn't come through."

"No, it didn't." He'd concede her point. Cell coverage was spotty at best. Not that he was letting her off the hook that easy. "And what's this about wandering around the woods?"

"Gary Torbin bought a property here, about seven miles from town. The real estate agent said he wanted water access with a dock, so it sounds like he—or someone—was planning on flying in a seaplane or bringing in a boat. Which I don't think he got around to doing."

"Glad to hear you're showing some common sense."

"Do I sense a 'for a change' to follow?"

"If the shoe fits."

She laughed, and the sound brought joy to his heart. "What news do you have?"

"Well, since you're not coming back tonight, I guess I can tell you." He filled her in on what he'd learned from Lockert—which wasn't much and wasn't very useful—and what Paul at the deli shop told him. "So I don't know how much that all helps us. Confirms that Gary wasn't a good character, and apparently he chose an attorney with the same moral compass as his own."

"Well, Mike, think about it. If you were trying to get away with something illegal, you wouldn't choose a lawyer who was on the up and up."

"I wouldn't know, since I don't do illegal stuff."

"And that's why I love you. Anything from the Feds?"

"Nope. But I'm going to ask around town, see what others think about Gary and what he was up to."

"Could you stop in and see Anne? I'm sure she'd love to see a friendly face."

"She'd probably rather see you."

"Tell her I'll come in as soon as I get back in town."

"Will do. Exactly how I want to spend my evening. At the jail."

"Well, at least you're not visiting me."

He laughed. "There is something to be said for that. Love you."

"Love you. Miss you."

He ended the call and stared at the screen for a moment, trying to imagine what pickle his wife had really gotten herself into. Wandering around the woods?

Glad now he'd indulged in the sandwich earlier, Mike checked email. Nothing from Walt Jamison. Thankfully nothing from Philip Osgood. As soon as he returned to Bear Cove, Mike would send a check—payable to Financial Freedom—returning the retainer. Cut all ties as soon as possible.

Since it was unlikely the company would put in a change of address with the post office, the check might well come back to him. But he would have done the right thing.

He shut down his laptop and closed the lid, noting the time. A couple of hours yet until dinner—assuming Anne's arrangements were still in effect. Time to walk downtown, ask a few questions, then visit Carly's friend, and still get back before dark.

So long as he didn't dawdle.

The main business section of town looked deserted with few pedestrians and fewer cars. He kept his eyes open for Loyola Lockert's SUV, but didn't see it. He checked in at the barbershop—even crooks needed haircuts—but the man trimming another fellow's beard shook his head and said he hadn't seen Lockert that day.

At the hardware store, the clerk admitted knowing the attorney, but again said he hadn't seen him. "Then again, he don't show his face around here much. Owes me money, and knows I won't give more credit."

Mike checked in with the garage and the only other diner in town and got pretty much the same answer. Loyola wasn't well-liked and not particularly welcome, unless he was coming in to pay a bill.

The other piece of information he gleaned was that most folks thought Lockert and Gary were two peas in a pod. Most of the town viewed both men as crooks because of their financial dealings, and several made comments about how badly Gary treated Anne. Apparently, their domestic problems were no secret, although nobody admitted to stepping in and helping Anne.

Which didn't really surprise Mike. Most folks might have an opinion, but few would intervene. Didn't want to get involved, they'd say if asked.

Next on his list was to visit Anne as promised. For that, he needed the truck since the state patrol substation was outside town on the highway. He returned to the B&B, picked up the vehicle, and headed out. Fifteen minutes later and he pulled into the near-empty parking lot. After parking in a visitor spot—of which there were about twelve, raising the question in his mind of why somebody would visit a state patrol office—he entered the building.

The front desk officer looked up as he crossed the small foyer. "Can I help you?"

Teleporting the Turnquists back home would be a help. If he could find Wilcox alive and well, that would be a great help. If he could release Anne, that would be a miracle.

But none of that was likely to happen.

Mike rested his hands—in plain sight—on the counter separating him from officer. "I was hoping to visit Anne Torbin."

The man checked a list of about twenty names—the state patrol arrest business was brisk these days—and nodded. "I'll bring her to the visitor center and then I'll come back for you."

Visitor center. Of course, that's why they needed visitor spaces, and so many of them. Folks coming to see their incarcerated loved ones—and perhaps not-so-loved ones. Mike shuddered, a tickle running down his back that brought chills. He'd only been inside a lockup a couple of times in his entire life, but he suspected there were folks who had seen the inside of various jails and prisons often during their lives.

Not a happy way to live.

About ten minutes later, the officer reappeared at a steel security door marked AUTHORIZED PERSONNEL ONLY and beckoned him through. Mike followed him down a long hallway with offices on both sides through a door at the far end and into a large room filled with tables, one chair on one side, two chairs on the opposite.

Anne, her normally perfectly-coiffed hair hanging limply, her face pale after only one day inside, sat at a table, her handcuffed hands resting on the table in front of her. She looked up, recognition lighting up her face. She glanced behind him then back at his face.

He offered her a weak smile.

The officer stood to one side and closed the door. "No touching. No raised voices. No cussing."

Mike nodded and sat opposite Anne. "Carly sends her love."

"Where is she?"

"Haglen. She went to follow up on why Gary had a train ticket there."

Dark circles ringed her red eyes, suggesting she'd spent a lot of time crying and not much sleeping. "Did she find anything?"

"Did you know Gary bought property there?"

She lifted one shoulder and let it fall. "I didn't even know he went there. But since we were divorcing, he needed to find a new place to live."

"According to Zach, he was fine with him. Didn't look like he needed to move anytime soon."

"Maybe he just wants—wanted a place of his own. That's how he is. Was." She swallowed hard, her bottom lip trembling. "Was. I still can't think of him that way. He was just so full of life." She glanced at her hands then back at Mike. "He could charm the birds out of the trees. It was part of his character, I guess."

"What do you know about Loyola Lockert?"

She didn't answer for so long he wondered if she'd not heard the question, but after several long minutes, she met his gaze again. "He's the lawyer who drew up our partnership agreement after we married. And our power of attorney documents. I never trusted him, so I actually took the papers to another attorney who found some things Lockert had written in legalese, trying to pull the wool over my eyes. I insisted he change them, which he did. I know Gary and he are—were—great pals."

"I just went to see him. He said Gary had lots of money. Paid all *his* bills. But folks around town say Lockert never passed that windfall along. Seems he owes everybody."

"Do you think he killed Gary?"

Mike shifted on the cold metal seat. "Doesn't make sense that he would." He leaned closer, and the guard cleared his throat. Mike sat back. "Do you think Gary would tell him what he was doing? Stealing from you? And if he did, would Lockert get involved?"

Anne crossed her arms over her chest. "I don't know. I never trusted him. There's just something smarmy about him."

Mike chuckled. "I know what you mean."

"Is everything okay at the house?"

"Meals are still magically appearing on the table at the prescribed hours. The Romers are still there, poking around. They are strange to say the least."

Anne smiled. "They were kind of evasive about their reason for staying with me, that's for sure. I never got a straight answer from them."

"Any ideas?"

She shook her head. "No. But they asked a lot of questions about the legend of the bodies in the basement. That seemed to invigorate them."

"Well, save that for when we can all gather around the table."

"Don't you mean if?"

He stood. "No. I mean when. With Carly on the case, no stone will be unturned. We'll figure this out and get you back home."

Anne's shoulders slumped. "I hope so."

"See you again soon."

Mike turned and headed back through the locked door and out into freedom. He stood outside the final door and breathed deep.

What was it about a jail that always felt like a coffin?

Chapter 15

Carly woke early the next morning after a restless night's sleep on a lumpy mattress. Hagen Nebraska was even smaller than Danforth Wyoming, which meant she had one choice of a place to sleep—a rundown motel near the edge of town. What with the less-than-desirable mattress and the slamming of doors along the townhouse-style cottages, she hadn't closed her eyes until after three.

But the sun on her face through the wimpy curtains was warm, lighting the dark room and lifting her spirits. Today she would get some real answers, and tonight she'd be back in Danforth, sleeping in the gorgeous room in Anne's house. With her husband.

Breakfast of weak coffee and a stale doughnut only served to promise her stomach that her throat hadn't been cut. Never mind. She'd have a more substantial lunch in town later, and a delicious dinner at the B&B.

Keeping as far to the right as possible on the often-narrow shoulder of the road, she walked to town and the train station. If Gary could rent a taxi for the day, maybe she could talk a cabbie into letting her borrow—uh, rent—his car for a few hours. She patted her purse. She had a couple of hundred dollars in case. That should be more than enough to buy the use of a car in a sleepy town like this.

At the station, she looked for the cab stand, and sure enough, one sat by the curb, the driver slumped in his seat, hat pulled low over his eyes. She stepped up to the car and tapped on the window. The driver opened one eye then tipped his hat back and sat up.

She glanced down the track. "Are you expecting a train soon?"

"If you need the train schedule, check inside."

"I don't need a train. I need a car."

He perked up. "I can drive you wherever you need."

"No, you don't understand. I just need to hire a car. How much for your car until about noon?"

"I don't know how many fares I might miss if I give you my car."

She leaned a hip against the door. "How many trains coming through between now and noon?"

"One."

A going business. No pun intended. "How much for that fare?"

He shrugged. "Depends on where they want to go. Out to the lake, forty dollars."

She tugged at her wallet and offered him twice that amount. "I'll pay you eighty now. And I'll have it back before the train after that comes through. Which is when?"

"Four. Heading west. To Danforth."

"I have to be on that train, so I'll bring your car back by then. Deal?"

He took the bills and nodded. "Deal. And don't forget to fill the tank."

He stepped out, and she slid in, adjusted the seat forward, and checked the gas gauge. "That's a good deal for you, since it shows only a quarter of a tank."

He tapped his temple. "I'm the smartest in my family."

She smiled and put the car in DRIVE then pulled away.

Following the directions the real estate agent gave her, she drove down the street and headed out on a narrow country highway. About two miles outside town, she turned off at the crossroad marked County Road 14A. Three miles along, the pavement ended, and she watched for her next turn.

Within twenty minutes, she pulled into a property marked 11410, the address for Gary's property. A gate barred her from pulling into the driveway, so she parked the car and climbed over. Birds sang from the trees, and a butterfly floated past. Grasshoppers and other insects chirped and sang, silencing as she neared, then resuming as she passed.

The house, a single-story bungalow, nestled in a clearing at the end of the drive. Curtains blocked her view into the structure, and no smoke emitted from the chimney.

Empty flowerboxes lined a gravel walkway, and round planters of soil and dead flowers rested on each side of the steps. Four steps up to the main door. Eight pots.

Carly chuckled at her subconscious counting. Anybody else would think her crazy if they offered her a penny for her thoughts.

She loved numbers. People might change, but numbers never do.

She headed up the steps and tried the door. Locked. Which didn't really surprise her. She'd have to ask the police if they'd found a key in his personal belongings. She cupped her hands around her eyes and peered in through the small window of the door, but couldn't see anything. Almost as though some kind of curtain or film on the inside blocked her view.

Seemed like Gary didn't want anybody looking in.

She retraced her steps and wandered around the small dwelling, hoping to find a window or another door unlocked, but her every effort netted her nothing. The rear of the house was dwarfed by a large evergreen tree that cast shadows, cones, and needles over the ground, muffling her steps and giving her the creeps. She wasn't certain she would want a tree this large looming over her house. One bad storm could bring it toppling down.

As she rounded the final corner, she came face-to-face with an old man. His shoulder-length grey hair, gnarled and knotted with leaves and other debris, framed his face like a cloud, and she wondered for one moment whether he was a ghost.

But when his face creased into a smile that revealed more space than teeth, she knew he was real.

She stepped back. "Sorry. Wasn't expecting to see anybody out here."

"S'okay. S'okay. I snuck up on you. Snuck up, I did."

His words reminded her of an Irish cadence, but one far removed from the Emerald Isle. "Do you live here?"

"Not here." He pointed off through the woods. "Over there. Over there."

"Do you know the man who owns this house?"

He dropped his gaze. "Not s'posed to be here. He said so."

"The man who lives here said that?"

He nodded vigorously, still not meeting her eyes. "The new man. Mr. Gary. Not the old man. Mr. Tom. Mr. Tom my friend. But he sold. And Mr. Gary moved in. He's not my friend. Not my friend."

"When did you see him last?"

He looked up at the tops of the trees and tapped an index on his chin. "Five days ago. Five days."

That sounded about right. Gary came here last week. And he'd been dead four days. "Have you seen anybody else around here?"

Finally, he pulled his gaze to her, and he jumped back as though seeing her for the first time. "Gotta go. Gotta go."

She clutched at his tattered shirt. "Please, have you seen anybody else?"

"Lights. Lights in the woods." He stretched out a hand and gestured to the woods around them. "When Mr. Gary came back. Came back again."

"Did you see anybody?"

He shook his head, sending leaves and tree needles dropping to the ground. "Just lights. Just lights. Like that story."

This caught her attention. "What story?"

"That story. That story."

She tried again. "What was the story about?"

"Bodies buried. Buried in a house."

"Where?"

"Danforth, of course." He clapped his hands in apparent glee. "Danforth, of course. That rhymes. I made a poem. A poem."

He turned on his heel and marched along a path only he could see, arms pumping, knees lifted high. As he headed away, in the singsong voice of a child, he called out at the top of his lungs. "Danforth, of course. Danforth, of course."

Carly watched until he disappeared but was still able to hear him singing.

As she headed for the car, she stopped short. What had the crazy old man said?

Something about bodies buried in a house in Danforth.

Could he be talking about Anne's house?

+++++

Mike's cell phone rang as he walked back from the jail to Anne's.

Walt Jamison of the FBI.

"Hi, Walt, how's it going? Any word on Riley Wilcox?"

A heaving sigh filled his ear. "Nothing yet. How about you?"

Mike filled him in on what they'd learned at the train station and found in the agent's suitcase. "Do you know anything about his case?"

"No, but I'm waiting for his CO to send me the case file. And then I'm heading your way. I want—no, I need—to get to the bottom of this mystery."

Mike chuckled. "Don't call it a mystery. That'll just validate Carly's curiosity and she'll get the big head."

"Is she listening over your shoulder?"

Mike sobered. "No, she took the train to Haglen. We found a train ticket and she insisted on going there. She was supposed to be back yesterday, but called to say she needed to follow a lead today."

"And you let her?"

Mike's insides clenched. What *had* he been thinking? "Didn't have much choice. She was a hundred miles away."

"Understood. I should be there tomorrow, so that will give us an extra set of hands and feet, not to mention a little more authority to push open some doors when needed."

"I'm pretty sure Anne has an extra room here."

"Sounds good. See you tomorrow."

"You're not taking the train, are you?"

Walt laughed. "No. Driving. I'll keep an eye out for crazies, don't worry."

The FBI agent ended the call, and Mike stared at his phone for several long moments.

Don't worry.

Famous last words.

+++++

Carly leaned her head back on the train seat and closed her eyes. After not sleeping well last night, she was tempted to nap her way back to Danforth.

But her mind wouldn't stop going round and round, taking what she knew and what she supposed and swirling them like a blender.

Instead of accomplishing something delicious like a milkshake or a fruit smoothie, all she had was a dull ache behind her eyes and a list of unconnected suspects and motives.

Maybe a little nap wouldn't hurt. . .

The train jerked to a halt, and Carly's eyes snapped open. She checked her watch. About a half hour since they'd left Haglen. She sat up straight. They were nearing the siding where the train she and Mike traveled on a week ago had pulled into a siding to allow the other train to speed past.

But she was on the wrong side of the train.

A quick check of the car she rode in confirmed there were several seats vacant across the aisle. She gathered her purse and jacket, and slid across to the window opposite. Dirt and grime obscured her view, so she lowered the window—after reading the instructions printed on a decal and stuck to the lower corner of the glass.

Who needs directions on how to operate a simple window? The train system,

171

apparently, since the process involved a complex combination of left- and right-hand levers.

Cool air blew across her face, riffling her hair and blowing tendrils into her eyes. As her train slowed, she studied the far side of the tracks. If a body fell off a train and hit the ground at a decent speed, perhaps a hat, scarf, shoe—something—was left behind.

But she couldn't see anything, not even a depression in the golf-ball sized gravel rail bed.

And unfortunately she couldn't see any blood splatters or hair or buttons on the rails, the ties, or the ground.

Which was probably just as well.

Asking a conductor to stop a second train in a week would be too much.

For the conductor. For the company.

And for her.

Not to mention Mike.

Chapter 16

Carly sat back from the dinner table. "That was such a good meal. I've been looking forward to this ever since I left yesterday." She patted her tummy. "Was it only yesterday? Seems like I've been gone a month."

Mike sipped his coffee and set the cup down. "To me, too." He waggled his eyebrows. "Time to make up?"

She pulled her brow down. "We didn't have a fight."

"We could pretend we did."

"I don't know. Isn't Walt Jamison arriving tonight?"

Mike slumped in his chair. "You're right." He sat up straight. "But that's later. Much later. Not until close to midnight."

"Guess he was anxious to get here."

"Yeah. Decided to drive straight through instead of stopping over and getting here early tomorrow." Waggle. Waggle. "But I wish he'd stuck with the original plan. Then we'd have the entire evening to ourselves."

"How about if we relax this evening instead?" Really, where did her husband get the energy? "I want to make some notes. Talk over what you learned, what I found out." She sipped her coffee. "Met an interesting old man in the woods."

"An old man?"

Now she had his attention. "Yeah, when I went to Gary's property. It was weird."

"You met a weird old man in the woods?"

She waved off his words. "Oh, I don't think he was weird. Just old. And dirty."

"You met a weird dirty old man?" He thumped the table with his palm. "That's it. Never letting you out of my sight again."

She opened her mouth to correct him then saw the laugh crinkles in the corners of his eyes. "Stop teasing."

He offered her another cookie. "Tell me about this man. I'm sure there's a story there somewhere."

Carly accepted the cookie and filled him in over their second dessert, making him laugh with her impersonation of this person who raised more questions than he answered.

Then she told him about the cabbie's reaction when she returned his cab. "I thought he'd be anxious to see his car back safe and sound. After all, it's his livelihood. But when I pulled up to the cab line at the train station around three, he wasn't even there. I found a porter, who called him. He was home sleeping. Which was funny, because he was asleep in his car that morning when I rented the car. And here he was still sleeping. Almost four in the afternoon. The porter, his cousin, apparently, said the man could sleep more than a sloth."

"I suspect he was glad you rented his car. Gave him some creds with his wife about why he wasn't working."

She peered at him. "Should I be worrying about the amount of time you spend asleep on the sofa while insisting you're programming?"

"I am programming."

She laughed. "I don't know about that. Seems suspicious. Maybe I should check with the cabbie's wife and see if she's seen some of the same symptoms."

"You probably won't find her."

"Why?"

"She's likely out working three jobs to keep a roof over their head because her lazy husband can't support them."

She nodded, thinking back to her first husband, who sounded like the twin of this man. Then again, the cab driver hadn't smelled of booze, as her late husband had. A drop of compassion for the cabbie and his wife tickled her conscience. "Then again, maybe he has a health issue and can't help it."

"True. Well, let's go to our room and make our lists and figure out who our number one suspect is."

"Sounds like a plan."

Carly stood and Mike clasped her hand, and together they made their way up the stairs. It was good to be home. Sort of. If only Anne was here, too. They'd gather in the front room and chat about their day. Talk about what else Gary was doing. Brainstorm Mike's computer program.

But Anne was in jail.

And Gary was dead.

And Mike's computer program was history, along with his contract.

And perhaps his reputation.

Would she turn into the cabbie's wife, working three jobs to support them?

Carly wrapped her arm around his waist. No, that wasn't Mike.

And it wasn't her, either.

At the top landing, she hesitated.

Mike turned to her. "Don't be afraid to come into my parlor." He held up his hands like claws, and twisted his face in all directions. "Said the spider to the fly." An evil laugh emanated from the lips of the man she so dearly loved. "Come in."

She mock-punched him. "Your Vincent Price impression needs work."

He lowered his hands. "What Vincent Price impression? It was supposed to be Bella Lugosi."

"Then that needs work, too." She turned to head downstairs. "I forgot something."

"What?"

"My purse. It's on the chair next to me at dinner."

"Leave it. It'll be all right until tomorrow."

"But my phone is in it. If someone calls, I don't want to have to go downstairs in the middle of the night."

He sighed. "Fine. But I'm waiting up for you."

She laughed. "The last time you said that, I saw a body thrown from a train."

He ran a hand over his face. "Don't remind me." Mike shooed her down the stairs. "Go, get your purse, but hurry back. I still say we have time before the Feds arrive."

She hurried downstairs, across the darkened foyer, and into the dining room. In just the few minutes since they left, somebody cleared the table and set it for breakfast.

Now, that's efficient.

Her purse lay exactly where she'd left it, and she gathered it under her arm and headed for the stairs.

Movement from the hallway leading to the kitchen—and the basement stairs—

caught her attention.

She paused and eased back into the dining room doorway.

Somebody was there.

Carly held her breath and eased her nose through the opening. Two people emerged from the door to the basement. She stepped out and flipped on the light switch.

The figures froze like they were statues.

The Romers.

And with dirt smudging their faces and their knees, they weren't simply taking pictures.

They *were* up to something.

She'd been right all along.

After a moment of panicked whispering between the two, he grabbed her arm and practically dragged her to the back door and out.

She waited until they exited before proceeding down the stairs, making certain to turn on the lights as she went.

At the bottom of the steps, two shovels and a pickaxe leaned against the wall. Drying dirt covered all the tools.

Carly headed further into the basement, the Romeros' tales of mice and spiders fresh in her mind.

Maybe she should go for Mike.

She clicked on the final switch, then stared.

Holes pockmarked the hard-packed dirt floor.

Someone had been digging down here.

And not just in one place.

A quick count revealed thirteen separate sites.

What were they looking for? None of the holes was more than a foot deep. If they expected to find a body or buried treasure, they weren't going down far enough. If they were well diggers, why not simply say so? And they weren't likely to find water in that shallow of a hole, either.

Carly retraced her steps up to the main floor, shut off the lights, and closed the door behind her.

The only way to know for certain what the Romers was up to was to ask them.

She scurried down the hallway and out the back door, pausing to let her eyes adjust. Low voices filtered across the yard from over near the garage. She headed that way, tripping in a rock along the way. The chickens, shut up in their hutch for the night, cluck-clucked as she passed.

She fell to her knees. "Ouch."

The voices stopped.

She stood, brushed off her pants, checked her palms for scratches—nothing, thankfully—and continued her trek to the source of the voices.

The man door was open, casting a rectangle of light on the otherwise dark yard, and she headed that way.

Inside, the couple sat on overturned five-gallon buckets, their faces turned toward her, looking as guilty as if she'd caught them with their hands in the cookie jar.

Well, she'd get the truth out of them this time. "What are you doing?"

George, to his credit, stepped forward as though protecting his wife from her. "None of your beeswax."

Forcing herself not to smile at the schoolyard expression, Carly maintained her most stern expression. "It is my beeswax. Anne is my friend and she's not here to ask questions."

Nancy's top lip lifted in a sneer. "Killed her husband, didn't she? She wouldn't have the nerve to ask us questions. What's she going to do? Call the cops?"

"Maybe she wouldn't, but she didn't kill her husband." Carly took a step toward them. "And I won't hesitate to call them."

Nancy whimpered, and George moved to stand beside her. She whispered something Carly couldn't make out. George gave a quick shake of his head, and his wife gripped his hands, imploring him to do something.

Carly stepped back. Here she was out in the garage with a couple of desperate strangers. Mike had no idea where she was. She wasn't armed.

What had she been thinking?

She hadn't been thinking, that's what.

No wonder he said she was a full-time job.

Then George's shoulders slumped and he nodded. He faced her. "We are ghost hunters."

Whatever she was expecting, that wasn't it. "What?"

"We visit houses with a reputation for being haunted, and prove or disprove the presence of spirits."

"Does Anne know why you're here? I can't believe she didn't say anything to me."

He shook his head. "We don't tell people in advance. We don't want them to stage an appearance. Or change something that might send the spirit away."

"So why this house?"

"We've read several accounts of a little girl who appears whenever cookies are being baked."

Carly leaned against the wall. "And you believe this stuff?"

Nancy stood and gripped her husband's hand. "It doesn't matter if we believe it or not. The fact is that some houses contain the spirit of someone who lived or visited there in the past. There are many documented cases all around the world."

"So why all the digging?"

"Along with the appearance of Rosalind, there are also stories of bodies in the basement. We were looking to see if they were true."

This was getting weirder and weirder by the moment. "Rosalind?"

George nodded. "Her family owned the house originally. She was an only child and loved cookies. So her parents ordered their cook to bake a fresh batch every day and let her eat as many as she wanted. Unfortunately, she was also a juvenile diabetic, but they didn't know it. She died at the age of seven. Her parents were distraught. They sold the house, fired the cook, and left for New York, but were killed along the way by bandits. The little girl appears whenever there are cookies around."

"I've never seen her."

Nancy sat again. "You aren't around much."

"What does she look like?"

Carly couldn't believe she was asking these questions. As if she expected to see the ghost of a child dead over a hundred years.

George held out a piece of stiff paper. "This is the only known photo of her."

Carly accepted the picture. A little girl wearing a white ruffled dress, with ribbons in her light hair, sat on a chair, a doll clutched in one hand. "She's so pretty." She handed back the image. "But you can't really believe she's haunting the house?"

George tucked the photo into his pocket. "Not haunting, at least not like you'd see in movies. Spirits tend to appear and disappear when triggered by specific events. In Rosalind's case, cookies."

"But what about the bodies in the basement? You didn't dig deep enough to find them, if they're here at all."

Nancy dug into a canvas rucksack and pulled out a square box. "We didn't want to disturb them if they are there, so we used highly technical electronics to pinpoint their location first. We had to penetrate the hard-packed top layer first. Which is why we had to dig holes."

"Did you find anything?"

"Not yet."

"Don't you have to ask permission to tear up a person's house?"

If that law wasn't on the books, it should be.

"If we don't find anything, we'll put it all back the way it was. And if we do find bodies, the homeowner is usually so grateful they don't care how much we dig."

"Usually? You've done this before?"

Nancy nodded vigorously. "Oh, yes. It's how we make our living."

Now it was beginning to make sense. "So when you identify a house with spirits, and you tell the homeowner, they pay you?"

George sat beside his wife. "But of course. These houses are now much more valuable. Homeowners can open up their houses to paid tours, which we can help them promote. In an area with multiple spirit domains, we can assist homeowners with setting up a neighborhood or community spirit walk. There is a lot of money to be made."

Mostly for people like the Romeros. "Sounds like it."

George's brow pulled down. "Skeptics like you are the reason why people like us stay quiet about what we're doing."

"Tell me about the bodies."

George shrugged. "We haven't proven that story yet."

"Who is supposed to be buried there?"

"Well, we heard stories about a man who disappeared and was never seen again. He was a Revenuer during Prohibition who came here to arrest the man of the house who brewed bootleg liquor. When he disappeared, another agent was sent, and he disappeared, too. Neither men were ever seen again. But the owner of the house removed wheelbarrows of dirt from the basement around that same time."

Carly cast a glance back toward the house. "And you think he buried the men down there?"

George stood. "Most people don't stop to consider that burying something displaces more dirt than the thing they buried because the compression on the soil is different now. Most bodies found buried in the woods, for example, are located because of the soil displacement and its different properties."

This was getting too creepy for even Carly. She quirked her head toward the door. "I suggest you check out and leave. After you fill in the holes."

George spluttered but she remained firm.

"Anne has enough to think about without worrying about her house being torn apart by ghost busters."

Nancy paused at the door. "That movie did more to harm our business than you might thing. It's why we don't tell people what we're doing until after."

Carly knew how they felt.

Sometimes she just jumped in and hoped for the best, too.

+++++

Despite his best attempts to convince—or trick—Carly into leaving work until the next day, Mike found himself still at his computer as the midnight hour approached.

Not exactly the romantic reunion he envisioned.

However, he'd had several texts from Walt Jamison indicating he was nearing Danforth, so it was probably just as well.

He glanced over at the other table where Carly sat, furiously scribbling notes, studying the words, then scratching out something that didn't meet her approval. She was hard at work and wouldn't appreciate an interruption.

He rubbed tired eyes and stared at his computer screen. Jamison should be arriving any minute—

The doorbell rang.

The man was punctual, to be certain.

Mike grabbed the file from Wilcox's suitcase, headed downstairs to the front door, and welcomed the agent inside. Jamison set down his small travel bag—very similar to the one Wilcox carried on the train—and followed Mike into the dining room.

A lump formed in the back of Mike's throat. The missing agent would likely have no need for his suitcase or its contents. This was followed instantly by the realization that he'd not asked about the agent's family.

He would rectify that at once.

Jamison sat on one side of the table and opened the folder in his hand. "I have the original case notes here, as well as some follow-up notes since Agent Wilcox took over. How about we trade files and see if there's anything different or that we might have missed. Sometimes just having the pages in a different order can spark a thought."

Mike slid his folder toward Jamison. "You sure you don't want to leave this until the morning?"

Jamison shook his head. "I'm pumped on caffeine right now. Don't think I'd be able to sleep, so I'd just wear myself out tossing and turning."

"Understood."

For the next twenty minutes or so, the two sat in silence and read the files. Jamison was correct. Wilcox had reordered his file according to some system, but seeing the reports and other notes in chronological order gave him a new understanding of the file.

He sat back and closed the folder. "Looks like the initial investigation was surface only. A few phone calls to local law enforcement. Three telephone conversations with the victim. And a call from one of her daughters."

Jamison crossed his arms over his chest. "Right. Not a lot there. The local LEOs didn't know this was going on right under their noses."

"It's interesting because it's another credit card scam."

"Right."

"Yeah. The ghost module I discovered accesses credit cards using small amounts under a shell company. Using authorized recurring charges, Mirrored them."

Jamison nodded. "But you brought that with you, didn't you? It's not like it was operating out of this area."

"True. But the pattern is so similar. I hope I didn't press Osgood too hard." I didn't care."

"Not much you can do about that. They've probably already disconnected their phone and disabled their email."

None of which made Mike feel any better. "I'm sorry. I should have kept my cool, but I'm not good at this subterfuge stuff. I'd never make a good undercover agent."

"Most people wouldn't. And it's not your fault. The plan sounds similar, that's true. But in this case, personal contact was made with the victim. And she's not the only one. She said she has several friends who were approached. But she was the only one who took the bait."

"And what was that?"

"A sad story that if he didn't make a sale, he's lose his job and his company-provided housing, putting him, his very pregnant wife, and their three kids out on the street. So she bought a small item, a magazine subscription, I believe. He swiped her card in a tablet reader. When she didn't get her magazine, she called the publisher. They didn't know anything about a sales team in the area."

Mike snorted. "And they don't provide company housing."

"And they don't work with any sub-contractors who do. But when the victim got her credit card statement, she was shocked to see it was run up to its limit. When she checked her credit report, she learned there were three more credit cards issued in her name by different companies, all maxed out. She didn't want to tell her family, because she didn't want them to think she was a foolish old woman, but she had to say something when she couldn't make even the minimum payments. That's where we came in."

"Similar mechanism, different sources."

"Right." Jamison chewed his bottom lip. "How about if I take a look at that program you were working on? Maybe there are other connections. I've seen a lot of these scams."

"I'll get my laptop. Back in a flash."

He took the stairs two at a time and entered the room he shared with Carly, expecting to see her hunched over the table.

But she wasn't.

He glanced at the bed.

She lay on her side, knees pulled up, eyes closed, still fully clothed.

Tempting as it was to crawl in beside her, he resisted and grabbed his computer then headed downstairs.

They could sleep in tomorrow.

Chapter 17

Simply sitting at a table laden with food and getting up when she was done was heaven to Carly. If she never had to prepare another meal, she'd get used to it pretty quick.

And whoever Anne hired to keep the meals and clean-up flowing along was doing a great job. She—or he—was as invisible as the child ghost the Romers told her about.

Speaking of which—

Carly filled Mike and the FBI agent in on what she'd learned from the strange couple. Both men agreed the two engaged in a strange occupation, but when Carly asked about whether their tactics might border on fraud, Jamison said that might be difficult to prove.

"The ability to convict is founded almost entirely on intent." He shook his head. "It's unfortunate, but if they simply tell the homeowner what they believe they found, it's up to the owner to decide if they want to pay to build a business around that information. Buyer beware and all that."

Carly wasn't mollified. "Seems to me there should be something we can do about it."

Mike patted her hand. "Who is this we? You and the mouse in your pocket?"

She laughed. "You're right. If I think something should be done, I should be willing to step up and do it. Not depend on someone else."

Jamison nodded. "That's what we try to tell folks. If it's something you're passionate about, do it. Grassroots efforts always have more impact than Big Government coming in and telling folks what to do. A blog about this will reach a lot more people than a bulletin from the Feds."

"I'll have to give that some thought. Starting with telling everybody I know. Not that I'm a social media guru or anything like that. But I know some folks who are."

"That's always a good place to start. Now, back to this mystery."

Mike set his cup down. "Or mysteries. Seems like we have several players but no script. We can't tell who is related to who or what."

"Where are you going to start?" The agent clicked his pen a couple of times. "I'm going to go visit the victim and see what she has to say. Where can I rent a car?"

Mike chuckled. "Not in this town. But maybe you could borrow the pickup Anne lends to guests. You're a guest."

"Speaking of which, it seems strange staying here when I didn't sign anything."

Carly clasped her hands to her chest. "If you can't trust the FBI, who can you trust?"

The men laughed, brightening the atmosphere in the room.

Carly continued. "Seriously, take the truck. Mike and I are going to Haglen for the day. If you could drop us at the station, we'll call you with our return time. If you're not available, we can walk."

"Sounds like a plan."

They spent the next few minutes discussing the case, when Mike slapped his palm to his forehead.

Carly stared. "What?"

"I meant to ask this before. Did Wilcox have any family?"

Jamison's smile dropped away. "He does. Parents, siblings. Not married."

Mike sat back. "I feel bad we didn't ask that before. Do they know he's missing?"

Jamison nodded. "Not the whole story. They know he's out of communication on an undercover assignment. He's done those before, so they know they can't call him. We simply told them it was deep undercover and that someone would get in touch with them when it's safe."

Carly sighed. "That must be so hard on them."

"At this point, they don't know enough to worry. Like I said, he's done these kind of incommunicado details before. It's the storyline we use when we don't have enough details. Which we don't right now."

Carly stood. "Time to go, I guess." She glanced at Mike and then held Jamison's gaze. "Just promise me that neither of you use that storyline on me. I want to know the truth if something happens."

Mike crossed his heart with an index finger. "I promise not to keep the truth from you if you promise the same thing."

She gripped his hand and squeezed. "You know I never knowingly withhold the truth from you."

"No, but sometimes you forget to tell me crucial details."

"*Moi?*"

Mike pulled her close. "Beware a woman who uses a foreign language as an avoidance technique."

He knew her too well.

+++++

Mike smiled at his wife. She seemed to enjoy the trip to Haglen with him. As they passed the rail siding that marked the spot along the tracks where she saw Gary toss who she believed to be Agent Wilcox overboard, they now had two sets of eyes studying the rail bed. And even though the train didn't slow, they had a good view confirming what she'd seen before.

No evidence a body had ever been there.

In town, Mike showed the station master a newspaper photo of Loyola Lockert he'd found—a grainy, low resolution image in a cheesy ad touting Loyola "The Bulldog" Lockert as the attorney to make sure his clients got what they deserved.

If his clients were anything like him, he sincerely hoped so.

The stationmaster peered at the image for a long time, and with each passing second, Mike's hopes dropped.

But then he nodded. "Thought it was the same guy, but I wanted to be sure. He came through here just the one time."

Mike peered at him. "And you remember him?"

"Sure." The man smiled, his teeth showing white against his ebony skin. "He asked about Gary Torbin, and the funny thing was, Gary came in on the train before his. I saw him tipping the porter for carrying his packages. I told this man that."

Carly edged forward, practically pushing Mike aside. "Did he say why he was looking for Gary?"

"Nope. And I didn't ask. He did ask if I knew where Gary lived, but I didn't. Still don't. Send him to the town office. They record all property purchases, so I figured they could point him in the right direction."

Mike thanked the man for his time and the information, then they headed for the line of cabs. Carly made a beeline for the fellow she'd rented from before and introduced them. The two men struck the same bargain, and within a few minutes, Mike and Carly headed out of town toward Gary's place.

There wasn't much to see along the way—just more of the same rolling prairie, the occasional tree, a few small creeks, and lots of cows. Carly suggested that it might be a nice place to live, but Mike still didn't see the attraction of living in the middle of nowhere—particularly if the kids weren't living nearby.

Even a simple Christmas get-together would entail a lot of travel.

Carly was uncharacteristically quiet and him do most of the talking. She'd bantered with him and Jamison at breakfast, but he suspected the news about Wilcox's family had sobered her, as it had him. Still, the information that he wasn't a married man with children was some consolation. But the idea of not telling the family the whole truth so they could prepare for the worst seemed wrong.

Then again, if they found the agent living it up in Vegas, perhaps it was for the better.

Not that he thought that was bound to happen.

Knots formed in his gut. He might not want to believe that Carly saw what she said she saw. He might think she let her imagination run away with her common sense once in a while.

Okay. More than once in a while. A lot.

But she had such a vivid recollection of the struggle on the train, and then she'd immediately identified Gary and Wilcox from their photos, that he'd resigned himself to accepting her story.

He glanced in the rearview mirror and then at the hand-drawn map in her hand. "How much further?"

She shrugged. "A mile or so. Why?"

"There's a car coming up fast behind us. I don't think he'll be happy that I'm sticking to the speed limit."

Carly twisted in her seat as far as her seatbelt would allow then faced front. "He doesn't look like he's going to slow down."

Mike nodded. "I'll pull over to the edge of the shoulder as much as possible so he can go by."

She gripped his arm. "He's coming fast. And close!"

He jammed on the brakes and veered to the gravel shoulder as the SUV passed them, leaving but a hairs width between the two vehicles. The rear of their car fishtailed as the front tires dug in. Carly braced her hands on the dash, and he gripped the wheel as the car bucked and skidded like an unbroken bronco.

And then they were stopped, enveloped in a cloud of dust.

Carly, her face white and mouth pulled into a hard line, stared straight ahead at the SUV screaming down the highway. "What an idiot. He didn't even slow down to see if we were okay."

Mike held his tongue as his breathing slowed, and after a long moment, he released the steering wheel and dropped trembling hands into his lap. They were safe. Their car wasn't wrecked. And they hadn't had to confront the driver.

Because without a doubt, he was fairly certain he knew the person behind the wheel of that vehicle.

The only navy blue SUV in Danforth.

While they weren't in Danforth, the coincidence seemed too great to ignore.

+++++

Carly indicated the turn with a tense nod of her head. Mike complied then slowed when the pavement ended. This area was a little more populated, with numerous drives leading away from both sides of the road. Fences and gates, NO TRESPASSING signs, and the occasional glimpse of a house or a vehicle through the woods confirmed that many folks lived in the area. Just like the real estate agent said.

They hadn't spoken much since the incident on the highway except for Mike to express his suspicion that Gary's crooked lawyer was driving the SUV, and Carly didn't push the matter. They both needed time to decompress, and a quiet drive through the woods should do just that.

It's not like they lived high-action lives and were almost run off the road every days.

Yes, they'd been threatened before in various ways, but they'd been kind of expecting something like that in those instances.

Not in the sleepy town of Haglen Nebraska, however.

And surely not for something as minor as a few missing paintings and some money.

Mike made the final turn and pulled to a stop at the gate, then turned in his seat. "So what's the plan?"

"I thought you might have an idea of how we can get inside."

"You really mean you're hoping I'll be able to break in where you couldn't?"

She smiled, half-hearted, to be sure, but a smile nonetheless. "I wasn't tall

187

enough to see in through all the windows." She dug in her purse and pulled out a couple of mini Maglites. "It's kind of dark in the back. And the house is dark."

He flicked his flashlight on and off. "And we want to look inside."

Now she tossed him a full-wattage smile. "What a great idea."

She slid out of the car and led the way around the house. The front door and windows were still locked, and no matter how they angled their lights, they couldn't see inside. She ventured around the back and flipped on her flashlight. Mike followed close behind, and at a look from her, he checked the windows, particularly the ones she couldn't reach.

Still nothing.

She sighed, disappointment coursing through her like a wet blanket. They'd wasted their time coming here. Except for the information that Lockert had come to Haglen asking for Gary, they were no further ahead. And she wasn't certain how that piece of information helped them at all.

She looped her arm through Mike's and they headed around the side of the dwelling toward the car.

And almost ran into the old man from her previous visit.

She took a step back, tripping in a tree root, glad that Mike was there to catch her. "Nice to see you again."

Mike stared at the recluse. "I thought you were exaggerating."

"Really?" She batted her eyes at him. "Like I ever do." She turned to the old man. "Seen anybody around here lately?"

"I did. I did."

Her pulse quickened. Maybe this was the breakthrough they needed. "Who?"

"You. You were here yesterday." He leaned closer. "Don'cha remember?"

She held her breath to avoid the odors of unwashed clothes and body, and the overwhelming pervasive smell of alcohol—mixed with something else? Berries?—on his breath. "Besides me."

The old man stared at Mike. "Who's he? Who's he?"

"My husband Mike."

The old man's expression relaxed, and he tossed a near-toothless grin at Mike. "Glad to meet'cha." Then he returned his attention to her. "Saw somethin' else, I did."

"What?"

"Light. Like yours."

"When?"

His brow drew down as though the process of concentrating hurt. Then he brightened. "Last week. Last week." He leaned closer again as though sharing a confidence. "Thought it was leprechauns, I did. Thought it was. Wanted their treasure, I did. Snuck up on them." He straightened, his face serious. "Only way to trick them, you know. Sneak up."

"And who was here?"

"A leprechaun, I tell you. A little man. Carried a light. Carried a sack. A bag of coins, he did."

Certain the alcohol influenced his recollection, Carly figured there was no harm in humoring the old man. "Did you talk to him?"

The man's head bobbed several times, and a couple of small twigs and a leaf fell to the ground. "Said he was rescuing the treasure from an evil leprechaun. Said it wasn't his."

That part was likely true. "Then what?"

"He opened the bag. Untied the string, he did. Gave me a reward for not telling. For not telling, he said." He clamped a dirty hand replete with too-long nails over his mouth. "Uh-oh. Broke my promise, I did."

"But we're friends with all the leprechauns in these woods." Mike winked at the old man. "They all know us. They won't mind you telling us."

"They won't?" The old man's brow drew down again. "He said not to tell anybody. I don't know." A dirt-encrusted finger scratched his head. "Nobody."

Carly smiled and patted the same tattered shirt the old man still wore. "But I'm not anybody. We're friends, aren't we?"

"Carly." Mike's low growl was almost too soft to hear. "Careful."

She dropped her hand to her side. "Show me what he gave you."

The recluse hesitated so long she was certain he would deny her, but then he turned his back to them, reached into a pocket in his cargo pants, and pulled out something that he examined for a moment before turning back to them, his hand outstretched. "No touching."

A gold coin glinted in their flashlight beam.

Mike peered at it. "1869. Gold double eagle."

"I think it's one of Anne's. She had a list of missing coins." Carly turned back to the old man. "And you say he had a bag of these?"

More nodding. "But they weren't his. He said so. He did."

She leaned close to Mike, inhaled his clean smell, and whispered. "Maybe he used the money he stole to buy more coins, because she didn't say a sack was missing." She turned back. "What did this leprechaun look like?"

"Are you going to look for him?" His brow drew down. "He wouldn't like that. Told me not to follow him."

"No, we're not going to look for him." She had to come up with a story. And quick. "We're just wondering if he was the same leprechaun we saw last week. He had blond hair."

The old man studied her as though peering into her soul, and she worried he might be more capable than she was giving him credit for, but then he shook his head. "Not the same one. Didn't look like that."

"You know what this means, don't you?"

He shook his head again. "What?"

"There could be two leprechauns in these woods. With two treasures."

"Two treasures? Two treasures? Maybe I could find him."

"What did your leprechaun look like?"

"Short. Shorter than you." He pointed to her. "Dark hair. Little beard here." His fingers caressed his chin. "Eye specs."

Carly turned to Mike. "Sounds like Lockert."

Mike nodded. "You're right. But now what?"

Carly addressed the recluse. "Thank you for your help. Keep that coin safe. It might be worth a lot of money."

"More than five dollars?"

"For sure."

"More than ten dollars?"

"Absolutely."

The old man beamed. "Long time since I had more than ten dollars. More than ten dollars." He clamped the coin between his two front teeth. "Tastes like gold."

"Yes, it is."

Brian tucked the coin back into his pocket and fastened the buttons. "See ya. See ya later, alligator."

"In a while, crocodile."

And like a puff of smoke, the old man trotted down another path only he could see and blended in with the trees.

Just like the leprechauns he sought.

Chapter 18

Having spent overly long at Gary Torbin's house, Mike and Carly missed the last train back to Danforth. Mike called Walt Jamison. "We're staying in Haglen tonight. Did you learn anything today?"

"No. The woman who reported the fraud isn't around. Spent most of the day chasing my tail, answering emails, fielding calls from the office. You know how it is."

Mike did. Seemed most of his days were like that. "I'll call tomorrow when we head back to let you know our ETA."

"Sounds good. Say hi to Carly for me."

"Will do." Mike hung up and turned to Carly, who was in the midst of finishing her coffee at dinner in the only restaurant in town that stayed open for the evening meal. "Walt says hi."

She nodded toward his cell phone sitting on the table. "Hi Walt." She swiped the chintzy paper napkin across her mouth. "Unremarkable food, to say the least, but at least I won't die of starvation tonight."

Mike patted his stomach. "Feels like the meatloaf is sitting like a brick. Hopefully there's more nutrition than that, or I might die of hunger."

She chuckled. "Like trying to live on a diet of cotton candy."

"Exactly." He scrolled through his list of contacts and paused at the name he sought. "Before we go, let me make one more call."

"To who?"

"I know a fellow in New York who collects coins. I was hoping he could tell me how much that double eagle could be worth."

"Good idea. I bet it's more than ten dollars, and I'd hate to see our elusive friend spend it like real money. Or for someone to take it from him. An old man like that could get hurt."

"Right." Mike pressed the icon to dial the number and waited through several rings before the call was answered. "Chuck. Mike Turnquist. Not too late to call?"

"Not at all. Where are you? You sound like you're in a barrel."

"Western Nebraska."

"What are you doing there?"

"Too long a story to tell right now. I'll fill you in later. Need a favor."

"So long as it doesn't include bailing you out of jail, I'm in."

Mike turned his shoulder to his wife. She had the hearing of a teenager, and there was no way she needed to know about this. "It doesn't. I need to know how much an 1869 gold double eagle is worth. Rough estimate."

"Mint condition?"

"No. But the edges were crisp, the engraving clear. No obvious scratches or rubbing."

"Ah. I see you have been listening to me yammer on all these years. So it's used but good shape. In the current market, about five thousand dollars. Maybe more. I'll give you that for it right now, sight unseen."

Mike whistled, and Carly scooted her chair closer. "Thanks, Chuck. It's not mine, but I'll let you know if the owner is interested in selling."

"Good to hear from you. Everything good with you and Carly?"

"She's practically sitting in my lap here."

"TMI. Talk to you soon."

Mike rang off and turned to his wife. "He says it's worth about five grand."

Now it was Carly's turn to whistle. "Wow. I hope nobody else learns he has the coin."

"I agree. They might try to take it from him by force. Which wouldn't turn out well for the old man."

"I'll bet Lockert stole them from Gary. Do you think he might have killed Gary?"

Mike shrugged. "Maybe. But why? And if this was such a secret thing Gary was doing, why would he have confided in his attorney?"

"Good question. What next?"

"Let's go check out our motel room."

Carly held up one hand and checked off on her fingers. "Lumpy mattress. No hot water. Nasty carpet. Walls as thin as tissue paper. And stale doughnuts for breakfast."

He laughed. "I was thinking no big deal until you got to stale doughnuts."

"No big deal? Mike, we won't sleep a wink in that dump."

He waggled his eyebrows at her. "Good. I was hoping for a romantic reunion sooner rather than later."

+++++

Regardless of what Mike thought was going to happen, it wasn't going to be in this dump. But they had no choice, because it was the only motel in town. And she didn't relish paying for a cab ride to the next town to check out the motel there.

So when they got to their hotel room, Carly steered Mike toward the shower. "Go in there and take a cold one while I call the jail in Danforth. I want to ask Anne a question."

One side of her husband's mouth lifted up. "You exaggerated how good this place was."

"I know. Makes you want to sleep on the bench outside."

"Which I might do if it wasn't so cold." He heaved a sigh. "Maybe I should take the blanket and sheets in with me, introduce them to the concept of washing. But how would we dry them?"

"I think the bed is okay. Just lumpy."

"Not so sure, but I'll take your word for it. And why a cold shower? Other than the obvious romance squelcher."

"Because you're unlikely to get any hot water."

He removed his shoes but kept his socks on. "I don't want to walk on this floor barefoot."

"Don't blame you. Now go."

He disappeared into the tiny bathroom and she soon heard the sound of running water and a sharp intake of breath as he stepped under the stream.

She perched on the edge of the bed and dialed the jail, then asked the deputy to take a question to Anne. Thankfully she'd reached a man who agreed without hesitation, and said he'd call her back in a few minutes.

Carly scrolled through the six television stations while she waited, but it seemed every station conspired to coordinate its commercial breaks so all she saw were snippets of the same car and furniture ads. She sighed and turned the set off, and the phone rang just a moment later.

She answered. "Carly here."

"Deputy Unger, ma'am. She says she had ten of those coins, which her husband took. As well as the paintings by some guy named American Masters. Worth about half a million dollars."

Carly smiled at the deputy's misunderstanding of Anne's message describing a type of painting, not the artist's name. "Thanks, Deputy."

"No problem. Enjoyed getting away from the desk for a few minutes. Need anything else, call. I work most nights."

Mike emerged from the bathroom wrapped in a once-white towel that was now a dingy grey. "What did you find out?"

Carly filled him in. "I knew Gary had taken a lot of stuff, but I hadn't gotten to the valuation part of the job, which isn't really part of the job but—"

"I know. You like to do a thorough job."

She smiled. "Actually, I was going to say I'm nosey, but yes, your response is true, too." She stared into a corner of the room where an enormous spider hunched as though waiting for an unsuspecting victim to wander near. "Seems like Gary was determined to drive her into bankruptcy."

"And if the police find out, they'll have more motive than they need."

"They already think she killed him, so they aren't looking anywhere else."

He sighed. "Which means we need to keep looking."

That was one thing she loved about Mike.

Even when he didn't want to do something, he would because it was the right thing.

+++++

The next morning, Mike learned that Carly had also under-described the staleness of the doughnuts.

But with the meatloaf from the previous night still sticking to his ribs and the rest of his insides, he didn't want to hazard a stop at the diner. Instead they bought a couple of hot dogs from the convenience store at the gas station. Filled a hole, that was about it. Good thing they'd be home by dinner tonight.

A wave of envy rose in him like a flood as he envisioned the breakfast Walt Jamison feasted on at Anne's.

He should have packed a picnic basket for this trip.

Back to the train station, deal with the cabbie, and they were soon on their way to Gary's. This time, however, the trip was uneventful, except for the amount of time he spent with his eyes glued to the rearview mirror. But no SUVs, navy blue or otherwise, tried to run them off the road.

Perhaps Lockert had returned to Danforth.

Maybe it wasn't Lockert, just some West Nebraska yahoo who wasn't accustomed to seeing other cars on the road.

Once again, they checked the perimeter of the clearing the house sat on, fully expecting to run into the old recluse again. But he was absent. Hopefully at home— wherever or whatever that was—sleeping off his previous binge.

At the rear of the home, a basement window stood slightly ajar.

Carly pointed. "I know that was locked yesterday."

He nodded. "I checked all the windows." He bent over and looked in. "I think I could get in there. Then I'll come up and open the door."

"Be careful, Mike. It could be a trap."

He chuckled. "If you were here on your own, you wouldn't think twice about sliding in through that opening. Probably without even checking to see how long a drop it is."

"You're right. I'll meet you at the back door."

He slid in through the window, glad for the solid workbench to bridge the distance between the opening and the floor. Within two minutes he appeared at the door, opened it and stepped aside for her to enter, and then they both went downstairs.

At the bottom of the steps, he held up a hand to stop her. "I didn't spend much time looking around, but I think you're going to be interested in what's in here."

She pushed ahead then stopped. Small mounds of dirt, similar in size to the ones the Romers created in Anne's basement, dotted the dirt floor. A shovel rested in a larger hole, flung aside as though the digger was interrupted and left suddenly.

"Come on, Mike. Let's see what they were looking for."

"I don't know, Carly. I think we should call the police."

"And tell them what? Gary was planning to grow mushrooms in his basement. There's no law against that."

Mike gestured to the disarray. "This doesn't look like a mushroom farm."

"You know what I mean." She picked up the shovel and lifted several loads of dirt out of the hole. On her next thrust, a hollow sound echoed back. "Found something. Help me."

Mike sighed but stepped down into the hole with her. On their knees, using their bare hands, they scraped at the dirt until they revealed a square outline.

Mike straightened and dusted off his hands. "Let me see if I can get this out. You wait up there. And don't get into trouble."

Carly scrambled out of the hole to give him space to work. He shoveled out more dirt, grunting with the exertion, until he'd dug around the box. Using the shovel as a lever, he rocked the box until it broke free.

He swiped at sweat running down his forehead. "Find a piece of rope so we can haul this thing out of here."

She searched a worktable on the wall under the window, returning with a length of nylon rope. Mike tied it to the handles at each end, then he climbed out, and together they huffed and puffed until they lifted the box to the basement floor. Using an oversized screwdriver, they pried open the latches.

Mike mock-bowed. "Do the honors since you found it."

She lifted the lid and the piece of velvet material inside.

And gasped.

A painting depicting a buffalo hunt, its colors vivid in the dim light.

Underneath it, another in the same style.

She shone her Maglite into the box.

These were the missing Nortons on Anne's inventory.

And beneath these was a canvas sack tied with a string.

Her fingers trembling, she undid the bag and poured its contents onto the length of velvet.

More gold coins.

"Oh, my," she whispered. "Gary has been a very busy boy."

She sifted the coins through her fingers like sand a couple of times. "Imagine using these as real currency all those years ago. Just feel them, Mike." She dropped several into his hand. "I feel rich just touching them."

Mike handed back the coins and gave her time to relish their find, before pointing to an alcove. "Looks like something has been buried over there, too. The soil looks disturbed."

She stood and brushed off her jeans. "Maybe he's got more treasure. Let's go."

But less than two minutes of digging and scraping later, she stared at the ground. "Oh, no."

"Oh, no is right." Mike leaned the shovel against the wall. "An understatement, in fact."

Three fingers lay visible in the turned soul at their feet, looking like something from an Edgar Allan Poe story, trying to climb out of its grave.

Chapter 19

Two hours later, and Carly shuffled out to their rented car. The cabbie was going to be so mad at her. She'd missed his return time by hours—through no fault of her own. In fact, she was surprised he hadn't sicced the cops on her, claiming she'd stolen his car.

Then again, maybe he was still home, sleeping.

His poor wife.

She slid into the passenger seat and laid her head back, then straightened. If she closed her eyes, she'd be asleep in minutes. And they still had places to go and people to see.

Mike opened the door and sat, started the engine, then looked at her. "If I never find another body in a basement, it will be too soon."

She giggled, more from nervous tension than because the matter was funny.

In fact, the matter was definitely not funny.

Without much doubt, the body belonged to Riley Wilcox. The police pathologist's guesstimate was that he died from blunt force trauma, likely from falling from the train. He'd been buried shortly after that. About six days before. Which coincided with his disappearance and what Carly saw.

She laid a hand on his forearm. "Sorry. Nerves."

He nodded. "Where to next?"

"Are you up to a drive?"

He nodded, weariness drawing deep lines around his mouth and eyes. "As long as it's no further than Connecticut."

"It isn't. First, let's head to town. I need to check with the cabbie if it's okay to keep his car just a little while longer."

She needn't have worried. When she looked for him at the train station, the porter directed her to his house, where his haggard-looking wives tried to corral three toddlers and reassure her that her husband didn't need his car—he'd gone fishing for a few days with his buddies. Mike paid her a little extra for the inconvenience, and she told them to leave the car in the station parking lot.

They returned to the depot, where Carly had Mike pull in at the cabstand. "Set the trip meter so we know how far we're going."

"And that's important why?"

"You'll see."

He did as she asked by pushing the little knob on the dash, and they headed out of town in the opposite direction—west. The highway ran roughly parallel to the tracks, at one point running almost directly next to it. At milepost 136.5, Carly had him pull over.

When the car came to a stop, she peered over at the numbers on the dash. "How far from town to here?"

"This says eighteen miles."

She did a quick calculation. "Perfect."

"What did that number tell you?"

"The cabbie said Gary put fifty miles on his cab the first time he rented it. He left town, was gone a while, then came back to pick up his packages, then left again. It's eighteen miles to here, so thirty-six round trip to town. Seven out to Gary's, and seven back when he returned the car."

"Accounting for the fifty miles." He reached across the front seat and pulled her close. "You are so smart."

"Just numbers, my dear Watson. Just numbers."

Mike peered through the windshield. The headlights cast long shadows down the track. A rabbit hopped from the underbrush and stopped, caught in the glare of the lights. "But I don't see anything. Why did Gary come here?"

"Because this is where I saw him toss Riley Wilcox off the train. He came out to retrieve the body before the railway police searched here. But he hadn't taken the time to load his packages, so he returned to town to get the paintings and coins he'd stolen. Then he went to his cabin in the woods and buried it all in the basement. He returned the car to the cabbie then got on the next train back to Danforth as though nothing happened."

Talking about a dead man's crimes helped her keep her emotions at bay, but speaking of the agent as "the body" was getting more difficult. She swallowed past a lump in her throat. "Let's head back to town. We'll need to spend another night in that horrible room because there aren't any more trains tonight."

Mike yawned. "I think I'm tired enough to sleep on a flagpole. Which might be more comfortable than that mattress."

+++++

The only thing that kept Mike going the next day on the return train ride to Danforth was the thought of sleeping in his own bed that night. Well, not exactly his own bed, but a very comfortable bed he had every intention of getting to know much better by spending many hours luxuriating in the firm mattress, clean sheets, and quiet environs.

Judging by how many notes Carly was writing, she had no intention of joining him.

At least not in the near future.

He sighed. This was not the vacation he'd envisioned. Not even the working vacation he'd hoped for. Between bodies on—make that off—trains, clients involved in illegal activities, hidden assets, and unscrupulous lawyers, he hadn't had a moment's peace.

In fact, the only good thing so far was that their time here was nearing an end.

But not before Carly proved her friend innocent.

Carly called ahead to make an appointment with the state patrol detachment in Danforth, and Mike arranged for Walt Jamison to drive them to the substation. But once that was done, Mike had every intention of taking a long nap.

After lunch.

And waking in time for dinner.

Then back to sleep. Eyebrow waggling or not, this was about as unromantic as life got.

When he called Walt, he learned something else. The agent, bored with waiting around time, decided to delve into Mike's program, being a bit of a programmer himself. What he found confirmed Mike's suspicions.

Financial Freedom was up to no good.

The long arm of the law was within Jamison's grasp, and he had access to contacts that Mike didn't, so he put in a call to the Minneapolis office to send an agent to Financial Freedom's offices and talk to Philip Osgood.

When the agent arrived, the place was empty except for an overheated shredder and an empty desk.

As Jamison suspected, they had cleared out, obviously destroying whatever records they didn't want to take with them.

The agent questioned the leasing office, who were surprised—Financial Freedom moved out during the night, leaving them stuck with six months remaining on the lease.

Mike wasn't particularly surprised. Once Jamison told him what companies like this usually did, he tried to call Osgood. The number was disconnected, and the email he sent returned as undeliverable.

Osgood was probably lounging on a beach somewhere, enjoying his ill-gotten gains.

Or, more likely, simply moved on to another scam in another city under yet another name.

And Osgood may not have been his real name, either.

The horn sounded, signaling Danforth ahead. Mike sighed and glanced over at Carly. Apparently her late nights and lack of sleep had caught up with her, too. Her head rested on the seat back, and her closed eyes gave her a peaceful and innocent expression.

Except he knew the real Carly Turnquist was anything but.

He nudged her arm, and she opened her eyes and turned to face him. "Go 'way."

"You are so grumpy when you first wake up."

She smiled at him, warming him from the inside. "Am not."

He planted a kiss on the end of her nose. "We're pulling in to Danforth."

She snapped to attention and gathered her notes, dropping her pen in the process. "Oh, my. I intended to think through what I need to tell the state patrol, and now I've lost my thoughts."

"Just tell them the truth."

She waggled her head from side to side like one of those bobbing dogs in the back windows of cars. "Easier said than done."

"Is there something you aren't telling me?"

She stared at him a long moment before relaxing. "I thought you were serious there for a minute."

"I am serious. Why should telling the police the truth be easier said than done?"

"Well, I don't want to overload them with facts and suppositions, but I don't want to leave out anything relevant."

"Let's just see how it goes, okay, before we worry about overloading them."

Still not sure why Carly was nervous about meeting the state patrol, Mike waited until the train came to a complete stop before standing and collecting their few carryon items. Their small suitcase could wait at the station for them.

The FBI agent waited for them, a friendly face in what turned out to be an unfriendly world. He led them to Anne's old pickup and chattered like they'd been away for a week instead of just one day.

Jamison needed to get out more.

The drive to the state patrol substation was short, and soon they paraded into the office and asked for Special Investigator Markwood. Within minutes, he ushered them into his office. A few minutes of rearranging furniture to make room for an additional chair, and the four sat, if not exactly comfortably.

Markwood waited with his hands clasped together easily on his desk, looking from one to the other. After a long moment, he cleared his throat softly. "Which one of you wants to start?"

Mike and Jamison both turned to Carly, who sat between them. She smiled at each in turn, and then leaned forward. "I guess that's me."

Markwood picked up a pen. "Go ahead. Ready when you are."

"We believe—we know Gary Torbin stole from his wife then hid it to keep it from being included in the divorce."

Scritch-scratching filled the room as Markwood wrote furiously on a pad of paper.

Carly continued. "We met a man at Gary's house in Haglen Nebraska who described another man lurking around the house. This description matches Loyola Lockert, Gary's attorney."

Markwood paused in his note taking. "Why would Lockert go to Haglen to meet Gary when they saw each other around town every day? Or could have?"

Carly tapped the desk with an index finger. "Exactly my thoughts. I—we think he went there to either deliver more hidden assets, or maybe to try to blackmail Gary into giving him a share of the loot."

A smile tickled the deputy's mouth, and Mike commiserated with the man. He likely didn't hear the word used as often as Carly might think. At any rate, and to his credit, he didn't interrupt her.

"We know he had possession of at least some of Gary's loot because he gave a coin to our witness. He showed it to us. An 1869 gold double eagle, worth about

$5,000."

"That's a lot of money." The SI continued writing. "Why would he give him something worth that much?"

"Our witness is a little bit simple. Maybe Lockert didn't have any cash on him. Maybe he thought the old man would never spend it. The old man thinks Lockert is a leprechaun, you see."

"A leprechaun?"

"Yes."

"One of the wee people?"

Carly sighed. "Yes."

"Just how credible is this witness?"

"We weren't out there looking for credibility. We were looking for information. And just because he drinks and hasn't taken a shower in a year doesn't mean—"

She paused when Mike laid his hand on her arm. Forget the old man's credibility—Carly's was about to go down the drain.

Mike scooted his chair a millimeter closer to the desk. "What my wife means is that this information led us to look inside the house, where we found a body. It's the missing FBI agent. And we found more paintings and coins buried in the basement. The whole place has turned into a crime scene."

Markwood nodded. "Let me make a phone call to check out your story. If what you say is true, then it's looking less and less like Anne Torbin killed her husband. And we never thought she killed the agent."

He ushered them into the waiting area. "Hang on here until I talk to the Haglen chief."

The three sat dutifully like kids called to the principal's office.

About ten minutes later, Markwood returned. "Haglen chief confirmed what you told me. And he said dental records confirmed that the body is Riley Wilcox."

Carly stood. "I'm glad that's over."

Markwood held up a hand. "Not quite. We've still got to hear Lockert's side of the story. Then it should be over."

Despite the confirmation of the identity of the body, Mike was glad to hear those words.

Over and done with.

Chapter 20

Anne exited the jail side of the substation and rushed into Carly's arms, who enveloped her once-incarcerated friend and hugged her close. "Anne, I'm so glad to see you on this side of the prison bars."

Anne sobbed into her shoulder, shaking with emotion. "Me, too." She held Carly at arm's length. "Thank you for all you've done for me." She released Carly and turned to Mike. "And you, too. I know you took a lot of chances for me, and I appreciate it."

Carly turned to Agent Jamison. "Anne, this is Walt Jamison of the FBI. He helped too."

Anne extended a hand, which Jamison shook. "Good to meet you, Mrs. Torbin."

Anne shuddered. "Please, just Anne. I'm going to change my name as soon as possible. I don't want to be reminded of that man or our marriage."

Carly turned toward Anne's truck. All she could think about was getting back to Anne's, having dinner, and then going to sleep. She was beat.

A police car pulled into the parking lot, its lights lit. Two officers stepped out and one opened the rear passenger door.

Loyola Lockert, hands shackled behind his back.

Deputy Markwood met his prisoner at the entry to the jail. He handed the man off to another officer, then waved Carly and her little group over. "We're taking him in for questioning. Want to watch?"

All exhaustion slipped away, and she nodded. "Love to."

Mike laughed and Jamison groaned.

She turned to them. "C'mon guys, it isn't every day we're invited to a police interrogation. I've always wanted to see one." She turned back to Markwood. "From the police side, of course."

He chuckled. "Of course." He gestured them in. "This way."

When Anne hesitated, he smiled. "No worries. If you are a little jail-shy, we understand."

Anne nodded. "I think I'll head back home, if you don't mind."

Markwood beckoned to an officer. "Please drive Mrs.—Anne home."

Carly waited until she was certain her friend was in good hands before joining the others inside. Markwood led them down a hallway to a room marked INTERROGATION 1. He paused. "I'll be in there with Lockert." He pointed to a doorway just past this one. "That's an observation room. You can see and hear him, but he won't know you're there."

Carly rubbed her hands together. This was going to be fun. She'd watched scenes like this on television crime shows, both fact and fiction. This was a dream come true.

Whatever she'd been expecting, what followed was neither as exciting or dramatic—or indeed fun—as she'd imagined. Instead, Loyola Lockert sat slumped, hands shackled in front of him on the table, as he answered questions.

The man was completely defeated.

Within less than an hour, the attorney confessed that Gary about what he was doing and where he'd hidden the assets. Lockert decided to blackmail him for half the money, knowing Gary couldn't go to the cops. But Lockert wasn't foolish enough to go to that meeting unarmed. He saw Anne check the glove box of her truck when she went downtown to run some errands, noticing the revolver. Nobody locked anything in Danforth, so he simply took the gun. When Gary put up a fight, Lockert shot him, leaving the gun to implicate Anne. Gary told him of their argument the previous evening, and Lockert knew spouses were always the first suspects. Lockert forged the necessary papers to gain control of her estate once she went to prison for Gary's murder.

The man recited his confession in a matter-of-fact way that chilled Carly to the bone. He might have been reading a news story for all the emotion he displayed.

After the statement was typed up, Lockert signed it, and they led him away.

Markwood nodded to the threesome behind the glass, obviously satisfied with the conclusion.

But the outcome was anything but satisfactory for Carly.

Two men were dead, another faced a long prison sentence, and her friend's life was torn apart.

+++++

Over dinner that night—which Carly worried wouldn't happen because of all the emotional turmoil of the day—the four discussed the remaining facts of the cases. Because without a doubt, although everything seemed to dovetail perfectly, there were a few loose ends.

Mike made a follow-up call to the Haglen chief and asked about developments there. As they'd presumed, Gary traveled to Haglen because it was along the train route to and from Danforth, meaning he could move the stolen items with ease and hide them in a secluded place. He bought the property under his assumed name, and traveled under that same identity on the train, which ultimately made it easier for the police to confirm their suppositions.

On one of the trips back to Danforth, it appeared Gary met Agent Wilcox. Once the conductors were shown a picture of both men, they recalled the two sitting near each other in the same car and eating at the same table in the dining car. One waiter heard Wilcox tell Gary he was traveling to Danforth to investigate a fraud case, which was probably the instigator for their tussle that ended with Wilcox going overboard.

Gary thought Wilcox was there to investigate him.

Gary got off the train in Danforth and caught the next train east, which came along just a few minutes later. He rented the cab, drove out to the spot where the body lay, and then carried Wilcox to his cabin and buried him. By the time Carly convinced the railway police to look into her allegations, Gary had already removed the body.

Apparently, Lockert went to the house after he killed Gary to retrieve the coins and paintings, fully intending to fence them then disappear with the money to warmer climes, but the old man appeared and almost gave Lockert a heart attack. Lockert gave him the coin and told him to keep it a secret. The last thing he needed was for word of gold coins in the area getting around.

Mike sat back and crossed his arms. "Well, that seems to cover everything."

Jamison leaned forward. "Not quite everything. Because of the hinky way Financial Freedom cleared out their office and bank accounts, leaving hundreds of thousands of people without recourse to clearing up their charges, I was able to get a subpoena issued for his arrest. But when agents went to his last known address, he'd already vamoosed. The only person there, a butler-cum-gardener, said he'd left the country."

Carly wiped at her mouth with a much more substantial napkin than the Haglen diner boasted. "Did they find him?"

Jamison shook his head. "We traced his flight plan and learned the Coast Guard was also looking for him in the Gulf of Mexico. Apparently, his private plane sent out a Mayday then disappeared from radar. To date, they think he went down. No survivors or wreckage have been spotted, but they're in the midst of a bad hurricane out there right now."

While he definitely deserved prison, he didn't deserve to die.

Carly turned to Anne. "So there's just one more thing."

Jamison groaned.

Mike laughed. "With Carly, there's always one more thing."

The front door opened and footsteps crossed the foyer.

Carly turned.

The Romers.

Standing in the doorway like redheaded step-children, unsure whether they were invited to the party.

Anne stood and waved them in. "Come in, please." She glanced at the others around the table. "I asked them to come because I think we all got off on the wrong foot."

George sat beside Mike, and Nancy sat next to Carly, who smiled at the woman. "Let's start again. Welcome. I'm Carly."

The woman nodded. "Nancy."

Jamison, Mike, and George soon completed their introductions, and then Anne stood to serve dessert. Once everybody had a plate of hot apple pie and sharp Cheddar cheese to go with their coffee, she looked to Nancy. "Now, perhaps you can explain what you do and why you wanted to do it in my house?"

Nancy's face reddened and she set her fork down. "We're ghost hunters."

Her husband piped up. "We look for spirits in houses."

Anne nodded. "So, why didn't you simply tell me what you were doing here?"

Nancy dropped her gaze to her hands. "When people find out who we are, they don't want anything to do with us. They think we're weird."

Carly chuckled. "I know exactly how you feel?"

Nancy tipped her head in question. "You do?"

"Yes. When people find out I'm an accountant, their eyes glaze over, and they don't want to talk to me because they think I'm boring. Just a bean counter."

Mike leaned forward. "But let me tell you, she is anything but. Carly has made it her life's purpose to prove to people that they are wrong when it comes to thinking accountants are boring."

"Not true, Mike. Not true."

He held up one hand and began checking items off by folding down one finger at a time. "Let's see. She found her boss in a furnace. She was almost run off the road. People threatened her by fax and by a note left on her car." He continued until one hand was filled out, then started on the other. When he got to two hands completed, he turned to George. "Can I borrow your fingers to prove my point?" He glanced at Jamison. "And maybe yours, too."

They all laughed, Carly the hardest.

But that wasn't the end of it yet. Not to her satisfaction, at least.

She stood and waited until everybody stopped talking. "Anne, where did these stories about bodies in the basement start?"

Anne's half-smile indicated her reluctance to take the stage, but when the others urged her to continue, she stood while Carly sat.

She laid her hands flat on the table. "I don't know if this story is true, mind you. But folks around here believe it, and that's all I'll say about that." She sipped her water and set the glass down. "Many years ago, about fifty or so, long before I owned this house, a man, his wife, and their child lived here. By all accounts, they were a happy family. Until he lost his job. Folks didn't see them for a while. One day, a neighbor noticed the newspapers were piling up, so he came over to check."

She sat and clutched her hands in front of her. "He found the wife and child dead in the basement, huddled in a corner, shot through the heart."

Carly shivered and leaned against Mike. She glanced at the Romers. George wore a satisfied smile while Nancy took notes. She shook her head.

Ghouls.

Anne continued. "The husband was arrested and convicted, but found to be insane, and was institutionalized for life. About thirty years later, he escaped and was never seen again."

"Oh, how horrible." Carly sat up. "So that's where the story comes from."

Anne held up a hand. "But there's more."

Nancy flipped a page in her notebook. "Please continue."

"He'd be in his seventies now, if he were still alive. And people say they've seen him wandering in the woods between here and Haglen."

Carly looked at Mike, and Mike stared at her.

No. It couldn't be. . .

A long silence ensued, and then Jamison cleared his throat. "Well, on that note, I think it's time to hit the sack. We all have long days ahead of us."

Mike stood. "Right. Coming Carly?"

Anne chuckled. "Seems my story made you nervous."

Carly smiled. "No, not at all." She gripped Mike's hand then turned to her friend. "He wasn't from Ireland by any chance, was he?"

"The murderer?"

"Right."

Anne shook her head. "Iowa, I believe."

Carly exhaled. "Oh, that's okay then."

Anne stood at her side. "Why Carly, you look like you've seen a ghost."

Mike wrapped his arm around her. "Not a ghost. Just a page out of history."

Carly leaned into him. Mike was right.

She *was* a full-time job.

As they headed upstairs, Mike paused. "I'm glad we're going home soon."

"Why's that?"

"Maybe in Bear Cove you won't find ways to get into so much trouble."

She smiled. Sure, let him think that just because the town was small there were no mysteries, no crime. Hadn't he learned anything in the last few years?

Other books in this series

No Accounting for Murder
Missing money. Carly's daughter accused of stealing. A mystery numbered company that threatens her when she turns down a job offer. A disappearing mayor. All of this adds up to murder.

There Was a Crooked Man
A working vacation—working for Mike, who's been hired to create a program for a dude ranch in New Mexico, vacation for Carly. But before they get off the plane, she's solved one murder, and is primed for solving more mysteries.

Unbalanced
When Mike's long lost brother turns up days before son Tom's wedding, Carly is suspicious. But when the brother disappears and leaves his own young son behind, her mystery sensors are on high alert. Add in a bank robbery nobody else saw, and Carly can't just sit by and wait for the other shoe to drop.

Five and Twenty Blackbirds
When a former acquaintance of Carly's is blown up in the middle of Mike's 25th college reunion, Carly knows something is wrong. And when a mobster threatens to kill her, she knows she can't sit by and hope the police solve the crime.

Broke, Busted, and Disgusted finds Carly and Mike back in Bear Cove Maine again, where they hoped to find the rest and relaxation they never seem to enjoy while on vacation. But when Mike's client ends of murdered, and he's missing, he becomes not only the prime suspect—he's the only suspect. Carly discovers their bank accounts are drained and their credit cards maxed out—are the police correct in thinking Mike has skipped out on her, leaving her to pick up the pieces? Or is something more nefarious at work here?

About the Author

Leeann Betts writes contemporary suspense, while her real-life persona, Donna Schlachter, pens historical suspense. She has released six titles in her By the Numbers series. In addition, Leeann has written a devotional for accountants, bookkeepers, and financial folk, *Counting the Days,* and with her real-life persona, Donna Schlachter, has published a book on writing, *Nuggets of Writing Gold,* a compilation of essays, articles, and exercises on the craft. She publishes a free quarterly newsletter that includes a book review and articles on writing and books of interest to readers and writers. You can subscribe at www.LeeannBetts.com or follow Leeann at www.AllBettsAreOff.wordpress.com

All books are available on Amazon.com in digital and print, and at Smashwords.com in digital format.

Facebook: http://bit.ly/1pQSOqV
Twitter: http://bit.ly/1qmqvB6
Books: http://amzn.to/2dHfgCE

Please leave an honest review at Amazon.com and Smashwords.com